DEF

OF EAGLES

DEFIANCE
OF EAGLES

William W. Johnstone
with J. A. Johnstone

PINNACLE BOOKS
Kensington Publishing Corp.
www.kensingtonbooks.com

PINNACLE BOOKS are published by

Kensington Publishing Corp.
119 West 40th Street
New York, NY 10018

PUBLISHER'S NOTE
Following the death of William W. Johnstone, the Johnstone family is working with a carefully selected writer to organize and complete Mr. Johnstone's outlines and many unfinished manuscripts to create additional novels in all of his series like The Last Gunfighter, Mountain Man, and Eagles, among others. This novel was inspired by Mr. Johnstone's superb storytelling.

All Kensington titles, imprints, and distributed lines are available at special quantity discounts for bulk purchases for sales promotions, premiums, fund-raising, educational, or institutional use. Special book excerpts or customized printings can also be created to fit specific needs. For details, write or phone the office of the Kensington special sales manager: Kensington Publishing Corp., 119 West 40th Street, New York, NY 10018, attn: Special Sales Department; phone 1-800-221-2647.

ISBN-13: 978-0-7860-3130-6
ISBN-10: 0-7860-3130-1

First printing: August 2013

10 9 8 7 6 5 4 3 2 1

Printed in the United States of America

First electronic edition: August 2013

ISBN-13: 978-0-7860-3131-3
ISBN-10: 0-7860-3131-X

PROLOGUE

General Fielding called Colonels Cahill and
Hamilton to the cabin of the riverboat, where around
a map spread out on a table, they discussed the
details of a strategy Fielding had put together that
very morning. After giving everyone their orders,
the officers left to meet with their subordinates, and
from there, the plan was dispensed to the next level
of commanders.

Colonel Edward Hamilton, in charge of the Third
Cavalry from Fort Ellis, Montana, had given the
assignment of marching up the Yellowstone and the
Bighorn to be in position to block the Indians should
they try to run, and, if Indians didn't try to run, to
assign someone to move quickly to join with Cahill
in the attack.

The officer Edward assigned for the task was Major
Boyd Ackerman.

"You will proceed down the Yellowstone with all

due speed," Edward told Ackerman. "Continue until you either encounter the Indians or hear the sound of guns. If you hear the sound of guns, move as quickly as possible to provide support."

Ackerman saluted, then, with two hundred men, started down the river. He sent two Arikara Indian scouts ahead of his column, and, on the afternoon of the 21st, the two scouts came galloping back. They were so excited, and were speaking so rapidly, that Ackerman couldn't understand them, so he had his chief of scouts translate for him.

"They say that there is a big Indian village ahead of us. Cahill has already had some of his men attack at the south end, and he is coming to attack at the north end of the village."

"How big is the village?" Ackerman asked.

"Very big, many, many lodges," one of the scouts answered. "And many warriors. More warriors than all the bullets in all the guns here."

"And that fool Cahill is attacking?" Ackerman asked.

"He isn't there yet," Captain Lindell said. Lindell was Ackerman's second in command. "If we hurry, we can join with him before he attacks."

Ackerman shook his head. "This is insane," he said. "Cahill has no business committing his troops under these circumstances. He studied tactics at the Academy just as I did. You don't commit to battle until you have the advantage."

"Major, I believe he is expecting us to join him," Captain Lindell said. "Our orders were to proceed at best possible speed until we either encountered the Indians, or heard the sound of guns."

"Have we encountered any Indians, Captain? Have we heard the sound of guns?" Ackerman asked.

"Not exactly, but our scouts have encountered the Indians."

"Our orders are also to block any possible retreat of the Indians. We will take up positions here, so that we can do that."

"With all due respect, Major, if there are that many Indians, they won't be retreating," Captain Lindell said.

"You have my orders, Captain," Ackerman said. "Put the men in position to block the retreat of the Indians."

Lindell stared at Ackerman for a long moment.

"Follow my orders, Captain, or I will relieve you of your position, now!" Ackerman said angrily.

"Yes, sir."

Over the next few minutes, Captain Lindell put his men in position to block any Indians who might try to run from the battle. No sooner were they in position than they heard the sound of guns.

"Major, the sound of guns!" Lindell said. "Shall we proceed?"

"We are in position now; I hardly see what purpose would be served by abandoning good defensive positions on what might well prove to be a futile effort. Scouts, proceed forward until you can see what is happening, then return with your report."

The sound of the guns continued, and even from here, they could see dust and gun smoke rising into the air. They could also hear the Indians' shouts and yells.

The scouts rode ahead, and the sound of the guns

continued in their absence. Then, the intensity of the gunfire began to lessen.

"Do you hear that, Captain? It was probably no more than a brief skirmish. When the main attack comes, the Indians will be coming this way, and we must be ready for them."

"That is the main attack, Major," Lindell replied in a clipped voice.

When the scouts returned, they gave their report.

"The soldiers are like pebbles in a creek. The Indians are like the water flowing around the pebbles," they said.

"Now just what the hell is that supposed to mean?" Ackerman asked.

"Major, it means that Cahill is in trouble. Big trouble. We have to go to his support, and we have to go now!" Lindell said.

"I've heard enough from you, Lindell. If Cahill was foolish enough to attack before we were able to join with him, then his fate is his fault. I'll be damned if I'll risk my life to save some arrogant bastard who got himself into trouble."

By now the shooting was sporadic at best, then it stopped altogether, and the only thing that could be heard were the yelps and shouts of the Indians.

"My God!" Lindell said. "Listen to that! What do you think that means?"

"I think it means that Cahill turned tail and ran," Ackerman said.

"Major, permission to go ahead with the scouts to see what I can find out?"

"Permission denied," Ackerman said. "We will stay

here, in a blocking position, until we know, without a doubt, that the Indians aren't coming this way."

Ackerman kept his troops in position for the rest of the day, and into the night. They made cold camp that night, Ackerman refusing to allow any fires to be built. For supper they ate hardtack and beef jerky, and they chewed coffee beans.

They stayed in position all through the next day, again hearing gunfire, but this time from farther away than it had been the day before. Just before nightfall of the second day, they saw a huge cloud of smoke, billowing into the sky, and though Captain Lindell asked, again, to be allowed to go forward and see what was going on, Ackerman again refused to give him permission.

Finally, on the morning of June 23rd, their positions were approached by Colonel Hamilton.

"Where is Cahill?" Edward asked.

"I don't know, sir, I haven't seen him," Ackerman replied.

"What do you mean, you haven't seen him? Weren't your orders to join him? What have you been doing all this time?"

"Colonel, I deemed it more prudent to establish a blocking position, should the Indians try to escape."

"Join your men with my column," Colonel Hamilton said.

"Yes, sir."

Twenty minutes later the large column continued toward Crooked Creek. As they approached the battlefield, they saw a lot of white objects lying around on the ground.

"What is that?" Ackerman asked.

"God in heaven," Edward said. "It is bodies. They are soldiers who have been stripped naked."

As the men rode through the battlefield, looking down at the naked and the dead, not a word was spoken. The bodies were arrayed in skirmish formation, which meant that they had been able to mount a defense. Tom Cahill was found, facedown, scalped, his skull crushed, dozens of arrows bristling from his body.

As Colonel Hamilton moved through the strewn corpses, he saw Falcon MacCallister with Captain Rawlings, walking among the dead.

"Falcon?" Edward said, completely shocked to see his brother-in-law. "What on earth are you doing here?"

"I was in the area when I heard the sound of guns. I investigated, and, quite unexpectedly, found myself in the middle of an Indian battle."

"Were you with Cahill?"

"No, I wound up with Captain Rawlings. We were engaged a little over a mile away," he said.

Falcon and Edward stepped over to one side of the battlefield and looked out at the many soldiers from both Reno's and Hamilton's commands, the living among the dead.

"How's my sister?" Falcon asked.

"Megan is doing well."

"And my niece?"

"Growing into a beautiful young woman," Edward said. "Though I may be a bit vain in saying so."

"What do you have to be vain about? It's the MacCallister lineage," Falcon said.

Edward smiled. "I suppose it is." He shook his

head. "It doesn't seem right, carrying on small talk here, in the presence of men who have given their last full measure of devotion to their comrades, their commander, and their country."

"No, I guess it doesn't."

"I sent two hundred men to join with Cahill. They were under Ackerman's command."

"Two hundred men? It's too bad they didn't get here in time. That would have doubled Cahill's command and changed the outcome."

"They would have been here in time, if Ackerman had carried out my orders," Edward said. "He stopped, not two miles from here. Captain Lindell tells me they heard the sound of battle, but Ackerman refused to advance."

"Refused, or couldn't?"

"There were no Indians that prevented it. He just refused. Tell me truthfully, Falcon, if Ackerman had followed orders, if he had joined with Cahill, do you think the outcome of the battle would have been different?"

"Yes, I think it would have been. As I said, that would have doubled Cahill's strength, and reinforced, he could have put enough pressure on the Indians to the north of the village that Rawlings could have left their entrenchment and advanced from the south. With Ackerman from the north, and Captain Rawlings from the south, it would have made a huge difference."

"Would you be willing to testify to that?"

"Testify?"

"At Ackerman's court-martial. I intend bringing charges."

CHAPTER ONE

Fort Ellis, Montana Territory

The officers who were to hear the general court-martial filed in and took their seats. Because Boyd Ackerman was a major, the jury was made up of his peers, majors and lieutenant colonels.

The chief witness against him was his commanding officer, Lieutenant Colonel Edward Hamilton. Edward was sworn in and the trial counsel, a captain, began to question him.

"Colonel Hamilton, you are the one who brought charges against Major Ackerman, is that correct, sir?"

"That is correct."

"And would you tell the court what position you held, relative to the events of this trial?"

"I was commanding officer of a detached element of the Third Cavalry, under the command of General Fielding during the Battle of Crooked Creek."

"And, for the record, that would be the campaign in which General Cahill, and all who were with him, were killed?"

"Yes."

"And what was Major Ackerman's position?"

"Major Ackerman commanded two troops of the Third Cavalry, two hundred men."

"So he was subordinate to you?"

"He was."

"And would you state for the court, Colonel Hamilton, what charges you have filed against Major Ackerman?"

"I will. I have filed charges against Major Ackerman to the effect of dereliction of duty and willful disobedience of a direct order. He was ordered to proceed with his two cavalry troops, with all due speed, to join with Colonel Cahill in the campaign to force the hostiles back to their reservation. His failure to repair resulted in the annihilation of Cahill and all the men with him. I could have charged him with cowardice had I so wanted."

"Objection," the defense said. "If the charge of cowardice wasn't made, it has no relevance in this testimony."

"Objection sustained," the trial judge said. He looked over toward the panel of officers who made up the jury. "The panel is instructed to disregard any consideration of cowardice, as that is not a part of the charge."

The trial judge turned his attention back to the trial counsel. "You may continue with your examination."

"Colonel Hamilton, you have accused Major Ackerman of willful disobedience of a direct order. Are you certain that the disobedience was willful, and not caused by something beyond Major Ackerman's control? By this I mean did he try to effect a junction with Cahill's troops, but was unable to do so because of circumstances?"

"It was willful disobedience."

"And why are you sure?"

"Major Ackerman made a statement, overheard by two other officers who will testify in this trial, that he had no intention of risking his life to save the life of, and I quote—that arrogant bastard—end quote, referring to Cahill."

"Your witness, Lieutenant," the trial counsel said, walking away from the witness chair.

The defense counsel approached.

"Colonel, is it not true that if Major Ackerman had led his men into Crooked Creek valley on that fateful day that he, and all his men, may also have been killed? Shouldn't he be credited with saving his command?"

"Anytime you commit troops to battle, you run the risk of sustaining casualties, sometimes very heavy casualties. It is my belief that had Major Ackerman carried out his orders, it would have saved lives, specifically those brave soldiers who were with Colonel Cahill. If you don't commit your command to battle when ordered to do so, it isn't a question of saving the men, it is a question of failing to carry out your duty."

"Do you actually believe that if Ackerman had joined Cahill, that the outcome would have been different?"

"Colonel Cahill had two hundred and ten men with him. Had Ackerman joined him as ordered, it would have doubled his strength. Military strategists have made the observation that an additional two hundred men would have changed the outcome of the battle."

"With all due respect, Colonel, those so-called strategists weren't there. I was," Ackerman called out from his position at the defendant's table.

The trial judge struck the table with his gavel. "You have not been given permission to speak," he said.

"I have no further questions of this witness," the defense counsel said.

"Your Honor, prosecution calls to the stand Falcon MacCallister."

Falcon approached the witness stand.

"Do you swear to tell the truth, the whole truth, and nothing but the truth, so help you God?" the trial counsel asked, administering the oath.

"I do."

"You may be seated."

Trial counsel waited until Falcon was seated, then he began the examination.

"Were you present during the battle at Crooked Creek?"

"I was."

"How is it that you, a civilian, happened to be there?"

"You hit on it. I just happened to be there. I was in the area, totally unaware of any Indian unrest. When I heard all the shooting, I knew that it had to be a battle of some sort, so I rode to the sound of the guns."

"And, as I understand, you wound up with Captain Rawlings's command, did you not?"

"Yes."

"In your opinion, and based upon your firsthand

knowledge of the battle, could Major Ackerman have reached the battlefield? Or were the Indians so positioned that it would have been impossible for them to do so?"

"All of the Indians were either engaged with Cahill, or were keeping Captain Rawlings's command pinned down. A relief element from the north could have reached Cahill."

"And had that relief element united with Cahill, do you think it would have made any difference?"

"I think it would have made a great difference," Falcon said. "It would have greatly increased the numbers, and they would have approached the Indians from a side they weren't expecting. I believe it would have broken the Indian attack."

"Thank you, no further questions."

The defense council approached Falcon.

"You were with Captain Rawlings. Did you attempt to relieve Colonel Cahill?"

"We did."

"And what happened?"

"We were forced back by the Indians."

"No further questions."

"Redirect?" the trial judge asked.

The prosecutor rose, but did not approach the witness. "From which direction did Captain Rawlings try to effect his relief effort?"

"From the south."

"And were there any Indians between you and Colonel Cahill?"

"Yes, the entire Indian force was between Captain Rawlings and Colonel Cahill."

"And from which direction would Major Ackerman's relief column have come?" the prosecutor asked.

"From the north," Falcon said.

"Were there Indians between where Colonel Cahill and his gallant troops made their last stand and any relief element that would have approached from the north?"

"There were none."

"So, in your opinion, a relief element from the north would have been able to reach Cahill?"

"There is no doubt in my mind."

"Thank you, Colonel MacCallister. I have no further questions.

The case for prosecution and defense was concluded by the middle of the afternoon, then the jury retired to reach their verdict. They came back in in less than half an hour and when called up by the trial judge delivered the verdict of guilty.

"Would the defendant please stand?" the trial judge said.

Ackerman stood.

"You have been found guilty of dereliction of duty, willfully disobeying a lawful order, and failure to repair. You are hereby sentenced to be stripped of all rank and U.S. Army accouterments, and to be dishonorably discharged from the service."

Immediately after the court-martial proceedings were adjourned, an armed escort was assigned to

Major Boyd Ackerman, and he was marched out into the middle of the parade ground where the entire complement of the post had been called to formation. Ackerman, by order of the commanding officer of the post, was in full dress uniform, complete with sash and saber. Colonel Hamilton, Ackerman's commanding officer, made the first cut, snipping off both epaulettes. That was followed by other officers of the regiment, until not one gold thing remained on Ackerman's uniform, but lay instead in pieces around him. The last thing to be taken from him was his saber.

"Sergeant Major!" Colonel Hamilton called.

Because a noncommissioned officer cannot be in command of a detail that contains commissioned officers, when the sergeant major was summoned, those officers who were standing in front of their commands quickly left their formations. Their places were taken by the various first sergeants.

The sergeant major came to the front of the formation and saluted sharply.

"Sergeant Major, dismiss the command and escort Private Ackerman off the fort."

"Yes, sir. Private Ackerman, you will remain in position," the sergeant major called. "First Sergeants, dismiss your troops!"

"Troop!" the first sergeants called. "Platoon!" came the supplementary commands of the many platoon sergeants.

"Dismissed!"

The formation broke up quickly, and as the men returned to their duties, many looked over toward

Ackerman, who, until he was escorted off the post, was still in the army, and still standing at attention. But he was no longer a major. Now, he was a private, and all those he had once ranked now outranked him.

Major Ackerman had been an overbearing, and much disliked, officer who was routinely cruel to his men. Now, "Private" Ackerman was jeered by most of the men who passed by him.

"Hello, Private Ackerman!"

"Too bad you're about to be kicked out of the army, Private. I'd love to see you on stable duty."

"Hey, Ackerman, you want to inspect me now?"

The derisive remarks continued, to the laughter of the men who were gathered around to watch the degradation of the former major.

After several minutes of the mocking, the corporal of the guard then took charge.

"Ackerman, until we reach the front gate, you are still in the army, and you are a private. At my command, forward, march!"

With the entire post laughing, and shouting insults, Private, formerly Major, Ackerman was marched to the front gate, shoved through, then the gate closed behind him. The moment he stepped off military property, he became a civilian.

One week after Ackerman had been dishonorably discharged, he returned to Fort Ellis in the middle of the night. Although Fort Ellis had a front gate, it was not surrounded by a high stockade fence, but was an open installation. Its security was maintained by a detail of sentries who walked a prescribed route along their guard post. Ironically, it had been Ackerman's duty to establish the routes the sentries would take, so he knew exactly when he could be at certain parts of the post undetected. He slipped in behind the stables, then, waiting for the sentry to pass, moved from the supply room to the post guardhouse. There were three men in the guardhouse, Sergeant Jay Casey, Corporal Clyde Jones, and Private Marv Boyle. All three men had been tried and convicted for the murder of a saloon keeper in nearby Bozeman. They were to be hanged the next day.

Ackerman had keys to the guardhouse, which he used to slip inside. Then, in the dark, he moved up to the cell where all three men were sleeping.

"Casey, Jones, Boyle," Ackerman said. The words were louder than a whisper but quiet enough that if anyone happened to be passing by they wouldn't hear.

"What?" Casey replied. "What is it? Who's there?"

"Come over to the cell door," Ackerman said.

By now the other two had been awakened.

"What's going on?" Jones asked.

"I'll be damned! It's Major Ackerman," Casey said.

"You mean Private Ackerman, don't you?" Boyle said.

Ackerman showed them a key. "I am willing to let you men out, if we can come to an agreement."

"What? Hell, yes!" Casey said. "Anything you say."

"I intend to form a group of irregular soldiers, similar to that commanded by Quantrill during the war. The only difference is, whereas Quantrill made his raids in support of the South, our raids will be completely self-serving."

"What does that mean?" Boyle asked.

"It means that any money we take, we keep."

"Yeah!" Boyle said. "Yeah, I'm for that."

There were five more men in the guardhouse, all five serving a penalty of six and two-thirds, meaning six months in confinement and forfeiture of two-thirds of their pay. At the conclusion of the six months, they would all be dishonorably discharged.

Ackerman freed them as well. Then Ackerman, and the eight men he had freed, took horses and tack from the stables and rode off.

They rode through the rest of the night, so they were twenty miles away by the time any of them were missed back at the fort. Ackerman called them to a halt, then told them his plans for the band.

"As long as you men are with me, we will conduct ourselves as a military unit," Ackerman said. "You will address me as Major, and you will regard me as your commanding officer."

"Oh, hey, I don't know about that," one of the five six and two-third soldiers said. "I didn't mind bein' in the stockade all that much, seein' as I was goin' to be discharged."

"If you went back now, your sentence would be increased from six months to two years for unlawfully leaving custodial confinement. Would you want that?"

"Well, no."

"I want you to join my army," Ackerman said, holding up his finger. "But in my army, you'll be paid a hell of a lot more money than you've ever made before in your life."

"Yes, sir, Major Ackerman!" Casey said. He saluted. "I'm proud to serve you!"

The others, seeing Casey come to attention and saluting, did so as well. Ackerman, too, came to attention, then returned the salute.

"Men, with your loyal service, I hereby give birth to Ackerman's Raiders."

CHAPTER TWO

Fort Ellis

"I hate to lose you, Colonel Hamilton," General Terry said. "You have been an outstanding officer, with a long and dedicated service. I would say that it is a shame you are leaving the army before you are eligible for a pension but . . ." Terry chuckled, "in your case, I don't suppose that matters. I hear you've bought a ranch as large as Texas."

Edward laughed. "Not quite, sir."

"But it is one-third the size of Rhode Island, I'm told."

"Even that is a gross exaggeration, and Rhode Island is a very small state."

Terry laughed again. "It is indeed, Colonel, it is indeed. I know your circumstances, Colonel, and I know that you could have left the army at any time you wanted. Why now?"

"My daughter was born on an army post," Edward said. "She's eighteen years old now. I think she should have the opportunity to see something of this world from other than a military perspective."

"Well, I can't say as I blame you," General Terry said. "Mary Kate is a beautiful young woman. No doubt you would be fighting off second lieutenants soon. But of course, she is your wife's daughter. How could she be anything but beautiful?"

"Or strong willed," Edward added.

"Well, what do you expect?" General Terry asked. "She is a MacCallister, after all. And the MacCallister family is, quite possibly, the most storied family of the West. From the Alamo, to the major battles of the Civil War, to the Battle of Little Bighorn, there has been a MacCallister involved."

"Yes, I'm well aware that Falcon MacCallister kept Gatling guns from falling into the hands of the Indians during that battle. Had he not done so, Reno and Benteen's men might also have been massacred."

General Terry took out his watch and opened it. "Perhaps we had best go out to the parade grounds. Your retirement parade is set to begin in five minutes."

General Terry and Lieutenant Colonel Edward Hamilton left the Headquarters Building and walked out to the parade grounds, where the entire complement of Fort Ellis was standing in formation under the flagpole. A reviewing stand had been erected, and Edward's wife Megan and their daughter, Mary Kate, were already there, seated on the stand. Neither General Terry nor Edward would be seated, but would stand at the front and return the salutes of the soldiers as they passed in review.

"Regiment! Pass in review!" the regimental commander ordered, and as the band played stirring marches, the soldiers, company by company and troop by troop, passed in review. When the parade was over, General Terry presented Edward with his honorable discharge papers.

One of those watching the parade was Boyd Ackerman. He wasn't recognized, because he wearing a beard that he had not worn while he was in the army. He was dressed in coveralls and a plaid shirt and was wearing a straw hat with a broad brim that shielded the top part of his face. He couldn't help comparing the dignity and honor of the event that was ending Colonel Hamilton's military career with the ignominious end of his own army service.

"Enjoy it while you can, Edward," he said. "You will pay for what you did to me."

He watched as first Colonel Hamilton's wife, and then his daughter, gave him a hug.

"You will pay," he said again.

Deer Lodge, Montana Territory

The train ride from Bozeman to Deer Lodge took six hours, but it was six hours of luxury because Edward had secured tickets in the Palace Car. Unlike the day cars, which had facing seats on either side of the aisle, the Palace Car had big, uncrowded, overstuffed, reclining chairs. They ate in the dining car, their meal served on shining china, with real silverware and sparkling crystal goblets.

When they reached Deer Lodge, Edward secured a two-room suite on the second floor of the Deer

Lodge Hotel. They remained as residents at the hotel for the six months it took to build the house at Brimstone, an exact replica of Denbigh Castle, Edward's ancestral home in England.

Eagle County, Colorado

The metal bit jangled against the horse's teeth. The horse's hooves clattered on the hard rock, and the leather saddle creaked beneath the weight of its rider. The rider, Falcon MacCallister, had a weathered face and hair the color of dried oak. But it was his eyes that people noticed. Deeply lined from hard years, they opened onto a soul that was stoked by experiences that would fill the lifetimes of three men. His boots were dusty and well-worn, and the metal of his spurs had become dull with time. He wore a Colt .44 at his hip, and carried a Winchester .44–40 in his saddle sheath.

Falcon dismounted, unhooked his canteen and took a swallow, then poured some water into his hat. He held it in front of his horse. The horse drank thirstily, though Falcon knew that the small amount of water did little to slake the animal's thirst. The horse drank all the water, then began nuzzling Falcon for more.

"Sorry, Lightning," Falcon said quietly. "But that's the best I can do for now. We'll be in town in about ten more miles. We'll spend the night there before we go out to the ranch, and I promise you, once I get you there, you'll have all the water you can drink; I'll get you some oats and put you up in a nice comfortable stall. But don't go flirting with any young filly you might see in there. We won't be staying but one night, and all you'll do is wind up breaking her heart."

The horse whinnied.

"Don't tell me no. I know you. I know you better than you know yourself. I tell you what, why don't I just walk you for a couple of miles, then ride the last eight? How would you like that? You wouldn't have to carry my carcass as far."

Lightning whickered, and nodded, and Falcon reached up to squeeze his ear.

"All right, let's go."

Falcon had walked for no more than a mile when he heard whistles and a loud popping sound behind him. Looking around, he saw a stagecoach coming down out of the high country and rolling across the flats, the six-horse team maintaining an easy lope. The wheels of the swiftly moving stage kicked up a billowing trail of dust to roll and swirl on the road behind it, making it easy to track its path.

As the coach drew closer, Falcon stepped to one side, intending to let it pass, but the driver pulled the coach to a stop as he approached.

"Whoa! Whoa there, horses!"

The driver set the brake as the trailing dust now came forward, overtaking the coach. Falcon heard some coughing from inside.

"Falcon MacCallister," the driver said. "I thought this might be you when I seen you from way back there. I told Darrell it was you. Didn't I, Darrell? Didn't I say that I believe that feller walkin' up there is Falcon MacCallister?"

"Yes, sir, that's what you said all right," the shotgun guard answered.

"Hello, Green. I thought you'd given up driving stagecoaches," Falcon said.

"Yeah, well, ever' thing else I tried was just too damn borin'. What you doin' out here walkin'? Lightnin' gone lame?"

"No, I was just givin' him a break."

"Why don't you give him a real break? Tie him on to the back, then climb in. You can ride the rest of the way with us into town, and maybe buy me 'n Darrell a drink."

"Sounds like a deal that's too good to pass up," Falcon said. "I will just take you up on the offer."

Falcon tied Lightning on to the back, then climbed into the coach. One of the passengers was a notions drummer, going to MacCallister to sell his wares to the merchants there. The salesman was short, with a narrow, pockmarked face and a hooked nose. The second passenger was overweight, red-faced, and sweating a lot. Falcon recognized the lone woman passenger. It was Karen Bobe, a very pretty blonde who was accompanied by her eight-year-old son, Sterling.

"Are you the cause for our stopping in the middle of nowhere?" the overweight man asked angrily. "It's bad enough with the dust coming in through the windows as it is, without having to stop to pick up some saddle bum."

"I'm sorry you were inconvenienced, sir," Falcon said, speaking pleasantly despite the harshness of the man's words. "But Mr. Orr is a good driver; he'll have us in MacCallister on time."

"No thanks to you," the sweating man said. "You may be assured, sir, that I will complain to the management about this, and I've no doubt but that I can get the driver fired."

"Hello, Mr. MacCallister," the young mother said.

"Hello, Mrs. Bobe," Falcon replied, touching the brim of his hat. "I hope John is doing well. Hello, Sterling," he added, speaking to the young boy.

"Hello, Mr. MacCallister," Sterling said.

"MacCallister?" the overweight bald man said. "Your name is MacCallister?"

"He's Falcon MacCallister," Sterling said. "I've read books about him."

"Oh, well, uh, look, Mr. MacCallister, about what I said about you being a saddle bum, I didn't mean anything by that. I hope there are no hard feelings."

Falcon nodded, but purposely didn't respond. Instead, he looked out the window at the passing countryside.

"Mr. MacCallister, what's a fella like you ridin' in a common stage for?" the drummer asked. "Why, I'd think you'd be ridin' in your own private coach."

Falcon chuckled. "In a way, you might say I am doing that, since I own this stage line."

The drummer laughed as well. "I reckon you got a point there."

"You own this stage line?" the overweight complaining man said.

"Yes."

"Well I, uh, of course, understand why the driver would stop for you."

"Mr. Orr is a good man," Falcon said without further elaboration.

* * *

Three miles ahead of the coach two men, Harvey Hood and Mo Fong, stood behind a rock, just at the top of a long grade.

"I gotta take a leak," Hood said, stepping to one side.

"Damn!" Fong said. "You have to piss uphill from me? It's running over my shoes."

Hood laughed. "You coulda moved."

"You should 'a pissed downhill."

"How much longer 'til the stagecoach gets here?" Hood asked.

"How the hell do I know? Fifteen minutes, half an hour, an hour maybe. I just know it normally gets into MacCallister around noon."

Hood looked up at the sun. "Looks to me like it ain't that far from noon now."

"Then it shouldn't be too much longer."

"How much money do you reckon that coach is carryin'?" Hood asked.

"How much money you got now?" Fong replied.

"I ain't got no money a' tall right now. I couldn' even buy a beer if we was in a saloon."

"Then it don't really matter how much the coach is carryin', does it? Whatever it is will be more than we have."

"You got that right."

"Wait a minute," Fong said. "I just seen it around the bend down there. It's got to climb up the hill, but it won't be much longer."

By now they could hear the sounds of the driver urging the team up the grade.

"Heah! Get on up there now!" the driver shouted.

"Get ready," Fong said.

Hood and Fong pulled their masks down over their faces and waited. Then, just as the coach reached them, Fong stepped out in the road and fired his pistol. The guard dropped his shotgun and grabbed his shoulder. Hood pointed his pistol toward the driver, and the driver pulled back on the reins, bringing the team to a halt.

Inside the coach, the passengers heard the sound of gunfire outside and felt the coach rumble to an unscheduled halt.

"What is it?" the sweating fat man asked in fear. "What's going on?"

The sweating man looked back toward the seat that had been occupied by Falcon; it was empty, and the door was open.

"Where did he go?"

"He jumped out when he heard the shot," the salesman said.

"You mean the great MacCallister has left us to our own devices?"

They heard loud angry voices outside, but at first they couldn't understand what was being said. Then someone appeared just outside the stage. He was wearing a wearing a hood over his face, and he was holding a pistol in his hand.

"You folks in the coach," he shouted in a loud, gruff voice. "Climb on out of there!"

"Look here! I paid for my passage in this coach and I will not be ordered out by some road agent," the sweating man said.

"Mister, you'll either climb down on your own, or I'll shoot you and drag your fat ass out by your heels."

The man got out, followed by Mrs. Bobe and her son, Sterling. The salesman was the last passenger to exit.

In addition to the masked man who was rousting the passengers, they could see that a second masked man was holding his gun on the driver. The shotgun guard was bleeding from a wound in his shoulder.

"Driver, throw down the mail pouch," the dismounted highwayman said.

"I'll throw you down the mail pouch," the driver said. "But I'm tellin' you now, there ain't no money in it. There ain't nothin' but letters. I know, 'cause I loaded it myself."

"All right, we'll just have to take what we can from your passengers. What about you, lady? How much money do you have?"

"Twelve dollars," Mrs. Bobe said.

"All right, I'll take that money. And that broach you're wearin'. We ought to be able to get somethin' for it."

"You can have the twelve dollars, but you're not getting the broach. This was my mother's broach."

"Yeah? Well, ain't that sweet. It might have been your mama's broach, but it's mine now."

"Leave the lady alone," the salesman said. "How much is that broach going to be worth anyway? It obviously has more sentimental value than actual value."

"Who asked you to butt in?"

At that very moment, Falcon was clinging to the boot of the coach. He hadn't jumped down when he heard the shot, he had merely climbed out the side of the coach, opposite from the road agents. Now slowly, and quietly, he eased himself up onto the top of the coach, keeping behind the luggage and cargo that was there. Then, when he was in position, and with his pistol in hand, he raised up just high enough to see over the top of the luggage. He could see both agents, one still mounted and holding his gun on the driver and wounded shotgun guard, the other on the ground with the passengers he had just forced out of the coach.

"I said give me that broach!" the man on the ground said. "Keep 'em covered for a moment," he said to his partner, and he put his own pistol back in the holster.

That was all the opening Falcon needed. He stood up with his gun pointed toward the man on the horse.

"Drop your gun, mister!" he said.

"What? Where the hell did you come from?"

"I'm not going to ask you again," Falcon said, cocking his pistol and extending his arm toward the mounted road agent. The road agent dropped his pistol and Falcon turned quickly toward the one on the ground who, abandoning his quest for the broach, had started for his own pistol.

"That would be a very bad mistake," Falcon said.

The road agent stopped.

"You," Falcon said to the fat, sweating man. "Take his pistol from his holster."

"I would have to get close to him to take his gun. No, sir, not me. I'm not risking my life," the sweating man said.

Karen Bobe reached for the gun. "I'll get it," she said resolutely.

"Good for you," Falcon said.

"Darrell, how are you getting along?" Falcon asked the wounded shotgun guard."

"It ain't that bad," Darrell replied.

"You," Falcon said to the salesman. "Do you think you could tie their horses on to the back of the coach?"

"Yes, sir," the salesman answered.

"Good man."

"Wait a minute here!" the fat man said. "Surely you don't intend for these two outlaws to ride the rest of the way into town with us? In the stagecoach? No, sir, I will not have it!"

"You can wait here alongside the road until the next coach comes along," Falcon suggested. "Of course, there might be someone in that coach who would object to picking you up. They might think you were a . . . what is it you called me?"

"I believe he called you a saddle bum," Karen Bobe said.

Falcon chuckled. "Yes, I believe he did. You two men, climb up here on top of the coach. We'll ride the rest of the way into town up here."

"Oh. Well if they are going to be up there . . . ," the fat man started, but the salesman interrupted him.

"Why don't you just shut up for a while? You have been boorish from the moment you got on this stage," the salesman said.

"Boorish?"

"I think that's the word," the salesman said.

"Yes, that is absolutely the word," Karen Bobe said.

"Well, I never . . ." the fat man blustered.

"I'm sure you don't," the driver said. "And if you don't shut up now, I'll have you ridin' up here with the outlaws."

When the coach rolled down Kate Street in MacCallister an hour later, the would-be road agents were sitting on top with Falcon, who had both under guard. Their horses were tied on to the back, alongside Lightning, and the unusual entry of the coach, with Falcon, who they all recognized, riding on top of the coach, holding his pistol on two men, was most curious. A crowd began to gather and they hurried alongside the coach, following it down the street. The coach stopped in front of the statue of the town's namesake, James Ian MacCallister, Falcon's father. By now the crowd had grown to a substantial number.

Like all the other residents of MacCallister, Sheriff Bill Ferrell had seen the rather unusual arrival of the stagecoach.

"Kelly," he said to his deputy. "Come with me; it looks like Falcon has got us a couple of prisoners."

Kelly took his hat from a hook, then joined the sheriff for the stroll down to the stage depot.

"Hello, Sheriff," Falcon called down from the top of the coach. "I brought you some company."

"I see you did. What happened?"

"They shot Darrell and tried to hold up the coach."

"Ha, and just their bad luck you happened along while it was goin' on."

"I didn't happen along, I was in the coach," Falcon

said as he jumped down. "I haven't gotten a name for either one of them."

"That's all right, I know them," Sheriff Ferrell said. "That one is Mo Fong, that one is Harvey Hood." He pointed to each man in kind. "Kelly, climb up there and cuff them."

"Yes, sir," Kelly said.

"You know there's a reward for these two galoots, don't you? A hundred dollars apiece," Sheriff Ferrell said.

"Is that a fact? I tell you what, Mrs. Bobe disarmed this one, so give her the reward for him. And since Darrell got shot, you can give him the reward for the other one."

"Mr. MacCallister, you don't have to do that!" Karen Bobe said, but the broad smile on her face displayed her pleasure over his act.

"Well now, thank you, Falcon," Darrell said. "A hunnert dollars damn near makes it worth gettin' shot in the shoulder."

From the *MacCallister Eagle:*

ROAD AGENTS THWARTED

Harvey Hood and Mo Fong will terrorize stagecoach passengers no more. On the 14th instant, the above mentioned brigands lay in wait for the Dixon to MacCallister stagecoach. As the coach approached they shot, from ambuscade, Darrell Bartmess, the shotgun guard. Green Orr, the coach driver, was forced to halt the team as the two outlaws, wearing masks, called upon the coach and its passengers to give up any money in their possession.

The outlaws did not count upon the presence of Falcon MacCallister who not only owns the stagecoach line, but had only a moment earlier, come aboard the coach as a passenger. MacCallister, upon perceiving that an attempted robbery was in place, secreted himself until the opportunity was presented for him to intervene. MacCallister, with the assistance of a brave lady passenger, Mrs. Karen Bobe, disarmed the would-be robbers.

There was a two-hundred-dollar reward being offered for the capture of Hood and Fong. At MacCallister's insistence, one hundred dollars went to Mrs. Bobe, and the other one hundred dollars to Darrell Bartmess, who is currently recovering from his gunshot wound in the shoulder.

Hood and Fong have both been tried, found guilty, and sentenced to twenty years in prison, each.

CHAPTER THREE

From the *Butte Daily Miner*, June 17, 1879:

ARMY OF DESPERADOES
TERRORIZING MONTANA

Boyd Ackerman,
Disgraced Major, In Command

Boyd Ackerman, late a major in the United States Army, has been riding roughshod throughout the entire territory of Montana. Ackerman was cashiered from the army for cowardice when he refused to come to the relief of the gallant Colonel Cahill and his brave soldiers. Ackerman's cowardice is all the more despicable when it is realized that he is a graduate of West Point, a school that hitherto could pride itself on the honor of its graduates.

Ackerman has assembled a large band of brigands thought to be former soldiers who, trained in military skills and tactics, have become a formidable gang of outlaws. Their action has been likened to the nefarious activities of the famous Rebel guerilla of the recent war, William Quantrill. Unlike Quantrill, though, Ackerman and his minions make no pretense to serve a cause other than their own.

Law officials have, so far, been rendered impotent in any attempt to deal with Ackerman because his army, which has earned the sobriquet Ackerman's Raiders, is much too large to be dealt with by any wearer of a lawman's badge.

Diamond City, Montana Territory—1880

The town was located alongside the Big Belt Mountain Range. It was built along Confederate Gulch Road running east and west, with four short, intersecting east and west streets.

Despite the size of the town, it had a bank, which flourished because of the success of a nearby placer mine. As a rule, they moved the money out as quickly as it came in because the town was too small for a city marshal, and with just over one thousand in the entire county, the sheriff's office consisted of one sheriff and one deputy to cover three thousand square miles.

On this sunny afternoon in early September, a formation of men riding in a column of twos was about a mile out of town when its leader, a tall, slender man with a Vandyke beard, held up his hand to call a halt.

"Corporal Jones, post," he called.

One of the riders pulled out of the formation, then rode up alongside.

"Yes, sir, Major Ackerman," Corporal Jones said.

"Reconnoiter the town, Corporal, then come back and tell me what you see."

"Yes, sir."

"Sergeant Casey, dismiss the men. Have them prepare a good meal. I don't know when we will be able to eat again."

"Yes, sir," Sergeant Casey said. Then, turning in his saddle, he gave the order.

"Look after your horses, and prepare your meal. Company, dismissed," Casey called.

"Hey, Waters," one of the men called. "You got 'ny that deer meat left?"

"You got 'ny taters?"

"Yeah."

"I think we can do somethin' then."

Ackerman had held back a couple of biscuits and bacon from this morning's breakfast, and he went over to sit down under a tree and eat them as his men built a cooking fire.

As Jones rode into town on Confederate Gulch Road, several people glanced at him, perhaps noting that he was a stranger, but paying no further attention to him. Jones rode from one end of the little town to the other. Some children were out on the playground of the school. Two women were standing together, talking, in front of the mercantile store. There was a wagon up on a jack-stand with one wheel removed, and somebody was replacing the iron band on the wheel. Two old men were sitting in front of the hardware store playing checkers.

Jones passed the saloon and got a whiff of the smell of beer. He almost went in to buy one, but he knew Major Ackerman wouldn't approve, and he didn't want to do anything to piss the major off. He learned a long time ago that it wasn't a good idea to get the major angry.

Reaching the far end, Jones turned around and rode back through the town. Not until he was out of town did he urge his horse into a gallop. He was met by the advanced picket when he returned to where the company had made its temporary bivouac.

"The major says to give him a report as soon as you get back," the picket said. "And Sergeant Casey, he fried you up a piece of ham."

Jones nodded, then reported to the major.

"How many armed men did you see?" Major Ackerman asked.

"Ten or fifteen."

"When I send you on a scouting mission, I want a precise answer. Ten or fifteen isn't good enough. Was it ten? Or was it fifteen?" Ackerman asked.

"I only counted ten, but they was the ones out on the street. I heard some sounds comin' from the saloon, I figure there's got to be one or two in there that's packin'. And in the stores and such, maybe two or three more. So I was saying fifteen, just to be on the safe side."

"Did you check the roofs of the buildings?"

"Yes, sir, I looked up at 'em, but I didn't see nothin' up there."

"All right, get the piece of ham Sergeant Casey cooked for you, and eat it quickly. I want to hit the town at exactly two o'clock."

It wasn't a casual decision to hit the town at two o'clock. Ackerman knew from observation that two o'clock was the hour that people seemed the most sleepy, and least alert.

In the Diamond City Bank, Joel Randall had just finished packaging the gold. By assay and weight, he had just over two hundred troy ounces of gold, processed from the nearby placer mines.

"How much is that worth, Mr. Randall?" someone asked.

"As of this morning gold was nineteen ninety-eight per ounce. That makes this shipment just under four thousand dollars."

"That's a lot of money."

"Yes, it is. I'll be glad when it's taken out of here. How many guards do we have, Mr. Sharp?"

"Well, for now, there's just me. But there'll be at least two guards once it gets on board the stage."

"Yeah, well, I don't care about it, once it leaves here. It's while it's here that I'm worried about."

"All right, men," Ackerman said, giving his command their last-minute instructions. "We'll ride into town quietly. But once we hit the bank, we'll make as much racket as we can while riding out. We'll ride out shooting up the town. I don't want to see any citizen on the street. I want windows shot out, I want roofs cleared. Any questions?"

"No, sir."

"Then let's go."

Ackerman timed their ride into town so that at exactly two o'clock they arrived at the west end of town on Confederate Gulch Road. The fact that there were nine of them, one rider out front and the other eight riding in a precise military formation behind their leader, got everyone's attention. It also seemed rather odd that, though the group was acting as if they were military, they were not wearing army uniforms. Not one person who saw them arrive connected this group of riders with Ackerman's Raiders.

"Road guards deploy!" Ackerman shouted as they came close to the bank.

Baker and Jerrod, the two men in the second rank, left the formation. Baker rode ahead while Jerrod took up a position behind the formation.

When they reached the bank there were only seven remaining of the original group.

"Corporal Jones, you, Smith, Powell, and Boyle will remain out here. Sergeant Casey, you and Waters, with me."

Not one man bothered to mask themselves. Ackerman knew that because of their modus operandi, everyone would soon figure out who did it.

With weapons drawn, Ackerman, Casey, and Waters burst into the bank. The bank guard went for his pistol, but he was shot down before he could even get his gun drawn.

There were three customers in the bank, two men and a woman. All three put their hands up in fear.

"Mr. Randall," Ackerman said. "I believe you have a gold shipment ready to go."

"What makes you think that?" Randall replied.

"Don't insult my intelligence, sir," Ackerman said. "I know you have a gold shipment all packed, and waiting for the stagecoach. I'll take it off your hands, now."

"You're Ackerman, aren't you?" Randall asked. "You're the one they call Major Ackerman."

"If you know that, you know that I do everything with military precision. And your hesitance over responding to my demand is putting this entire operation in jeopardy. I caution you now, sir, I will not let anything jeopardize my mission. You have to the count of three to turn over the gold, or I will shoot you."

"No! no!" Randall said. Picking up the packages from behind the teller's cage, he slid them through the window. "Here they are!"

"Thank you, you have been most cooperative," Ackerman said. The gold was in six packages, and he handed two to Casey and two to Waters, taking the last two himself. Then the three men started backing out of the bank.

It was at that precise moment that Randall brought a weapon up from its concealed position behind the counter. Ackerman shot him, then turned toward the three customers who had witnessed both shootings.

"Lie on the floor, facedown," he ordered.

"Please, mister, you're not goin' to shoot us, are you?" one of the men asked.

"You will address me as major," Ackerman said. "Make no move and you won't be shot."

Ackerman, Casey, and Waters backed out of the bank, then mounted the three horses that had been held for them by Jones, Smith, and Boyle.

"Sergeant Casey, recall the road guards," Ackerman ordered.

"Road guards, recover!" Casey shouted, and the four men who had been deployed to each end of the road galloped back to join the formation.

"Withdraw with fire!" Ackerman ordered. "Bugler, sound the 'Charge'!"

With Powell blowing "Charge" on the bugle, the mounted column galloped away, shooting as they departed. Three local citizens, with rifles, made the mistake of coming out into the street to challenge the bank robbers, but they were shot down. Ackerman and his men thundered out of town, leaving seven dead behind them. Two of the dead were a mother and her daughter, hit by stray bullets.

Centerville, Montana Territory

Just outside the town of Centerville, Ackerman paid off his men, then gave them "furlough" until he needed them again.

"Don't go into town in any group larger than three people," Ackerman said. "Otherwise you might arouse suspicion."

Centerville was on the Northern Pacific Railroad, which made it one of the more bustling towns in Montana. Primarily a mining town, its population base was made up of Irish and Cornish, and though there were no fights between them, neither did they associate with each other.

"What about findin' us some women?" Waters suggested.

"Women later, whiskey first," Boyle said.

"Where you reckon a saloon is?" Decker asked.

"Hell, it ought not to be hard to find one. Just follow your nose," Boyle replied.

As Boyle had suggested, finding something to drink wasn't all that difficult. Every other building, it seemed, was a saloon. With no predetermined purpose in mind other than to find drink, the three men headed toward one, identified by the sign out front as the Hard Rock Miner.

Although it was early afternoon, the saloon was crowded with noisy customers. At the back of the saloon a bald-headed piano player was pounding away on a scarred, and out-of-tune, instrument.

"Bartender, bring us a bottle!" Waters said, shouting to be heard above the din. The bartender pulled a bottle from a shelf behind the bar, handed it to the customer, then accepted, as payment, a pinch of gold dust.

"You boys must've have good diggin's," the bartender said.

"Yeah, well, don't expect us to tell you where it's at," Boyle said.

The bartender chuckled. "Can't say as I blame you."

* * *

Ackerman had taken a hotel room, and, after a bath and change of clothes was now occupying a table in the Grub Stake Saloon. He stood out from all the others in the saloon because he was dressed like a gentleman, complete with a jacket, vest, and cravat.

"Oh, look at him," Diana said. Diana was a prostitute who worked the saloon for business. She got a share of all the drinks she could convince a customer to buy her, and the saloon got a share of her fees when she took a customer upstairs. The other bar girls sometimes called her "Diana Duh," because of her irritating habit of saying "duh" when she wished to make a point.

"What about him?" Susana asked.

"Well, duh! Can't you see that he is dressed differently from everyone else in here? You know that someone like that has a lot of money. And he is probably a gentleman, too."

"He's probably not interested in women, either," Susana said. "At least, not our kind."

"He's in here, isn't he? He wouldn't even be in here if he wasn't interested in our kind of women. Duh."

Ackerman was disappointed with the amount of money they had gotten at Diamond City. He had thought it would be much more than it was, but even taking thirty percent, he had only made twelve hundred dollars. There had to be a bigger score somewhere.

Ackerman had picked up a newspaper at the hotel desk, and as he sat at the table, he began to read.

ACKERMAN'S RAIDERS STRIKE AGAIN

The small town of Diamond City was terrorized Tuesday, when Boyd Ackerman and his group of former soldiers robbed the bank. They killed Joel Randall, the well-respected president of the bank, as well as Mitchell Sharp, the bank guard. Five more citizens fell before the bullets of this nefarious gang of outlaws, including Mrs. Coretta Cline and her four-year-old daughter, Amy.

Ackerman's Raiders are led by Major Boyd Ackerman, a disgraced army officer who has put to use, in the most nefarious way, his military training. He has been terrorizing Montana for the last four years with his brilliant military tactics and his skillful employment of well-disciplined military troops.

Ackerman smiled at the mention of his "brilliant military tactics," and his "skillful employment of well-disciplined" military troops.

"I see you are smiling," one of the girls of the saloon said, approaching him. "Is it because of me?"

Ackerman folded the paper over and looked up at the woman who had approached him. Though the dissipation of her profession had taken its toll on her, she was skilled enough with the artistic application of makeup and the provocative way of wearing her clothes that she could still elicit enough interest to do a brisk business as a prostitute.

"I might be," Ackerman said, smiling at her. He stood up and pulled out a chair for her. "Won't you join me for a drink?"

"Oh, such a gentleman you are," Diana said.

When Ackerman got up from Diana's bed half an hour later, her left eye was black and swollen nearly shut. Her lip was bleeding, both of her breasts were bruised, and she was crying.

"I suppose you won't be doing any more business tonight," Ackerman said.

"Please, mister, don't hit me again. Please," Diana said.

"How much do you get for overnight?"

"No, please, I . . ."

"Don't worry, I have no intention of spending the night with you. I just want to know how much you get for overnight?"

"Five dollars," she said.

Ackerman took some money from his wallet. "Here is ten dollars," he said. "Stay in your room for the rest of the night."

"Ten dollars? You're giving me ten dollars?" Diana asked, her demeanor changing.

"Yes, ten dollars. Unless you have a whore's code of honor that says you won't take the money unless you earn it."

"Well, duh, you beat me up. I'd say I earned it."

Ackerman dropped the money on the bed, then left her room. Diana grabbed the ten-dollar bill and held it tightly. She had never made this much at one time before.

CHAPTER FOUR

Falcon was following the White River north, not sure where it would take him and not particularly caring. The river snaked out across the gently undulating sagebrush-covered prairie before him, shining gold in the setting sun, sometimes white where it broke over rocks, other times shimmering a deep blue-green in the swirling eddies and trapped pools.

The Danforth Hills to the north were purple and mysterious, but the Great Hogback, a range of wild and ragged mountains to the west of him, were dotted with aspen, pine, cottonwood, and willow. There were bare spots on the mountains in between the trees. These bare spots of rock and dirt were sometimes gray and sometimes red, but always distant and foreboding.

Late in the afternoon Lightning scared up a rabbit, and it bounded down the trail ahead of him.

"How about that, Lightning, you just found my supper for me." He stopped, pulled his rifle from the saddle scabbard, looped his leg around the pommel, raised the rifle to his shoulder, rested his elbow on his knee, and squeezed the trigger. He saw a puff of fur and spray of blood fly up from the rabbit. The rabbit flopped over, then lay perfectly still.

Falcon made camp under a stand of aspens, started a fire, skinned and cleaned the rabbit, then skewered it on a green willow branch and suspended it over the fire between two forked limbs.

After his meal, Falcon lay down by the fire and watched while the red sparks rose on a heated column of air. There, the still-glowing red and orange sparks joined the blue and white stars that were scattered across the velvet black of the night sky.

Falcon had no particular destination in mind, and had no specific reason for leaving the last town. Nor did he have any reason for traveling around as he did. He owned a ranch, but it was being efficiently run by his foreman and cowhands. He was part owner of the MacCallister Stagecoach Line, but it was also being run by a manager. He had a producing gold mine, again, being managed by trusted associates. He had enough money to spend the rest of his days in a big mansion, tended to hand and foot by house servants if he wanted to.

But he didn't want to. Perhaps if his wife and children were still alive, he could be content in such an environment. But they weren't alive, and, as his brother Jamie Ian once pointed out, Falcon had an even worse case of wanderlust than had their father. He, too, had wandered around a great deal, but eventually he settled down.

"Are you ever going to settle down, Falcon?" his sister, Kathleen, asked.

"Probably not," Falcon replied, and she didn't question him. It was exactly the answer she expected to hear.

The country was beautiful, with unbroken grassland leading to the valley of the Yellowstone River, the mountain ranges making up the Bitterroot to the left, the Big Belt just ahead, as Johnny McVey drove the herd of five thousand north. He had brought the herd all the way up from Texas, supervising a crew of thirty cowboys. They had crossed the Yellowstone and were now following the Gallatin up into Montana.

Johnny had trained a guide bull, which he named Oscar. Oscar made the drive unbelievably easy. When cows strayed, his bawl and his bell brought them back. At night the cowboys muffled the bell and tethered the bull with the horses, feeding him corn from a skillet. The next morning, no matter what time they started, when the cows heard the bell they fell in behind their leader.

On the ninety-third day of the drive the herd reached the Powder River Basin, and Johnny was struck by the majesty of what he saw, not only the mountains, but the limitless prairie. There was buffalo grass, bluestem, slough grass, bunchgrass— miles and miles of it—and in some places it was as high as his horse's knees.

About midmorning, Johnny looked up to see several riders riding hard toward him.

"Hank," he called to one of his trail hands, "I don't know who these men are, but tell the boys to be ready for them."

"You think maybe they're rustlers?" Will asked.

Johnny pulled his pistol and checked the chambers to see that it was loaded.

"I don't know, but I've come this far, and I'm not taking any chances."

Because of the clear air, distances were foreshortened, and it was several minutes before the men were close enough to make them out individually. The man in the middle leading the others sat tall in his saddle. Johnny recognized him as Colonel Hamilton, but it was the rider next to him who caught his attention. At first he thought it was another cowboy. The rider was certainly dressed that way. But as they drew closer, Johnny saw that it was a young woman.

"It's all right, boys," he called to the others. "That's Colonel Hamilton."

Johnny urged his horse into a ground-eating lope, closing the distance between them. And Edward and Mary Kate, who was riding beside him, seeing Johnny coming toward them, galloped ahead of the others. They met in the middle.

"You're here! I didn't expect you for another two weeks, but one of my men told me he saw a herd moving this way and I knew it had to be you," Edward said, holding out his hand to clasp Johnny's. "Welcome to Brimstone Ranch."

"It's good to be here," Johnny replied, though he had not taken his eyes off Mary Kate, nor had she taken her eyes off him.

"Where are my manners?" Edward asked. "Mr. McVey, this is my daughter, Mary Kate."

"Pleased to meet you, ma'am," Johnny said, tipping his hat.

"And you," Mary Kate replied with a broad smile.

"Any trouble on the drive, Johnny?"

"No. It's been tiring for the men and the livestock, but we didn't have any real trouble."

"I'm running twenty-five thousand head now," Edward said. "But everyone I've talked to told me I needed to get some Texas beef up here to mix with my herd, so that's what I did. And my men will help drive them the rest of the way."

"How much farther is it?"

"You're almost there. Only a few more miles." Edward pointed to a hill just behind him. "Once you crest that rise, you'll be able to see Denbigh Castle."

"Denbigh Castle?"

Edward laughed. "Well, it isn't really Denbigh Castle. Denbigh Castle is back in England. But I got the plans and gave them to my builders here, so it is close as you can get to Denbigh Castle without being the actual building."

A few minutes later, Johnny, Edward, and Mary Kate were at the crest of the hill, and some few miles in the distance, Johnny saw the house. He had never actually seen a castle before, but anytime he had ever imagined one, it looked just like this.

Almost one thousand miles south of Denbigh Castle, Falcon MacCallister was just riding into a small town, and he checked the sign to see where he was.

WELCOME TO
MEEKER
Town of Friendly People

Falcon was impressed by the bustling activity of the small town. It was alive with commerce; from freight wagons lumbering down the street, to carpenters erecting a new building, to a store clerk who was sweeping the front porch of his place of employment. A black dog was curled up on the corner of the porch. The store clerk swept around him.

On either side of the street, well-maintained and clean boardwalks ran from one end of the town to the other. At a few places, there were planks stretched all the way across the road so that pedestrians could cross from one side of the street to the other without having to walk in the dirt or mud. Just ahead, Falcon saw a young woman and a small girl crossing, so he slowed the pace of Lightning to let them cross safely before he reached the plank.

When the woman and girl had successfully negotiated the street, Falcon clucked at his horse, and it stepped up the pace, heading toward the livery, a little farther down.

Then, quite unexpectedly, Falcon heard several gunshots from the other end of the street. Looking back toward the sound, he saw three men backing out of a building. A sign identified the building as the Bank of Meeker.

The three men backed out to a fourth man who was holding the reins to three more horses.

"Off the street! Everyone off the street! We're comin' out shootin'!" one of the men shouted, and he fired a couple of shots down through the middle of the street. With shouts and screams, the people who were on the street when the shooting started scattered.

The three robbers climbed quickly into the saddles. Mounted now, they started shooting up the town as they began their getaway, galloping in Falcon's direction.

"Halt!" a man shouted, stepping off the boardwalk and pointing a gun toward the four men.

The four riders fired at him, and the brave young man who attempted to stop them went down, twisting around as he fell. Falcon saw the sun flash off a badge on his vest.

Most of the townspeople had cleared out of the way, but looking across the street, Falcon saw the young girl who had been with the woman who crossed the planking just a moment earlier. Whether curious, or confused, Falcon didn't know, but the little girl had wandered out into the street.

"Rebecca! No! Come back here!" the little girl's mother shouted.

The window of the shop right behind the mother shattered as a bullet hit it, and great shards of glass came crashing down onto the boardwalk around her.

The woman screamed, but again, she called out to her daughter. "Rebecca, come back!"

Urging Lightning into a gallop, Falcon raced toward the little girl, bent down from the saddle, and scooped her up. Frightened, the little girl began crying, and Falcon galloped back over to the little girl's mother, dismounted, and handed the child to her.

"Keep her with you. Go back inside, now!" he shouted.

Falcon's immediate goal was to get the child and her mother to safety, but now he found himself in the path of the robbers' escape route.

Turning toward the robbers, he saw they were rapidly closing the distance between them and him. He didn't need to see the muzzle flashes and puffs of smoke to know that they were shooting. He could hear the bullets whizzing by his head so close that they were no longer zinging, now they were actually popping.

Raising his pistol, Falcon fired at one who was closest to him. He saw a puff of dust and a mist of blood fly up from the impact of the bullet. Then, even as that robber was tumbling from his saddle, Falcon aimed at the next nearest one, firing a second time. Again he hit his target, and this one fell to join the other in the middle of the street.

The remaining two robbers realized then that they couldn't continue to ride toward him, but there was no cross street for them to take, so their only option was to turn and gallop away in the opposite direction. Falcon aimed at them, but he didn't want to shoot them in the back. He didn't have to, because by now half a dozen of the men of the town were out in the street with rifles, shotguns, and pistols, all of them pointing toward the fleeing bank robbers.

The two remaining outlaws, realizing now that they had no place to go, reined their horses, threw their guns down in the dirt, and put their hands up. "No, no!" they shouted. "Don't shoot, don't shoot! We quit, we quit!"

With their surrender, the armed men of the town came running out into the street with their guns aimed at the two robbers.

"All right, you two, climb down off them horses," one of the armed men shouted in an authoritative voice. As Falcon watched from where he was, he saw a flash of light from the badge that was on the vest of the man giving the orders.

Falcon hurried over to the woman.

"Miss, are you and the child all right?" he asked. "Were you hit?"

"No, we're, we're fine," she answered in a weak and trembling voice. "Thank you, mister. Thank you."

At that moment another man came running up the street. He put his arms around the woman, then reached down and picked up the little girl. They stood there for a moment, then the man directed the woman and the little girl to go into the building that had had the window shot out.

The next person on the scene was the store clerk who had been sweeping the porch.

"Mister, I want you to know I ain't never seen nothin' like that in all my life," the store clerk said to Falcon. "I mean, the way you just stood out there in the middle of the street and faced down them four fellers like you done."

Falcon chuckled. "The way it turned out, I didn't have any other choice. All of a sudden I realized I was standing in the middle of the street with nowhere else to go."

"Yeah, well, that's not quite how it was," said the man who had come to embrace the woman and the little girl. "You were there because you went out to rescue my little girl. I don't know what would have happened to her if you hadn't done that, and mister, I can't thank you enough."

By now the sheriff had joined those who were congratulating Falcon. The two who had been captured were being led off.

"Mister, this town and this county owe you a debt," the sheriff said. "We recovered every dollar they took."

"How's Deputy Larson, Sheriff?" the store clerk asked.

"I'm sorry to say that he's dead," the sheriff replied.

"But at least two of his killers is dead," one of the men who had gathered around Falcon said.

"And if ever there was anybody that needed killin' it was them," the store clerk said.

"Too bad the other two weren't killed," the little girl's father said.

"They will be," the sheriff said. "They shot Dewey Larson down in front of the whole town. I don't reckon it will be very hard to get a conviction, and knowin' Judge Norton, those two galoots will be legally dangling from a rope within a week."

"And I'll be there to watch," someone said.

"Hell, more 'n likely the whole town will be."

"Are you just passing through?" the sheriff asked Falcon. "Or were you plannin' on stayin' here for a while?"

"I was planning on eating a supper I didn't have to cook, and sleeping in a bed instead of on the ground," Falcon said.

"Ha! Well, mister, I can guarantee you that we'll do

that for you. You can eat in any café you want, and the meal will be free. And you can stay free in the hotel as well. The town will pick up the charges."

"And if you're a drinkin' man, you're welcome in my saloon tonight," another man said. "My name is Tilsdale, and I own the Silver Strike Saloon. Come on down and visit us. The drinks will be on the house."

"Well you folks are being mighty kind," Falcon said.

"We owe it to you, mister . . . you know what? I haven't got your name," the sheriff said.

"It's MacCallister," Falcon said. "Falcon MacCallister."

The sheriff laughed. "I'll be damned. Well, I might have known that it would have to be someone like you who did all this. The name is Wallace. Harold Wallace," the sheriff said, sticking out his hand. "I reckon you'll be wantin' to board your horse tonight, too."

"Yes."

"Abner!" Wallace called, and a moment later another man, also wearing a badge, came trotting up.

"Yes, sir, Sheriff?"

"Has Dewey's wife been told yet?"

"Dewey's brother has gone down to tell her."

"That's good. She'll take it better from him than one of us, I expect. You tell Tom Nunlee that Dewey is to be given the best he's got."

"Yes, sir."

"This is the man who stopped them," Sheriff Wallace said. "His name is Falcon MacCallister. I reckon you've heard of him."

"Yes, sir, I sure have!" Abner said, sticking his hand out toward Falcon.

"I want you to put Mr. MacCallister's horse in our private stable behind the jail tonight," he said. Wallace looked over at Falcon. "You'll be wanting your saddlebags, I take it?"

"And my rifle," Falcon said, reaching for the items.

"What say we get you checked into your hotel first, then get you fed? After that, you're on your own. And whenever you're ready to leave, why, you can just come down and get your horse." Wallace pointed. "That's the jail down there. The stable is right behind."

"Thanks."

Falcon followed Sheriff Wallace to the hotel, where the sheriff checked him in and told the clerk that the city would be paying the bill.

"Take his saddlebags up to his room now, so I can take him over to Kathy's Café and get him a good supper."

"Oh, you'll like Kathy's place, Mr. MacCallister. She sets a real good table."

The food at Kathy's was good, but it was a little disconcerting with everyone pointing to him, and talking about him, very quietly. After a while Kathy came over to his table. Kathy was a tall, slender woman with dark eyes and black hair. She was, Falcon couldn't help noticing, a very attractive woman.

"I'm sorry about all this," she said. "I know that all the pointing and talking about you is making you uncomfortable."

"It's all right," Falcon said. He smiled. "I've been pointed at before."

* * *

After having his supper, Falcon went into the Silver Strike Saloon, where he was cheered by all the saloon patrons as soon as he went in.

Falcon smiled self-consciously and waved at the others, then he started toward the bar.

"No, sir, Mr. MacCallister," the bartender said. "You just have you a seat over there, and one of the girls will bring you anything you want to drink. Mr. Tilsdale, he told me you'd be comin' in here, and that I was to take good care of you."

"Well, I appreciate that, bartender," Falcon said.

"What will you have, Mr. MacCallister?" one of the bargirls asked.

"A beer," Falcon said.

Falcon had one beer, then, to the disappointment of all the customers who wanted him to "have a drink with them," begged off by explaining that he had been on the trail for a couple of weeks and was anxious to sleep in a real bed tonight.

CHAPTER FIVE

That night Falcon extinguished the lantern, shucked out of his boots, pants, and shirt, and climbed into bed. It had been two weeks since he had slept in a real bed. This bed had a mattress, springs, and sheets that were almost clean.

He didn't know how long he had been asleep when something awakened him. He lay very still, barely breathing, every sense on the alert as he listened. He heard the doorknob turn, ever so slightly, and he was up instantly, reaching for the gun that lay on a table by his bed.

He moved into the darkest corner of the room and waited there. It was more than just the doorknob turning, he could hear a key being pushed into the keyhole. The key turned, and there was a solid click as the tumblers were tripped. Naked, except for a pair of skivvies, Falcon felt the night air on his skin. His senses were alert, his body alive with readiness.

Outside the hotel Falcon could heard a tinkling piano and a burst of laughter coming from the nearby Silver Strike Saloon.

Slowly the door opened, and a wedge of light spilled into the room. Falcon pulled the hammer back on his pistol, the sear making a double click as it rotated the cylinder.

"Oh!" It was a woman's voice, and in the light that was now coming into the room, he could see that it was Kathy, from the café.

"Kathy?" Falcon called.

"Where are you?" she asked.

By now Falcon had lowered the hammer and put the pistol down on the table.

"I'm over here," Falcon said.

Kathy stood in the doorway. The hall lantern back-lit the thin, cotton robe she was wearing, and he could see her body in shadow behind the cloth. It was easy to see that she was wearing nothing underneath.

"Come on in," Falcon invited as he lit a lantern on the table nearwhere he was standing. Kathy closed the door behind her.

"Have I picked a bad time?" Kathy asked.

"A bad time? I don't know. What time is it?"

"It's one o'clock in the morning."

Falcon laughed. "Now, what can be bad about one o'clock in the morning?" he asked. "I do have a question, though. How did you know which room I was in? And how did you get a key?"

"I not only own the restaurant, I also own this hotel," Kathy said.

"My. You've done very well to be such a young woman."

"I haven't done well. I married well," Kathy said.

"You're married?"

"I'm a widow. Poor Mr. Wilcox passed away at the age of eighty-three."

"I do hope he died with a smile on his face," Falcon said.

"I did what I could to please him. You don't sleep in a lot, do you?" Kathy asked, looking pointedly at Falcon in his skivvies.

"Would you be more comfortable if I got dressed?" Falcon asked.

"No, that won't be necessary," Kathy said as she pulled her own gown off, revealing a naked body, shining gold in lantern light. "You would just have to get undressed again."

At this very moment, at the other end of the street from the Starlight Hotel, Dale and Travis Hastings were in the county jail. They were the only two survivors of the failed bank robbery.

"Who did the sheriff say that feller was that kilt Toby and Andy?" Dale asked.

"His name was MacCallister. Falcon MacCallister."

"Yeah, I thought that was what he said. I've heard of him before."

"Who hasn't? Hell, he's as famous as just about anybody you can name," Travis said.

"You know what we should have done, don't you? What we should have done is, we should've joined up with Ackerman when we had the chance," Dale said.

"Why? You remember him, don't you? He was the most overbearing, arrogant son of a bitch in the whole army. Why, he'd as soon put you in the guard-house as return a salute," Travis replied.

"That was then. Besides, me 'n you seen him get his comeuppance, because we was both there when they busted him down to private and marched him off the post. He ain't in the army no more."

"But you heard what Boyle said. He's runnin' his outfit like an army."

"So what if he is? It's workin', ain't it? Boyle said he's got more money now than he's ever had in his life."

"Yeah, well, that don't take all that much, does it? Boyle ain't never had more'n two nickels to rub to-gether in his life."

"Really? Tell me, Travis, how much money do we have now?"

"We don't have none."

"That's the point. Boyle's got a lot of money. And if we had gone with 'em, we would have a lot of money now, too. And we wouldn't be sittin' here in this jail. The truth is, if we had been with Ackerman when we tried to rob that bank, we would 'a got away with it. There ain't no doubt in my mind."

"Ain't no sense in talkin' about it now," Travis said. "We're in jail an' more 'n likely, we'll be goin' to prison for a lot of years."

"No, we ain't."

"What do you mean, we ain't?"

"We're goin' to bust out of here," Dale said.

"How are we goin' to do that?"

"They didn't search my boot," Dale said.

"The derringer?"

"The derringer," Dale replied, smiling and nodding his head.

"How are you goin' to use it?"

"All we got to do is get the guard in here."

"He ain't goin' to come in here just 'cause we call him."

"He will if you try to commit suicide."

"What?"

"Not really. But we're goin' to make it look like it. Start chokin' like you took poison or somethin'. Be grabbin' your throat and gaggin' when the guard comes in here."

"All right," Travis said.

"Get ready. Guard! Guard! Help! Help! Come in here, quick!" Dale started yelling.

"What the hell's goin' on in there?" a voice called from the front of the jail building.

"Hurry, get in here! My brother's dyin'!"

They heard the door from the front part of the jail being opened.

"Now!" Dale said.

Travis put both hands to his throat, rolled his eyes back in his head, stuck his tongue out, and started making gagging sounds.

"What happened? What's goin' on?" the guard asked.

"My brother! He took some kind of poison!"

The guard opened the cell door, then came in. "What did you do a stupid thing like that for?" He walked over to look down at Travis writhing on the bed.

"To get you in here," Dale said calmly.

"What?" The guard turned toward Dale and saw the derringer in his hand. "Where did you . . ."

That was as far as the guard got before Dale pulled the trigger. The .41-caliber bullet plunged into the guard's neck and he put both hands there, then began choking as the blood not only spilled through the fingers of his hands, but also drained back into his throat. He staggered back a few steps, then fell.

"Let's get out of here," Dale said.

The two men went into the front of the jail and started jerking open drawers until they found their pistols. Strapping them on, they went out back, found their horses and saddles, and fifteen minutes later were riding quietly out of town.

Falcon was reading the paper over breakfast in Kathy's Café the next morning.

GUNFIGHT HURLS THREE MEN TO ETERNITY

Deputy Dewey Larson Killed, His Widow Mourns

MURRAY JEFFERS AND CARL MALONE
ALSO SLAIN

World Is Better Off for Their Demise

Yesterday afternoon at a time lacking fifteen minutes of four o'clock, just before

the bank was due to close, four
desperadoes, Murray Jeffers, Carl
Malone, and Dale and Travis Hastings,
entered the bank and, at gunpoint,
relieved the bank of over three thousand
dollars.

Upon exiting the bank they turned the
streets of Meeker into a battlefield hoping
to cover their escape by shooting up the
town. When at last the smoke had cleared,
three men lay dead in the street, they
being the above mentioned Jeffers and
Malone, two of the outlaws, and Deputy
Dewey Larson, who courageously stepped
into their escape path to stop them.

Assisting Deputy Larson was Falcon
MacCallister, a well-known figure
throughout the West. It was fortuitous for
our fair town that Mr. MacCallister
happened to be passing through at this
time. By his courage, and the accuracy of
his shooting, the murder of Deputy Dewey
Larson was avenged, and two of the most
pernicious desperadoes of recent years
were dispatched to their Maker, whose
mercy they can only hope for, as no one
who remains on this mortal coil would
deign to lift a prayer on their behalf.

The remaining two would-be bank
robbers in attempting to turn away from
the deadly shooting of Falcon
MacCallister encountered several armed
citizens of the town who persuaded them
to give up their ill-gotten gains and
surrender. Dale and Travis Hastings are
now residents of the city hoosegow, where
they will remain until a jury of 12 men,

good and true, will find them guilty of
murder and Judge Norton will, no doubt,
sentence them to have their necks
appropriately stretched.

Falcon was just finishing reading the news article
when Sheriff Wallace came in to the café. He stood
just inside the door for a moment and looked around
until he saw Falcon, then he came walking quickly
over to his table.

"Good morning, Sheriff," Falcon said. "Won't you
join me for breakfast?"

"I can't, I don't have time. Last night those two
bastards killed my night jailer and escaped."

"The Hastings?"

"Yes, Dale and Travis. How did you know their
names?"

"In the paper," Falcon said. "But the paper didn't
say anything about them escaping."

"That's 'cause the paper didn't know anything
about it. I don't know how those two did it but when
Deputy Parker went in to relieve Abner this morning,
he found him lying dead in the empty cell with a
bullet hole in his neck."

"I'm sorry to hear that, Sheriff," Falcon said.

"I thought maybe I ought to tell you about it,
'cause I wouldn't be surprised if they didn't have it in
mind to come after you, seein' as you killed their two
partners yesterday."

"Yes, they might at that." Falcon, finished with his
breakfast, picked up his napkin and dabbed at his
mouth. "I appreciate the warning, and I will keep

my eyes open. Are you going back to the sheriff's office now?"

"Yes."

"I'll walk back with you to get my horse."

It took the Hastings brothers a month to reach the small town of Feely, Montana. Along the way they robbed two general stores, choosing them as their targets because even though there was little money involved, they were also easier to rob. They had just gone into a saloon when Dale reached his hand out to stop his brother.

"Travis, look at that man over there in the corner with them two girls around him. Ain't that Private Jerrod sittin' over there?"

"Yeah," Travis said. "Yeah, it is. I wonder what he's doin' up here?"

"Let's find out," Dale suggested.

Jerrod recognized the two men coming toward him, and he knew that meant that they also recognized him. Slowly, he pulled his pistol from its holster and held it under the table.

"You two git," he said.

"Oh, honey, you mean you don't want our company anymore?" one of the women asked.

"There might be some shootin'," Jerrod said, and with a quick look of alarm, the two women moved.

"Hello, Jerrod," one of the two men said.

"I don't know nobody named Jerrod."

"Come on, Jerrod. We're the Hastings brothers. We was in the same barracks with you."

"What do you want?" Jerrod asked.

"Nothin'," Dale said. "We just seen you over here and thought we'd say hello."

"Well, you've said it."

"What's wrong with you?" Travis asked. "How come you ain't bein' very friendly?"

"I got all the friends I need," Jerrod said.

"What about Major Ackerman? Does he have all the friends he needs?"

"Ackerman? What are you asking me about Ackerman for?"

"Boyle invited me and Travis to join up with him and Major Ackerman," Dale said. "And while he was talkin' to us, he happened to mention that you was one of them. Are you still?"

"What if I am?"

Dale smiled. "Then we've come to the right place."

"I'll ask you again," Jerrod said. "What do you want?"

"We want to join up with you," Dale said.

Jerrod drummed his fingers on the table for several seconds, then he nodded. "Stay here," he said. "I'll come back and let you know."

"They're good men, Major," Corporal Jones said after Jerrod brought Travis and Dale's request that they be allowed to join with the Raiders.

"I don't remember them that way," Ackerman said. "I remember them as real troublemakers."

Jones smiled. "Yes, sir, but ain't we all?" he asked. "Except for you of course, Major."

"All right, have Jerrod bring them to me," Ackerman said. "I'll talk to them."

"Here's the thing," Jerrod told the Hastings brothers. "When you are around Major Ackerman, you have to act just like you're still in the army. You have to say sir to him, and all that."

"Why?" Travis asked. "It was the yes sir 'n and no sir 'n and the salutin' and stuff that made us desert in the first place."

"How much money did you make as a private in the army?" Jerrod asked.

"Eleven dollars a month."

"We got three hundred dollars from our last job, and there ain't been a job yet that we didn't get at least a hundred dollars. And because we're an army instead of just a bunch of robbers, we ain't lost a man. There ain't no townspeople goin' to mess with us, there ain't no sheriff that's got enough deputies to stop us, and there ain't no posse big enough to come after us."

"That beats what happened back in Meeker, don't it, Travis?" Dale asked.

"Yeah, it beats it all to hell."

"What are you talkin' about, Meeker?" Jerrod asked.

"Four of us tried to hold up a bank there," Dale said. "Two was kilt, me'n Travis got away."

"With no money," Travis added.

Jerrod chuckled. "That ain't never happened with

us, and it ain't goin' to happen. Come on, I'll take you to see Major Ackerman."

Ackerman had rented a small two-room cabin just beyond the town limits of Feely. In the front room he had a desk, and on the wall behind him, a map of Montana. Except for the lack of uniforms and flags, it could have been the office of the commandant of any army post in the West.

As they had been instructed by Jerrod, both Dale and Travis Hastings came to attention when they stepped up to the desk. The two men saluted, and Dale rendered the report for both of them.

"Sir, privates Dale and Travis Hastings reporting for duty."

Ackerman returned the salute. "At ease, men," he said. "Have either of you ever heard of a man named Euripides?"

"Seems like I have, Major. Wasn't he with the Fifth Cavalry?" Travis asked.

Ackerman laughed. "No, Euripides was a trage- dian, a playwright from the fourth century B.C. And though not a soldier, he is credited with one of the most truthful maxims of the military art. '*Ten soldiers, wisely led, are worth one hundred without a head.*' Have you ever heard that quote?"

"No, sir, I can't say as I have," Travis replied.

"No, I wouldn't think so," Ackerman said. "It is, however, one of the core truths taught at West Point."

Ackerman smiled as he saw a complete lack of comprehension on the faces of the two men.

"We are shortly to undertake another operation,"

Ackerman said. "One that should make a lot of money for all of us. And, considering the comment of Euripides, it is quite fortuitous, I think, that the number of men in my battalion has just gone up from eight to ten, particularly as I am a wise leader. We are fulfilling the Euripides maxim. All right, men, you are now a part of Ackerman's Raiders."

Ackerman pulled open his desk drawer and took out two twenty-dollar gold pieces, giving one to each of the two brothers.

"This will tide you over until our next operation, which, I am convinced, will pay handsomely. See Sergeant Casey, and let him fill you in on what will be expected of you."

"Yes, sir, thank you!" Dale said, taking the money. He turned away from the desk.

"Aren't you forgetting something?" Ackerman asked sharply.

"What?" Dale asked, then, he remembered, and he saluted. "Sir, permission to leave?"

Ackerman returned the salute. "Permission granted."

"Is he really serious about all this salutin' and sir 'n and stuff?" Dale asked Casey.

"Yes. But it works. When we are out there, we are an army," Casey said. "Nobody dares to try and stop us."

"What is this next job that he's talking about? One that he says is going to make us a lot of money?"

"That's another thing. We never know what job we are going to do until we actually start it. The major says that, that way, there's no chance of anyone finding out about it."

CHAPTER SIX

Colonel and Mrs. Edward Hamilton
request the honor of your presence
at the marriage of their daughter,
MARY KATE MACCALLISTER,
to
JONATHAN WILLIAM MCVEY,
on Saturday, the 17th day of July,
at half past three o'clock in the afternoon,
Brimstone Ranch,
Deer Lodge, Territory of Montana.

It was fortunate that Falcon was in MacCallister when the invitation arrived. It was from his sister, Megan, who sent a letter with the engraved invitation.

Falcon, I haven't seen you in so long, please do come. Everyone else is coming, even Andrew and Roseanna. It would mean so much to me, and I know it would be important to Mary Kate.

Falcon sent a telegram to them.

BEST WISHES TO MARY KATE STOP I WILL BE
THERE STOP

"Do you have any baggage, Mr. MacCallister?" the
station agent asked.

"I want my horse to go. And my saddle and saddlebags," he said. "As far as I'm concerned, they can be
in the stock car with Lightning."

"What about your rifle?"

Falcon considered checking his rifle through, but
then decided against it.

"No, thanks, I guess I'll just keep it with me."

"Very good, sir, but I remind you that game cannot
be shot from the train."

"I'll remember that," Falcon said, wondering what
fool would even want to shoot game from the train.

The station agent wrote out the ticket and handed
it to Falcon. "The train should be here within the
hour," he said.

Falcon thanked him, then took a seat in the
waiting room. True to the station agent's promise, it
was just under an hour when he heard the whistle
of the approaching train. He walked out onto the
platform to wait for it.

The train swept into the station with belches of
steam and smoke, and a symphony of hissing steam
and rolling steel. It was a beautiful engine, painted a
forest green, with shining brass trim. The lettering
was yellow, and the huge driver wheels were red.

The engineer was hanging out the window looking
at the track ahead, in order to find where to stop. He

held a long, thin, curved-stem pipe clenched tightly in his teeth. The cars slowed, squeaked, and clanked as the couplers came together when it came to a complete stop. Even at rest the train wasn't quiet, as the overheated bearings and journals popped and snapped as they were cooling.

The conductor, who had been standing on the boarding step of the first car, stepped down onto the brick platform once the train came to a complete halt. At least half a dozen passengers got off.

"Grandma!" one little girl called toward one of the older detraining passengers. She ran to the woman, who received her with open arms.

Falcon always watched such displays with mixed emotions. On the one hand he enjoyed seeing happy families. On the other hand, he couldn't help thinking of his own life and the tragedies that had shaped it. His mother and father were both murdered. So, too, were his wife and children. The twins, a boy and a girl, would have been in their early twenties now, and he had no doubt that he would be a grandfather. Now he was a man alone.

No, that wasn't true. Falcon wasn't alone. He had friends, and siblings, a lot of siblings. Multiple births seemed to be the normal in his family. Among his siblings were the twins, Jamie Ian and Ellen Kathleen, the twins, Roseanna and Andrew, and Matthew, Morgan, and Megan, who were triplets. Falcon was one of three single births, the other two being Karen, who was murdered by bounty hunters when she was only five months old, and Jolene, who was the closest in age to Falcon. The MacCallister siblings were not only numerous, they were also a very close family. It would be good to see them all again.

Looking toward the attached stock car, he was satisfied to see Lightning being led up the ramp.

"Mr. MacCallister, it's good to see you, sir," the conductor said, smiling broadly. "It's been a while since you rode with us."

"Hello, Ralph. Yes, it has, hasn't it?" He left unstated the explanation as to why he was riding the train. Carrying his rifle low in his left hand, Falcon passed from the front to the rear of the car. Midway to the back, he saw a very pretty woman with dark hair, deep blue eyes, high cheekbones, and a smooth, olive complexion sitting next to a window. She noticed him looking at her and returned his gaze with a smile.

"Ma'am," he said, touching the brim of his hat and nodding as he continued toward the back of the car.

Falcon chose a seat that was unoccupied so he could spread out a bit. It wasn't that he was too big to sit in one half of the seat, it was just that he found it more relaxing if he could have the entire seat to himself. Putting his rifle butt down on the floor between his knee and the wall of the car, he settled back to get comfortable for the ride.

Just as he was about to get settled in, a harried mother with a young boy came on board, a late arrival. She was holding on to the boy with one hand and carrying a bag in the other. She was unsuccessful the first time she tried to put it in the overhead rack.

"May I help?" Falcon asked, reaching for the bag.

"Why, thank you, sir. That's very nice of you," the mother said as Falcon lifted it easily. Then, with a nod, he retook his seat and watched as the other passengers got settled. From outside he could hear the train whistle blow, then the train started forward with a jerk.

Falcon would be on board a train for thirty-six hours with no sleeper cars on any of them. His siblings, Andrew and Roseanna, who were well-known stage performers in New York, had complained bitterly the last time they came west, because once they got off the main line, they had been unable to get sleeping berths.

Falcon had slept in the saddle, in mud-filled holes during thunderstorms, in mountain blizzards, and, during the war, under artillery barrages. The prospect of spending thirty-six hours in a padded seat in a train car was, compared to much of his life, luxurious.

As Falcon sat here, looking through the window at the passing countryside, he realized that he had not seen Mary Kate too many times in her young life. He had visited his sister when she gave birth to the baby. The next he saw her was when she was twelve years old, already a beautiful young girl with a quick mind and a good sense of humor. Edward Hamilton was in the army then, stationed at Fort Halleck, Nevada. He had just been promoted to Lieutenant Colonel and, because Falcon was nearby, he was able to respond to Megan's invitation to "wet down the leaves." "Wet down the leaves" meant there would be a party at the Officers' Club where drinks would be hoisted as a toast to the new colonel.

That was also the last time that all the siblings had

been together, even Andrew and Roseanna. Andrew and Roseanna had put on a show, first for the officers only, then for the entire post.

"Falcon, I could certainly use you in the army," General Fielding had told him. "I could guarantee you a commission of at least a major."

"I appreciate the offer, General, but I don't intend to ever wear a uniform again."

"If you ever change your mind, let me know."

He had gone to Fort Ellis to testify in the court-martial of Major Ackerman, and had spent a few days on the post with his sister and brother-in-law before returning to MacCallister. Mary Kate was eighteen and had fulfilled the promise she had shown when twelve of becoming a beautiful young woman.

Just before the supper meal that evening, the pretty woman with dark hair, deep blue eyes, high cheekbones, and a smooth, olive complexion, who had been sitting next to a window a few rows ahead of him on the same car, stepped back to his seat, then leaned over. She smiled at him.

"Pardon me, sir, I'm sure you must think this quite the boldest thing you have ever seen, but I wonder if I might prevail upon you for a favor?"

"Certainly, if it's something I can do," Falcon replied.

"It's just that it is nearly time for supper. When I took my lunch in the dining car, there was a most unpleasant gentleman who made the meal most uncomfortable. I was wondering if you would take your supper with me."

Falcon smiled, broadly, then stood. "Yes, ma'am, that is a favor I would gladly do."

Picking up his rifle, he followed the young woman into the dining car, where they were met by one of the waiters.

"I have an empty table," the waiter said.

Falcon, and the young lady, who said her name was Sue Roussel, followed the waiter. The waiter held the chair out for Sue, and Falcon didn't sit down until she was seated.

Sue was on her way to Fort Laramie to get married.

"Your fiancé is a very lucky man," Falcon said.

Sue beamed under the compliment and explained that she had met the young man while he was still a cadet at West Point.

"I'm not sure I'm doing the right thing," she said. "I'm still very young, and now I'm about to commit myself to one man forever without the slightest taste of what life is all about."

"Life on an army post in the West can be most interesting," Falcon said. "I have many friends in the military. I'm sure you will be very happy."

"Yes," Sue replied with just a twinge of regret in her voice. "I'm sure I will be."

Falcon wasn't sure where Sue had wanted that conversation to go, but he was sure where he didn't want it to go.

"I'm going to a wedding myself," he said.

"Oh?"

"Yes, my niece is getting married. And she grew up on army posts; her father was a colonel."

"Was a colonel, but no longer?"

"He's out of the army now and is a rancher."

"Well, you must give the young lady my best wishes."

Falcon had been on the train for thirty-six hours when it pulled into the station at Deer Lodge City. Looking out the window he saw his siblings, the triplets, Matthew, Morgan, and Megan, as well as Edward Hamilton, standing on the platform waiting for him.

Falcon glanced over at the seat where Sue Roussel had been sitting when he first boarded. She had left the train in Cheyenne, stepping down with a final and obvious invitational glance. Had conditions been otherwise, had she not been going to get married, and had he not been going to his niece's wedding, he might have left with her. He was reminded of the passage from the Longfellow poem:

> *Ships that pass in the night, and speak each other*
> *in passing,*
> *Only a signal shown and a distant voice in the*
> *darkness;*
> *So on the ocean of life we pass and speak one*
> *another,*
> *Only a look and a voice; then darkness again and*
> *a silence.*

He smiled, then shook his head, and, carrying his rifle, stepped down from the train. Megan came toward him. "Hello, little brother," she said as she embraced him.

"Hello, big sister."

Matthew, Morgan, and Edward greeted him with extended hands.

"You brought Lightning?" Morgan asked.

"Yes."

"All right, as soon as you get him off-loaded from the train, we'll go out to Brimstone. Everyone else is already there."

"You mean I'm the last? Andrew, Roseanna, Jolene, they are all there?"

"That they are, little brother," Matthew said.

Falcon didn't even bother to saddle Lightning. Instead he hitched him on to the back of the carriage and rode the four miles from Deer Lodge out to Brimstone Ranch. Brimstone Ranch was a hundred-thousand-acre spread that was just outside Deer Lodge City, Montana.

General Terry had been accurate when he said that Colonel Hamilton would not miss his army pension. Edward Hamilton was the only son of the Earl of Denbigh, and after his father died, Edward inherited Denbigh Castle, which was located between Malmesbury and Chipping-Sodbury. He also inherited the title of Earl of Denbigh, but he would have to return to England to claim the title.

Having acquired American citizenship, he had no desire to return to England. He sold the land and the title to a second cousin and used the money, plus investment funds from English friends and relatives, to buy Brimstone. Once he had the land purchased, it was necessary to stock it, which he did, supplementing the cattle with Texas Longhorns, importing them for their genes for high fertility, their easy calving, resistance to disease and parasite, their longevity, and because they can live on coarse forage without any problem.

The cattle were driven all the way from Texas by Johnny McVey, a remarkable young man who so impressed Edward that he hired him away from the XIT Ranch. Johnny McVey so impressed young Mary Kate Hamilton that when he asked her to marry him, she accepted. That wedding had brought Falcon to Brimstone.

When Falcon saw the house he couldn't help commenting on it. The house was situated on a hilltop between Deer Lodge and Phillipsburg, overlooking the Hell's Gate River. It was one of the largest private homes he had ever seen.

"Is this a house or a hotel?" he asked jokingly.

"Welcome to Denbigh Castle, little brother," Megan said. "It is an exact replica of Denbigh Hall, where Edward was born and raised. And, since I have been there three times, I can attest to its exact detail."

"It is one impressive edifice," Falcon said.

Megan chuckled. "Edifice. Yes, that's an appropriate word. Denbigh Castle was one of the most significant Elizabethan country houses in England, representing one of the earliest examples of the English interpretation of the Renaissance style of architecture, which came into fashion when it was no longer thought necessary to fortify one's home."

"I'm disappointed. There's no moat or castellated walls for archers," Falcon teased.

"Tut, tut, little brother, don't be puerile. If you

want to hear about the house I'll tell. But if you are going to be snide about it, I'll just leave you to wonder."

"I'm sorry. No, I would like to hear about it."

"The original house was designed for the first Earl of Denbigh, Robert Smythson Hamilton, in the late seventeenth century and remained in the family until Edward sold it."

"Sold it? Looks to me like he just moved it," Falcon said.

The carriage rolled into a long, curving drive, glistening white with its cover of marble chips. The drive encompassed a beautifully manicured lawn. It stopped in front of the house.

"Moses, put Mr. MacCallister's horse and saddle in the stables," Edward said.

"Yes, sir," the white-haired, liveried, black carriage driver replied.

Denbigh Castle had its great hall built on an axis through the center of the house rather than at right angles to the entrance. It was three floors high, with a grand, winding, stone staircase that led up to a suite of staterooms on the second floor, including a long gallery and a tapestry-hung great chamber.

Falcon could hear music as they started up the staircase to the great chamber.

"I hear Roseanna," Falcon said with a broad smile.

"Yes, and Andrew is playing the piano. I tell you the truth, Falcon, those two got every ounce of talent that may have been allocated for this family."

"I can't argue with you on that," Falcon said.

Roseanna stopped in the middle of her aria when she saw Falcon. "Falcon!" she called, and she ran across the floor to embrace him.

Jamie Ian and Kathleen stood to greet him as well, and so did Jolene. Andrew finished with the song he was playing.

"That's Andrew for you," Roseanna said. "Ever the consummate entertainer. The show must go on, even if a relative he hasn't seen in a long time appears."

"Well, you have certainly seen Falcon since you saw any of us," Jamie Ian said.

"That's true. He is the only one who has ever come to New York to see us, more than once, I might add."

"Where is the star of this gathering?" Falcon asked after he greeted everyone. "Where is Mary Kate?"

"I don't know, we came to get you," Megan said. "Mr. Travelstead, where is Mary Kate?"

"She is downstairs in the library, mum," Travelstead said. Travelstead was a gentleman's gentleman, who had been with Denbigh Castle in England, but came to America at Edward's invitation when the estate was sold.

"The library is downstairs, at the back end of the great hall, last door on the right," Megan said.

"Thanks, I'll go say hello to her."

Falcon went back downstairs and, even as he reached the bottom step, heard the music start up again. He walked down the long hall and wasn't at all surprised to see at least six suits of armor, three on each side of the hall. He also saw a very large painting of Colonel Edward Hamilton in full dress uniform, sitting in a chair with Megan standing beside him, her white-gloved hand resting on his shoulder.

The door to the library was standing open and Falcon looked in. There was a bubble of golden light at the far end of the library and there, sitting in a high-backed leather chair, was Mary Kate. Falcon stopped for a moment just to look at her. If anything she was even more beautiful now than she had been when last he saw her. Her fiery red hair was gleaming in the light of the lantern.

"Mary Kate?" Falcon said, advancing into the library.

Mary Kate looked around, then, and as she recognized Falcon, her face became very animated.

"Uncle Falcon!" she said, and getting up from the chair she rushed toward him with her arms outstretched.

Falcon hugged her, then walked back into the library with her.

"All alone?" he asked.

"Yes. I'm just . . ." she paused for a moment before continuing, "thinking."

"That's understandable. You're taking a big step tomorrow. Are you nervous?"

"No, not nervous. Just thoughtful. Johnny is a good man. Wait until you meet him."

"I'm looking forward to it."

"Why didn't you ever get married again, Uncle Falcon?"

"I don't know. I guess the right woman never came along. Or, perhaps they did come along. I think, now, it is more a case of me not being the right man. I seem to have a difficult time settling down."

"It's not that. It's that you are too busy going all over the country to help people. I've read books about you. I remember, when I was a young girl living on army posts, I would hear about you, and be so proud that you were my uncle."

"Don't believe everything you read and hear."

"Still, if I ever got into trouble, and needed a knight in shining armor riding a white horse to come rescue me, promise me that you will do it."

Falcon laughed out loud. "Darlin', I'm not a knight and I don't have armor. In fact I am quite sure that I would not fit into one of those suits of armor out in the hall. Besides, Lightning is black, not white."

"But promise me if I ever need you, that you will come rescue me."

Falcon put his hand on Mary Kate's cheek, and she reached up to pull his hands over to her lips to kiss.

"Of course, I promise," he said.

CHAPTER SEVEN

Three quarters of the population of Deer Lodge County attended the wedding. Among the guests, it was a toss-up as to who made the biggest impact among the locals. There were many who had heard of, and were impressed by, Andrew and Roseanna, but just as many had heard of Falcon, and he was, after all, a Westerner, like them.

James Mills, the publisher and editor of the *Deer Lodge Examiner*, wrote of the wedding that it was "the biggest social event to happen in Montana since it was admitted as a territory to the United States."

Conveyances of all sorts, from private coaches, to carriages, surreys, spring wagons, buckboards, buggies, and even farm wagons had arrived for the event, until the area where they were parked covered two full acres. Special hitching racks had been built to accommodate the scores of horses that were here.

Edward had hired a band to provide music for the occasion, and on the patio behind his house, there were two steer halves and two pigs turning on spits over an open fire. The cooking had gone on for the entire night before the event, so that the area was permeated with the delightful aroma of barbecued meat.

The wedding was performed by Leigh R. Brewer, who was the Episcopal Missionary Bishop of Montana. The actual wedding was over rather quickly, then the new Mr. and Mrs. John McVey stood in a receiving line, greeting all the guests. Falcon was family and it wasn't necessary for him to go through the receiving line as there would be a private family reception later, but he decided to go through the line anyway.

"Uncle Falcon!" Mary Kate said, surprised to see him in the line. "I would like to present my husband, John McVey."

"I know we'll get to visit at the family reception," Falcon said, "but I thought I would sneak through the line and get a head start. I'm very pleased to meet you, John."

"I'm pleased and honored to meet you, sir. And most folks call me Johnny."

"All right, Johnny it is."

"Wow," Johnny said. "I've read about you for my whole life. I never thought I'd meet you, and now I learn that I've married into your family. Wait 'til I tell some of my friends back in Texas. Do you know anyone in Texas?"

"I know quite a few people in Texas," Falcon said, then with a smile he added, "but I wouldn't say that they are all my friends."

An easy smile spread across Johnny's face. "Truth

is, I can't really say that all the people I know in Texas are all my friends, either."

All the MacCallister siblings were sharing a table under a canopy in one corner of the patio. Jamie Ian and Ellen Kathleen were twins, and they were there with their spouses. They were the oldest, and Morgan and Matthew, who were the triplet siblings of Megan, made a big thing about escorting Jamie Ian and Ellen Kathleen, their "old" brother and sister, to their tables.

"If you two try something like that with Andrew and me, I'm going to hit you right upside the head," Roseanna said. "I'll have you know I'm not old, I am merely seasoned."

The others laughed.

Jolene and Falcon sat together, not only because they were the closest to each other in age, but also because they were the only surviving single births in the family.

After much visiting and eating, Edward had the band play a fanfare to get everyone's attention.

"My friends," he said, holding up his hands. "I thank you from the bottom of my heart for coming to help us celebrate the marriage of my daughter to a wonderful young man, Johnny McVey."

There was a polite applause.

"And now, Mary Kate, Johnny, if you would, please come up here? I would like to present you two with your wedding present."

Mary Kate and Johnny walked up to stand by Edward, responding with smiles and waves at many who called out to them.

"I have to say that I wasn't sure what kind of

wedding present I should get them," Edward said. "I thought about a silver hatband for Johnny, or maybe a new pair of boots. And I considered a silver bracelet for Mary Kate, but then I was afraid that Johnny might decide to go back to Texas and take Mary Kate with him. So, how could I keep him here? And then I got the idea. Johnny, Mary Kate, so that I know you will always be close, I am giving you twenty thousand acres of land, adjacent to Brimstone, and two thousand head of cattle."

"Wow!" Johnny shouted out loud.

"Oh, Papa!" Mary Kate said, giving her father a big hug.

The gift was greeted with applause and cheers from all who were in attendance.

"And I've been keeping this part a secret. I've already had a house, barn, smokehouse—which is stocked, by the way—and corrals built. Johnny, you'll be able to move in tonight if you want to . . . and it's so close that Mary Kate can come visit you every day. I intend for Mary Kate, of course, to continue to live here, with her mother and father."

"What?!?" Mary Kate screamed, and everyone laughed.

Finally the reception ended, and Johnny and Mary Kate climbed into the back of a carriage, to be driven by Moses to the railroad station. They were going to San Francisco for their honeymoon, and all the guests threw rice at them as the carriage drove away.

That night Falcon stood at the window of his bedroom. There was a bright, three-quarter moon, so the grounds were all in silver and shadow. He had enjoyed being with all his brothers and sisters; it was a very rare occasion for all of them to be together. He had enjoyed his talk with Mary Kate and was pleased that she was such a delightful young woman. But truth to tell, he could scarcely wait to leave. As big as this house was, he still felt restricted by it.

Encampment in the Elkhorn mountain range

"The sentries are posted, Major," Casey said.

"Who have you got out?"

"Jerrod and Smith are on the first relief. They'll stay on duty until midnight. The two Hastings brothers will go from midnight until four in the morning. Then Baker and Boyle until eight."

"Very good," Ackerman replied. He was scratching in the dirt, and though Casey wanted to ask him what he was doing, he knew better than to do so. With two men posted, that left eight in the encampment, and it was a real encampment with six two-man pup tents pitched in two neat rows of three. A campfire had been built, and Les Waters, who had become the company cook, was preparing a stew for their night meal.

"What's the major doing over there?" Travis Hastings asked.

"Whatever he's doin' ain't none of our concern," Casey said. "When he wants us to know, he'll tell us."

Throughout the next hour, as the men waited for their supper to be cooked, they played cards, or just talked, and except for the lack of uniforms, it was no different from a hundred bivouacs they had been on before. All the while they kept glancing over at Ackerman, who, as he was scratching in the dirt, often referred to a map.

"All right, men, gather 'round," Ackerman called.

When the men gathered around him, they saw what appeared to be a small road running between some large rocks that had been moved into place, with a small pile of pebbles stacked up at each end.

"This is Clancy," he said, pointing to the pile of pebbles at one end of the road. "And this is Deer Lodge. I've constructed this road here, exactly as the road is depicted on the map. And right here," he pointed to where the road went between some of the larger rocks he had put into position, "is Cutaway Pass. Now it will take two days for the wagon to get from the mine at Clancy, to Deer Lodge, where they will put the gold on the train. They will have five guards, two riding in front, one riding shotgun on the wagon, and two riding in trail. When they get right here, the road narrows and the guards can't scatter out. We will have the high ground, which is always a necessity when you are planning a military operation. We will also have more men than the guard detail, and we will have superior discipline and leadership.

"I anticipate no problems, but we will be prepared. Boyle, you will be at this position here, on Fish Peak, just as they enter the pass. We will have a good view of where you are. Using your mirror to catch the sun, you will flash us when you see them entering the pass."

"Yes, sir."

"All right, men, after you have supper, I suggest that you all crawl into your tents and get some sleep."

Ackerman had his own tent, and as he lay there in the complete darkness, he thought about the events that had brought him to this place and this time. He didn't know how much gold the wagon would be carrying, but he knew that the placer mine near Clancy had just about played out, and there could be as little as one thousand dollars with the shipment.

It almost wasn't worth it, but even if it was only a thousand dollars, his men would get eighty dollars each, and as all of them realized, that was much better than their army pay had been, and was even better pay than the area cowboys and miners were making.

Still, it did very little for him. He would take thirty percent, as he did from every operation, but he needed one big job somewhere . . . something that would net him several thousand dollars. He had a goal of ten thousand dollars. As soon as he got ten thousand dollars, he planned to leave the West and go back east, probably to New York.

He remembered New York from when he was a cadet at West Point. He had visited the city a few times and was taken with the excitement of it. There was also a lot more money available there, in a much smaller space. With ten thousand dollars working capital, and with his experience, he believed that he could turn ten thousand into a hundred thousand once he got there. And another good thing about it would be that, once he left here, nobody would have any idea of what happened to him. Nobody would think of looking for him in New York. And the chances were very good that nobody in New York had ever even heard of him.

San Francisco

From their hotel room Johnny and Mary Kate stood at the open window, looking out over the bay. They could hear the buoy marker bells and see the moonlight dancing on the surface of the black water. Several ships were at anchor and their lights were displayed.

On the cobblestone street below they heard the hollow clop of horse hooves and the ring of rolling, iron-rimmed wheels.

"Are you happy?" Johnny said, putting his arm around her and pulling her closer to him.

"I am deliriously happy," she said. "What about you, Johnny? Are you happy?"

"Yes, I'm happy. But I still have to pinch myself several times, just to make certain that it's real. I mean a cowboy marrying a rancher's daughter." He laughed. "I remember sitting around in the bunkhouse down at the XIT, that sometimes we would get in these fanciful conversations. And every now and then, someone would have this wild idea, dream, that they would find a woman they could love, who just happened to be the rancher's daughter. I never thought it would actually happen."

"Well, darling, you aren't just a cowboy, you know. You are a rancher yourself."

"I know," Johnny said. "That part's hard to believe, too."

"You know what I'm finding hard to believe?" Mary Kate asked.

"What?"

"That we are standing over here, looking out the

window, when we could be over there." She pointed to the bed.

"Yeah," Johnny said with a smile. "Why don't we do that?"

Ackerman encampment

"All right, men," Ackerman said the next day. "This is your final briefing. By the time the wagon gets here, the horses will be exhausted, so they'll have to stop to give the horses a blow before they start down the other side. I will put all of you in position so that we will have overlapping fields of fire. When I give the word, start shooting."

"Are we going to give them a chance to stop and just give us the gold?" Smith asked.

"No," Ackerman said. "Consider this to be a military operation where it isn't convenient to take prisoners. That means when we start shooting, we will shoot to kill. I expect all six men, the five guards and the driver, to be dead within thirty seconds after we open fire, so make your shots count. Jones, Boyle, and Smith, you three are my best sharpshooters. And since the trail guards will be the farthest away, you will take them. Waters, Baker, and Jerrod, you will take the two guards in front. Powell, you and the two Hastings will take the driver and the riding shotgun guard. Are there any questions?"

"No, sir," they all said as one.

"Major, Sergeant Casey just flashed at us," Jones said.

"All right, men, this is it. Everyone get into position, and do your duty," Ackerman ordered.

The men hurried to get into the positions they had already prepared by digging into the ground behind natural rock barriers. These would not only provide them with concealment, the rocks would also provide cover, though if the operation went as planned, there would be no need for cover because the likelihood of return fire was practically non-existent.

Ackerman also got into position, but he didn't intend to shoot unless it was necessary to clean up what one of his three shooting teams may have left. He could hear the wagon approaching before he could see it. The snaps and pops of the whip urging the team on up the pass, the whistles and shouts of the driver, the squeak and rattle of the harness and the wagon itself. He could also hear the clacking sound of the hooves of the horses as they struck the rocky ground.

Finally the two lead guards came around the bend, followed by the wagon, then by the two men riding trail. Ackerman had preselected the kill zone and had marked it with two sticks stuck in the ground to form a little pyramid. The men had been told to hold fire until the wagon reached that point.

The wagon labored on up the hill until the point was reached.

"Fire!" Ackerman shouted as loud as he could.

"What the hell?" one of the guards shouted in shock and fear. He was so surprised that he made no effort at all to go for his gun. Instead he twisted around in his saddle to see who had shouted.

That was his last move. Nine rifles began shooting at the same time, raining fire down, not only from above, but from both sides of the narrow pass. The driver was first to be hit, and he tumbled forward, falling from the wagon and being run over by it. The other five men went down within the next few seconds. Not one of them managed to even pull their weapons, let alone get off a shot.

The two horses that had been the mounts of the lead guards bolted ahead, and the horses pulling the wagon also tried to run.

"The team! Shoot the team!" Ackerman shouted, and after another half dozen shots, both horses fell in their traces. The two horses that had been ridden by the trailing guards, their saddles now empty, turned and galloped back down the pass, the sound of their galloping hoofbeats echoing and re-echoing back up the trail.

"Ya hoo!" Travis Hastings shouted, stabbing one hand into the air. "That was sweet!"

The wagon was carrying three hundred ounces of gold dust. At the going rate, that was six thousand dollars, which was better than Ackerman expected. He would clear eighteen hundred dollars, and the men would get four hundred and twenty dollars each. To a man, they were pleased with their take.

CHAPTER EIGHT

Although normally gold dust was easily negotiable, six men were killed in the robbery, and the story made front-page headlines in nearly every newspaper in the West. Included in the story was a caution to be very wary of anyone trying to pay for goods or services in gold, rather than in currency.

AN ACT MOST FOUL:
SIX MEN SLAUGHTERED!

Bodies Not Found for Three Days

On the 19th, instant, six men, good and true, were slaughtered, their bodies left in Cutaway Pass to be feast for carrion birds. Their remains too horrible to view, they were brought back to Casey from which they had parted but five days previous.

The men were employed by Mine Number Two, and according to Angus Hathaway, they were taking some three hundred ounces of gold dust to Deer

Lodge, to be placed on the train for shipment to Denver.

The perpetrators of this nefarious deed are not known, but it is believed that there were several involved, for a check on the weapons of the guards disclosed the fact that not one cartridge had been fired, which would indicate that they were fired upon from ambuscade. When asked if this might be the work of Ackerman's Raiders, Sheriff Tompkins stated that it could be, but he has no evidence to support that assumption.

Merchants are asked not to accept gold dust as the specie for any business transaction until its source has been verified by the sheriff's office.

"What are we going to do now?" Casey asked after he read the paper. "We've got all this gold, and it is worthless."

"I know where it can be exchanged, but it will cost us ten percent," Ackerman said.

"Ten percent. What does that mean?"

"It means that instead of getting four hundred and twenty dollars, you will each get only three hundred and seventy-eight dollars."

"Well, hell," Casey said, smiling broadly. "That's still a lot more money than any of us have ever got at once before. And it'll be money we can spend."

"Tell the others what I plan to do," Ackerman said. "And let them select from their number one man to come with me so that they will be satisfied that I am not cheating them."

* * *

The others agreed to go along with Ackerman's plan, and Jerrod was the one they selected to go with him. Ackerman and Jerrod traveled by train to Denver, where Ackerman contacted a man who, at one time, had been a sutler on an army base until he lost his contract because of suspected fraud. There, Ackerman offered him six thousand dollars in gold at a ten percent discount, and the deal was consummated.

Two weeks later, the men, with money to spend, were in Willow Creek. Ackerman, as was his custom, took a room in a hotel, then dressed in a suit, vest, and cravat, inquired at the desk as to what would be the finest restaurant in town.

"Why, that would be the Rustic Rock, sir," the desk clerk said. "It's just down to the corner on the same side of the street." He pointed.

"Thank you." Ackerman saw a pile of newspapers on the desk, and, paying for one, he picked it up and took it to the restaurant with him.

He could see where the Rustic Rock got its name. Although most of the buildings in town were of lumber, the restaurant was constructed of rock, hauled in from the mountains. The rocks were perfectly fitted together like pieces of a puzzle, and they were held in place by mortar. Every other diner in the establishment was dressed much as Ackerman was, verifying the desk clerk's assertion that this was a fine restaurant.

Ackerman ordered a meal of oysters on the half shell, baked stuffed trout, and a raw spinach and mushroom salad.

"And, for my drink, a Sauvignon Blanc," he concluded.

"Oh, my, yes. An excellent choice, sir," the waiter said obsequiously.

As he waited for his meal to be delivered, he read the newspaper he had picked up from the hotel.

COL. EDW. HAMILTON DONATES
TEN THOUSAND DOLLARS

Colonel Edward Hamilton of Brimstone Ranch, near Deer Lodge Lake, has donated ten thousand dollars to a fund with the idea of establishing an institute of higher education in the territory of Montana. "I feel that we cannot be seriously considered for statehood until we have an accredited university within our borders," Hamilton said.

Edward Hamilton, who was once the Earl of Denbigh, gave up his title to become an American citizen. He fought with honor and distinction in the American Civil War, and went on to command the Third Cavalry under the noted Indian fighter, General Alfred Fielding, in the Western campaigns. While still in the army he married Megan MacCallister, of the noted MacCallister

family. A few years ago, Colonel Hamilton
left the army to begin ranching. Colonel
and Mrs. Hamilton have one daughter,
Mary Kate, who, with her husband, John
McVey, own and manage Twin Buttes
Ranch, adjacent to Brimstone.

Well now, Ackerman thought, thumping the
article with his fingers. This is good to know. Yes, sir,
this is very good to know.

During his meal an attractive, and very well-
dressed, young woman walked by his table, where she
dropped something.

"Oh, dear," she said. "I've dropped my reticule."

Ackerman got down to help her pick up the items
that scattered, and while they were engaged, she
slipped him a piece of paper.

"Thank you so much," she said with a polite smile.

Not until the woman was seated at her own table
did Ackerman read the note.

My name is Molly. I live in a small house behind
Green Street. If you are interested in what I have
to sell, look back at me as you leave.

Ackerman smiled. The woman didn't look like a
prostitute. As he left, he made a point of looking back
toward her. She returned his look with a slight nod of
her head.

An hour later, having changed out of his suit,
Ackerman went into the Muddy Water Saloon. As he

expected, he saw Sergeant Casey and Corporal Jones sitting at a table in the back. Both men had a glass of beer sitting in front of them, and both were gnawing on pickled pig's feet. He walked over to them.

"Hello, Major," Clyde Jones said.

"Clyde, first names only in here, remember?" Jay Casey said.

"Oh, yes, I forgot. Sorry Maj . . . uh, Boyd," Jones said.

"I appreciate the courtesy," Ackerman said. "But Jay is right. When we are among the civilians, we must be very careful."

"Yes, sir," Jones said.

"I want you two men to take a look at this," he said, sliding the newspaper across to them.

"What is it? I don't see what you are talking about?" Casey said.

"This article," Ackerman said.

"Oh, about Edward? Yeah, I remember that son of a bitch. He was the one brought charges against me 'n Jones 'n Boyle. You, too, as I recall."

"Yes, but that's not what I'm talking about," Ackerman said.

By now Jones had seen the article as well. "What are you talking about?" he asked.

"I'm talking about money, Clyde, a great deal of money," Ackerman said. He smiled. "Money in negotiable currency, not gold dust, or gold nuggets, or anything we have to palm off. Cash. And, for all three of us, well, four counting Boyle, it will also be no small amount of personal revenge."

"Well, maybe I can see some revenge here," Casey said. "I mean if we go burn his house or something.

But I'll be damned if I can see where there's any money in it."

"There's money in it, don't you worry about that. There's a lot of money in it. And I'll explain it all when the time comes that it is necessary for you to know," Ackerman said.

"All right, what do we have to do?" Casey said.

"The first thing we have to do is get ourselves up to Deer Lodge."

"Can we go by train? I mean, we got a little money and it would be nice to go somewhere by train, I think."

"All right. But it would cause too much suspicion if all eleven of us went on the same train and sent our horses on the same train. I suggest we go up on four different trains, then rendezvous up there."

"Where, up there?"

"Spread out in the saloons when you get there. I'll find you. Casey, you get the schedule worked out as to who goes when. I'll be the last one to come up. We'll take at least a week to do it."

"All right," Casey said.

Two days later, Ackerman found a story in the paper that he had been looking for.

WOMAN FOUND DEAD
Throat Had Been Cut

A lady of the evening, known as Molly MaGee, though that may not have been her real name, was found dead in her own bed late last night by a gentleman caller. It is believed that she was killed by one of her customers, perhaps in a dispute over money. The sheriff has no leads and asks that anyone who may know something that could be helpful to contact him. Due to the sensitivity of the situation, the sheriff guarantees that the name of anyone who may provide him with information will not be released.

Ackerman smiled. There was nothing to connect him to the woman.

After all ten of his men had been dispatched to Deer Lodge, Ackerman, wearing a black shirt, clerical collar, and a low-brimmed hat, went down to the depot where he bought a ticket as "Father Thaddeus Sanford."

"Will you be startin' a new church up there in Deer Lodge, Padre?" the ticket clerk asked.

"I will see if there are any sheep up there that need my pastoral care," Ackerman said.

"Well, I've spent some time up there, and I tell you true, that's sure a town that can use a little pastoral care."

Shortly after arriving in Deer Lodge, Ackerman changed out of the clerical collar. He had a strict rule that no more than three of the men could ever be together at one time while in town. Too many men together attract attention, whereas two or three men don't. Because of his rule, the men were scattered out among three different saloons. He checked in with all of them to make certain they were ready for orders.

His next step would be to reconnoiter his target, and that meant he had to find out as much about Brimstone and Twin Buttes as possible. He accomplished that by going to the land officer under the auspices of wanting to buy land.

"Yes, sir," the real estate agent said. "We have some fine land for sale."

"Do you have a map? I would like to look at it on a map before I actually ride out to examine the land."

"Oh, yes indeed we have a map. Come over here, it's spread out on the table. Quite detailed it is, too."

"Will it tell me who my neighbors might be?"

"Oh, yes, I have all the owned property crosshatched. That means that anything that isn't crosshatched is available for sale."

Ackerman went over to examine the map. "Oh, my, this is a huge piece of property here," he said, pointing to one large area of cross-hatching. "Does all that belong to one man?"

"Yes, one hundred thousand acres belongs to Colonel Hamilton," the land agent said. "Oh, no, wait, that's not entirely correct. He deeded this part of it right here, twenty thousand acres, to his new son-in-law."

"New son-in-law?"

"Yes, Johnny McVey is his name, and he is as nice a young man as you ever will meet. I attended the wedding when he married Miss Mary Kate. Well, most of the county did. It was quite a large event. But what else would you expect from the largest landholder in the county?"

"What kind of neighbor would he make? Colonel Hamilton, I believe you called him? Is he in the army?"

"Not now, but he was in the army, and you know how these army colonels are. Once they get that title, it seems that they never want to give it up. Oh, and to answer your question, I believe Colonel Hamilton would make an absolutely wonderful neighbor."

"And this area here? This is the land you say he deeded to his son-in-law?"

"Yes, sir, twenty thousand acres."

"I see."

"Would you like to ride out there to look at some of the land?"

"No, not yet. I have some investors back in New York; I'm going to have to consult more with them before I can do anything else. But I do thank you for showing me the layout on the map. I'll get back to you soon."

"Very good, sir, I'll be looking for you," the land agent said.

CHAPTER NINE

Twin Buttes

"Mary Kate, hold that end up, will you?" Johnny McVey asked. McVey was putting in a new gate to the corral. He had the bottom hinge in place but needed the gate held up so he could get the top hinge.

"Your pa got on me last time he was here because I hadn't fixed this gate yet. I don't want him gettin' on me when he and your ma come for lunch."

"What are you talking about, Johnny? Papa didn't get on you. All he did was tell you that the gate looked like it needed some work."

"Sometimes I think he still thinks he's a colonel in the army and this ranch is an army post."

Mary Kate laughed. "I was born and raised on army posts. Believe me, this ranch is nothing like an army post."

Johnny chuckled, then started screwing in the first woodscrew. "Yeah, it is. This is Fort McVey."

* * *

Approximately one-quarter of a mile from the McVey place, Boyd Ackerman was surveying the scene through a pair of binoculars.

"Do you see anyone else beside them two there, Major?" Casey asked.

"No, there's just the two of them," Ackerman said as he lowered his binoculars.

"Well, then, let's just ride on down there and take care of business."

"We will 'take care of business' in the proper way," Ackerman said. "Sergeant Casey, take Jerrod and the two Hastings brothers, and using that ridge line for concealment, get around to the right side of the barn. Corporal Jones, you take Waters, Baker, and Powell, and, using the creek bed, go up to the left side of the house. When you are in position, send me a signal by flashing a mirror."

"Yes, sir," Casey and Jones answered.

"Boyle, Smith, when they are in position, you two and I will ride on down. McVey isn't likely to be spooked if he thinks there are no more than three of us."

Casey and Jones, with three men each, mounted their horses.

"And remember, don't hurt the woman. She's worth twenty thousand dollars to us, but this whole thing depends on her not getting hurt," Ackerman said.

"Give us about ten minutes, Major, and we'll be in position," Casey said.

"You will do it in five minutes," Ackerman said.

"Yes, sir, five minutes," Casey agreed.

Ackerman watched the two groups ride off.

"Tell me, Major, what makes that woman worth so much money?" Boyle asked.

"You remember Colonel Hamilton, don't you?"

"How can I forget the son of a bitch? He was the one that charged me 'n Corporal Jones and Sergeant Casey with murder."

"Well, Colonel Hamilton is a civilian now, and he is one of the wealthiest men in the state of Montana. The woman we are about to capture is his daughter, Mary Kate McVey. I intend to hold her for ransom. I've no doubt but that Hamilton will gladly pay twenty thousand dollars to get her back."

"What about the woman's husband?"

"We will dispose of him. He is of no use to us."

A couple of minutes later Ackerman saw first one flash, then another.

"They're in place," Ackerman said. "Let's go."

Ackerman, Boyle, and Smith started toward the ranch.

"There," Johnny said, testing the gate, opening and closing it. "See how smooth it is? The colonel can't complain about that."

"Oh, hush, Johnny," Mary Kate said with a little laugh. "You know Papa doesn't complain. He suggests."

"Might I suggest, young man, that when responsibility calls, you answer straightaway?" Johnny teased, perfectly mimicking Edward's accent, pronouncing the word answer as "ahnswer."

Mary Kate laughed. "Johnny, you're awful, making fun of . . ." she paused in midsentence. "Johnny, there's someone coming."

Mary Kate pointed to three men who were riding toward them.

"I see them."

"I wonder what they want?" Mary Kate asked.

"I don't know. Water maybe? Directions?"

"There's plenty of water all around, you know that. Johnny, I don't feel good about this."

"I'll see what they . . . damn!" Johnny said. "They're riding right through the garden." Angrily, Johnny called out to the two riders.

"What the hell is the matter with you men? Are you blind? Get out of there! You're riding right through the garden!"

The three riders continued through the garden without so much as an indication that they had even heard Johnny.

"Oh, my God, Johnny! It's Major Ackerman!" Mary Kate said.

"Are you sure?"

"Yes, I'm sure. I've known him for years!"

"What do you want, Ackerman?" Johnny called as the three men came through the garden, then rode right up to Johnny and Mary Kate.

"I want nothing from you," Ackerman said. He drew his pistol and pointed it at Johnny.

"Here! What are you . . . ?"

That was as far as Johnny got before Ackerman fired, the sudden and unexpected sound of the shot loud.

The impact of the bullet plowing into him felt like he had been hit in the chest with a hammer. The pain was excruciating, then it was as if he could feel his body flowing down, like water from a bottle, and the world went black as he collapsed.

Mary Kate saw Johnny slump to a sitting position against the gate.

"No!" Mary Kate shouted. "You shot him! Why did you shoot him? He was no danger to you!"

A weeping Mary Kate fell on her knees beside her husband. "Johnny! Johnny!" She put her hand on his cheek. "Johnny!"

"You're wasting our time," Ackerman said. "Tell me, Mary Kate, do you have a favorite horse?"

"What?"

"A horse. Do you have a favorite horse? If so, point him out. You're coming with us."

"Are you crazy? I'm not going anywhere with you," Mary Kate said. "I'm not leaving Johnny like this! Get out of here, now!"

Mary Kate turned and started back toward the house, only to be confronted by eight men who were approaching her. She stopped in her tracks.

"Cooperate and you won't get hurt. Resist and you will be. Either way, you will come with us," Ackerman said.

"Why are you doing this?"

"For two reasons," Ackerman replied. "One is economic opportunity. The other is to exact a bit of revenge for what your father did to me."

"Revenge? After all this time, you want revenge? It's been four years."

"According to the French novelist Pierre Ambroise François Choderlos de Laclos, 'Revenge is a dish best served cold,'" Ackerman said with an evil smile.

"My God," Mary Kate said, lifting her hand to her mouth. "You really *are* crazy!"

"Sergeant Casey?"

"Yes, sir?"

"Post the demand there on the fence above the body."

"Yes, sir."

Johnny regained consciousness, and he heard Ackerman tell someone to post something on the fence above the body. *What body? Is Ackerman talking about my body? Am I dead?*

Johnny wanted to call out to Ackerman, to tell him that he had better not take her, but he was unable to speak and unable to move. He saw them ride away, now many men, not just the three who had been here first. Again, he opened his mouth to shout, but no words came.

If I'm dead, why am I still hurting? I'm not dead. But if I die, how will anyone ever find out what happened to Mary Kate? They came for her, and they took her. Why?

Johnny remembered then that Colonel Hamilton and Mary Kate's mother were coming for lunch. They would be here shortly. He wouldn't have to hang on for much longer.

Brimstone Ranch

"Megan, if you don't hasten, we shan't be to Megan and Johnny's house in time for dinner, let alone lunch," Edward said.

"I'm hastening, I'm hastening, so that we shan't be

late," Megan said, teasing him by pronouncing the word as "shont." As she hurried out of the house she was carrying a basket.

"What's that?"

"Fried peach pies. You know how much Mary Kate loves them. Johnny, too."

"I thought they were going to feed us. I had no idea we were going to feed them. What if she's already made dessert?"

"Fried peach pies can keep for a long time," Megan said, climbing into the surrey.

Edward snapped the reins, and the team started out at a spirited trot.

"I wonder how long it will be before we have any grandchildren," Edward said.

"Oh, heavens, are you that anxious to make me a grandmother? I look old enough now."

"Nonsense, my dear, you are quite as beautiful now as you were the day I first saw you."

"As I recall I was with two of my brothers, and we were delivering cattle to Fort Collins. I was dressed just like them; how could you even tell I was a woman?"

"It was the way you were carrying yourself, my dear. You had a certain savoir faire about you that suggested, here was no mere cowboy. And upon closer examination I saw a beautiful young woman."

Megan laughed. "And you are as full of blarney today as you were then."

"The term blarney would bespeak an Irishman. I am English."

"Ho, and don't I know it. It's . . ." Megan stopped in midsentence and pointed to circling birds ahead. "Edward, what is that?" she asked.

"Birds."

"They aren't just birds, and you know it. They are vultures. Edward, what is it?"

"Don't get yourself all in a dither yet. I'm sure it's nothing more than a dead deer, or something."

"It's too near where the house is. They wouldn't let a dead deer just lie there."

Edward urged the team into a gallop, and, even before they got there, they could see Johnny sitting on the ground, supported by the corral gate.

"Oh, my God! It's Johnny!" Megan said.

"But where's Mary Kate?"

Edward pulled back on the reins and put on the brake, causing the surrey to slide to a stop. Jumping out, he hurried over to Johnny. Johnny was still alive, but barely.

"Good," Johnny said, barely able to speak. "You got to me before the buzzards did."

"Johnny, what happened? Who did this? Where is Mary Kate?"

"Ackerman," Johnny said, the words strained. "Boyd Ackerman took her."

"Ackerman! Are you sure?" Edward replied.

"Yes," Johnny said. "Boyd Ackerman." He let out one long, last, rattling breath, then his head fell to one side.

"My word, Megan," Edward said. "He's dead. It's almost as if he stayed alive just long enough to tell us about Ackerman."

"Ackerman? Major Ackerman from Fort Ellis?"

"I'm afraid it is."

"I've read that he has taken to the outlaw trail. But what would he want with Mary Kate?"

It wasn't until then that Edward saw a paper, posted on the fence just above Johnny's body.

"Perhaps this will tell us," he suggested, pointing to the paper.

Leaving Johnny, Edward removed the paper from the fence.

WE'VE GOT MARY KATE
SHE'S SAFE FOR NOW, BUT SHE WON'T BE
IF YOU DON'T COME UP WITH $20,000.
POST AD IN NEWSPAPER AND YOU WILL
BE CONTACTED

"My word! Ackerman has taken her for ransom!" Edward said.

Already more than five miles away from the ranch, Ackerman and his men were riding down the road in a military formation. The main body was riding in a column of twos, but Ackerman had one man riding a quarter of a mile ahead in point, and another a quarter of a mile behind, in trail. They were instructed to return to the main body immediately to report anything that might represent a danger to the formation.

Mary Kate had been wearing jeans while she was helping Johnny repair the gate, and because of that, she was able to sit astride the horse. Using a small piece of rope, Ackerman tied her hands to the saddle pommel. He had assigned Casey to ride with her and, holding the reins of her horse in his hands, Casey and Mary Kate were riding abreast, in the very first row.

They rode through the rest of the day, then just as the sun was a bright red disc balanced on the western horizon, they reached an arroyo.

Ackerman held up his hand. "Company, halt!" he called.

The column came to a stop.

"Bugler, sound 'Recall,'" Ackerman said, and Powell lifted his bugle to play "Recall."

Shortly after "Recall" was sounded, the two outriders returned.

"Sergeant Casey, post a guard detail. We'll spend the night here," Ackerman said.

"Yes, sir. Waters, Jerrod, you two will take the first relief."

The two men ground-hobbled their horses, then went out to assume guard.

"Say, Major, what are we going to do with the woman?" Travis Hastings asked.

"What do you mean, what are we going to do with her? We aren't going to do anything with her," Ackerman replied.

"The reason I ask is, I figure that as long as we got her, we may as well make the best of it," Hastings said. With a lascivious smile, he started toward Mary Kate, and she cringed back in fear.

"What do you think you are doing?" Ackerman asked.

"What the hell does it look like I'm doin'? I'm 'bout to have me a little fun."

"If you so much as touch her, I will have you shot," Ackerman said.

"Come on, Major, what would it hurt? I mean, she's here, why not take advantage of it?"

"The major is right, Hastings," Casey said. "Why take a chance on messing things up? With the money we're goin' to get from her, you can have the best-looking whore in all of Montana. Hell, you can have the two best-lookin' whores."

"No, he can't, Sarge," Dale Hastings said. "How's he goin' to have the two-best lookin' whores in Montana if I've got 'em?"

The others laughed then, including Travis Hastings.

"All right, all right, I'll wait," Travis Hastings said.

"Why are you doing this, Major Ackerman?" Mary Kate asked. "I remember you from Fort Ellis. You were always very kind to me. What happened to you?"

"Surely you remember the difficulty that occurred between your father and me."

"I know there was a trial of some sort. I didn't pay that much attention to it."

"You didn't pay much attention to it," Ackerman said scathingly. "Yes, there was a trial of some sort," Ackerman replied. "A trial that destroyed my military career. Unlike your father who had his commission given to him, I earned mine. I was a West Point graduate."

"I'm sorry," Mary Kate said.

"Yes, well, being sorry doesn't make me a colonel, does it?"

"What do you plan to do with me?"

"That depends upon your father."

"What do you mean?"

"I left a message for your father, explaining that he can have you released safely, in exchange for twenty thousand dollars in cash."

"Do you really think my father will give in to that kind of pressure?" Mary Kate asked.

"He will if he ever wants to see you alive again," Ackerman said.

CHAPTER TEN

Mary Kate had no idea what time it was, but the fire they had built when they first camped in the arroyo had burned down so that now there was nothing left except a few glowing embers, and a very thin rope of smoke that curled up into the night sky. All the men who had bedded down around the fire were now asleep, that fact verified by heavy snoring from so many.

If she was going to escape, now would be the best time to try. Quietly, barely daring to breathe, she got up on her hands and knees and began crawling away from the fire and the sleeping men. Not until she was about twenty yards away did she stand up.

Once on her feet she looked back toward the campsite. There still had been no movement among the sleeping men. She had made it! She felt such a sense of elation that it was all she could do to keep from crying out. Turning back away from the camp, she started to walk out of the long draw.

Suddenly Baker, one of Ackerman's men, stepped out in front of her.

"Where do you think you're going, missy?"

Baker grabbed her and then, to Mary Kate's horror, he started trying to tear off her clothes.

Mary Kate screamed.

"Here! What is going on?" Ackerman called from back at the camp.

"I caught her, Major. She was tryin' to escape!" Baker said.

"Bring her back."

"Yes, sir."

"He . . . he was trying to tear off my clothes," Mary Kate said. "I think he was trying to rape me."

"No such thing, Major. She was just fightin' me, that's all. Maybe some of her clothes got tore."

"You did a good job of stopping her, Private Baker. You are to be commended."

"Yes, sir, thank you, sir."

"Return to your post."

Mary Kate watched it all in disbelief. Not only the fact that Baker's obvious lie went unchallenged, but also the, she thought, ridiculous charade at pretending they were still in the army.

"Lie back down," Ackerman ordered.

"You know he lied, don't you?"

"Yes."

"He lied, but you did nothing about it. I thought you were his commanding officer."

"I am. But sometimes it is prudent to be flexible. I needed you back, and in one piece. And I advise you not to try this again. Conditions may be such that when the next man catches you, I might not be around in time to stop the inevitable unpleasantness. Now, I want you to promise me that you won't try anything like this again."

"What's going to happen to me, Major Ackerman?"

"It depends on your father, girl. If he cares for you as much as I think he does, he will do whatever it takes to get you back safely. And right now, that means he has to come up with twenty thousand dollars. And you, Miss Hamilton . . ."

"My name is McVey, Mrs. McVey," Mary Kate corrected.

"All right, Mrs. McVey. You owe it to your father not to try any more stupid stunts like the one you just pulled. I'm going to give you back to him once he pays the money, whether you are in one piece or not. For your father's sake, I hope you are as healthy when he gets you back as you were when we took you."

Brimstone Ranch—*two days later*

Megan put four shot glasses on a tray, filled them halfway with bourbon, then carried them into the parlor where the other two of her triplet siblings were seated. So, too, was her husband, Edward.

"As you suggested, we have not told the sheriff that we know who did this," Edward said.

"And there has been no further contact?" Morgan asked as he took his glass.

"There has been no contact of any kind," Edward said. "Nothing since the sign we found posted above poor Johnny's body."

"I see."

"I still don't understand why you suggest that we

not tell the sheriff that we know who did this," Edward said.

"If the sheriff gets involved, it will just make our job more difficult," Morgan replied.

"But wouldn't the sheriff be better equipped than just the two of you to handle this?" Edward asked.

"Tell him, Megan," Morgan said.

"Darling, if Mary Kate is still alive, and I pray God that she is, no law enforcement agency in the world would have a better chance of getting her back, safely, than my brothers."

"But there are only two of them, Megan. And God knows how many men were involved in this beastly affair. For all Ackerman's faults, I know that he is a skilled tactician. Also it has been said that he is traveling with his own private army now."

"We won't be alone," Matthew said. "We'll send a telegram to Falcon. That will make three of us."

"Knowing Jamie as well as I do, I know he would also want to take part in it, but the truth is, he is just too old," Morgan said, speaking of their oldest brother, Jamie Ian IV.

"Ha, I'd be willing to bet that Jamie doesn't think he's too old," Megan said.

"Which is precisely why we won't contact him," Morgan said. "I have no doubt but that Falcon will be here as soon as he can. So, like I said, that makes three of us."

"Four," Megan said.

"Four?" Morgan chuckled. "Surely, you aren't thinking about Andrew."

"No, I'm thinking about me," Megan said.

Both Matthew and Morgan shook their heads.

"No. You aren't a part of this. You are a woman," Matthew said.

"I am also a MacCallister. And beyond that, I am Mary Kate's mother," Megan added firmly. "So, if you think you are going to, somehow, keep me out of this, you have another think coming."

"I think you should listen to your brothers, Megan. What do you think you could do to help?"

"Come outside," Megan demanded. "All of you. Come outside."

As they started outside Megan reached into the front hall closet and took down a gun and holster set. She began strapping on the gun, buckling it up just as they reached the front porch.

On a tree limb, about fifty yards distant, there was a small Y-shaped twig.

"I'll take them off one at a time," Megan said. She fired twice, and both arms of the twig were severed.

Morgan chuckled. "She's been showing off like that since she was twelve years old."

"It's good that you sent word to Falcon to get him up here," Megan said. "But just remember, when you start after whoever did this, I'm going with you."

"I wish you wouldn't," Edward said.

"Edward, we've known her a lot longer than you have," Matthew said. "Believe me when I tell you that you aren't going to be able to talk her out of this. But I promise you, we will look out for her."

"There is no need for you to make such a promise," Edward said. "If Megan is going, then I am as well."

"Don't you think you would be better off staying here to run the ranch?" Matthew asked.

"I have enough hired men that the ranch will

practically run itself," Edward said. "And, if we arc going after Boyd Ackerman, you might find my presence helpful. Having once been his commanding officer, I know him quite well."

"Poor Mary Kate, to have watched her husband killed, and now be held by that evil bunch of bastards," Matthew said. "I'm going to take special delight in tracking down the sons of bitches who did this, and making them pay for it."

"What about Johnny's funeral?" Matthew asked.

"I've contacted his parents," Edward said. "They are amenable to having him buried here, in the local cemetery. Unfortunately, I'm afraid they won't be able to get here in time for the funeral."

It rained on the day of the funeral, and the preacher continued the service for as long as he could, hoping that the rain would stop before it was time to go out to the cemetery. His ploy worked, because by the time the church service was over and the coffin moved into the hearse, the rain had stopped and the sun was shining.

The sun might be shining, but the roads and grounds of the cemetery were filled with mud, which made it difficult for the few people who actually showed up at the funeral.

"Poor Johnny," Morgan said. "He has no relatives here, and with Mary Kate gone, there are very few to mourn for him."

"Wrong," Megan said. "I am mourning for him as much as if he had been my own son. And I know that Edward is mourning, as are his friends. And as you can tell by the number of people who have come, despite the rain, his friends are legion."

"Yes, I can see that now," Morgan said. "That was a foolish comment for me to make."

The sheriff came to the funeral and he stood quietly until the coffin was lowered into the grave. Then he came over to talk to Edward, Megan, and her two brothers.

"I'm sorry to say that we still don't have any idea who did this," Sheriff Tompkins said. "We've been over the McVey Ranch with a fine-tooth comb, and we've found no clues. You're sure you don't have the slightest idea of who might have done this?"

"No idea," Edward replied.

"I mean, there's nobody that you know of that was mad at your son-in-law, someone who might have wanted to kill him for revenge?"

"Not unless it was someone who came up from Texas," Edward said. "As you know, Constable, he had not been up here for so very long. And all the people he met since he arrived were friends. Johnny was a most affable person. He made friends quite easily."

"Yes, well, I can attest to that," Sheriff Tompkins said. "I met Johnny shortly after he arrived with the herd. He had, as I recall, a rather large number of men riding with him, and not a one of them caused us any trouble. He had them well under control."

"If your investigation turns up anything, you will let me know, won't you?" Edward asked.

"Yes, well, to be honest with you, Colonel, I don't even know where to go from here. I know that whoever did this has your daughter, but until something else turns up, there's nothing I can do."

"We understand, Sheriff. And thank you for coming to the funeral," Edward said.

"Yes, well, comin' to the funeral is about the least I could do," Sheriff Tompkins said. "I reckon I'd better get back to the office. Again, Colonel, Mrs. Hamilton, you have my condolences."

Tompkins touched the brim of his hat and walked away.

"I hated lying to him like that," Edward said. "But I think you and your brothers are correct. I don't believe there is anything that the sheriff or his deputies can actually do, and having him involved would only get in our way and make our own investigation and rescue operation more difficult."

Megan leaned over and kissed him.

"I'm glad you see it our way, dear."

"Might I suggest that we send the telegram to Falcon?" Morgan offered.

"How are we going to do that without the telegrapher knowing that we know who did it?" Megan asked.

"Simple, we will just send a nonspecific telegram asking Falcon to come, telling him that Johnny was killed and Mary Kate taken, but we won't mention Ackerman's name," Morgan said.

"Good idea."

CHAPTER ELEVEN

It was four days now since Johnny McVey had been killed and Mary Kate taken. And during that time Ackerman and his men had been holed up at the Helmville way station, a gray, weather-beaten building that sat baking in the afternoon sun. A faded sign just outside the door of the building gave the arrival and departure schedule of stagecoaches that no longer ran, for a stage line that no longer existed. The stage line had been abandoned when the railroad had gone south, rather than north, of the Rattlesnake Mountains.

The roof and one wall of the nearby barn were caved in, but there was an overhang at the other end that provided some much-needed shade for their horses. Ackerman had posted guards east and west of their position because the north and south approaches were blocked by mountains.

Inside the building in what had been the waiting room, Mary Kate McVey sat in a chair in the corner. Ackerman sat at a table in the middle of the room, while Casey had biscuits in the oven, and bacon, twitching in the pan, on the stove.

"Do you want something to eat?" Ackerman asked Mary Kate.

"No," Mary Kate answered.

"You've eaten so very little since you joined us that I'm afraid if you don't start eating, you might get ill."

"Since I *joined* you? What do you mean, since I joined you? I didn't join you, you brought me here against my will. After you killed my husband."

"I'm sorry about your husband," Ackerman said. "But having him here with us would only complicate things. Sometimes people have to be sacrificed for the success of the overall operation. You might say that he was a tragic, but necessary, casualty."

"Major, I don't know what you have in mind, but believe me, it isn't going to work."

"Oh, I think it will."

"How can you do this? You and my father served together."

"We didn't exactly serve together, as you recall. I served under him. He was commanding officer of the Third Cavalry when, by all that is right, I should have been given that command."

"Really? As I recall, you were kicked out of the army. My father left with honor."

"You talk too much," Ackerman said. Getting up from the table, he stepped out onto the front porch of the way station, leaned against the supporting pillar of the porch roof, and stared out at the Rattlesnake range.

* * *

Ackerman's promise to the men he had "rescued" after his expulsion from the army was that if they rode with him, they would be well paid. His proposal was cheered at the time, and so far he had made good on his promise, their operations earning much more money than any of them had ever earned before. And this latest project, if all went well, stood to earn them, even after Ackerman took his thirty percent cut, over one thousand dollars apiece.

"Major, your supper's ready," Waters said, sticking his head out the front door.

"Thank you, Private Waters."

"I'll take some out to the guards."

"Yes, do that."

When Ackerman went back into the way station, he saw Mary Kate just as he had left her, still sitting in the chair. At the moment, she wasn't tied. She had complained, earlier, that the narrow rope Ackerman was using to bind her was cutting into her wrists and making her hands go numb, so he had untied her.

"You know, Miss Hamilton . . ."

"Mrs. McVey," Mary Kate said. "My name is Mrs. McVey."

"Yes, but now that your husband is dead, I'm pretty sure you don't have to use the name McVey anymore if you don't want to."

"What makes you think I don't want to?"

"Nothing, I was just telling you of your options. Now I'm going to ask you again to eat. I'm asking it nicely, and this is the last time I'm going to ask you." He carved open a biscuit and lay a piece of bacon inside.

"Here, eat this."

"No!" Mary Kate shouted loudly, and she knocked the biscuit from his hand.

In an almost instantaneous reaction, Ackerman slapped her.

"I told you, that would be the last time I was going to ask you nicely," he said angrily. "Women are all alike," he said in a hissing tone. "You can't be nice to them. Try it, and they'll go out of their way to try and belittle you. Well, believe me, girly, I've shown a woman or two that they can't do that to me and get away with it. Now I'm going to pick that biscuit and bacon up and give it to you again. You will either eat it, or I will stuff it down your throat."

"I thought officers were supposed to be gentlemen," Mary Kate said.

"I'm sorry," Ackerman said in a flat voice. "When they stripped me of my rank, they also stripped me of my gentlemanly decorum."

Ackerman retrieved the biscuit and bacon and brought it back to her. Because the biscuit had been on the floor, it had smudges of dirt on it.

"Eat it," he said.

"The biscuit is smudged. It's dirty," she said.

"That is your fault. You should have eaten it the first time it was offered to you," Ackerman said. "Now eat it!" he shouted at the top of his voice. Gone was the well-modulated dulcet voice he had been using with her.

With tears streaming down her cheeks, Mary Kate began to eat the biscuit.

* * *

"The hell you say. He slapped her?" Powell asked Smith. Powell and Smith were watching Dale and Travis Hastings, Bob Jerrod, and Corporal Jones playing poker for rocks. At the moment Marv Boyle and Waters were on guard. Baker and Maxwell were getting ready to relieve them.

"Yep," Smith answered. "He asked her to eat, she wouldn't, so he slapped her."

"I'll be damned. And here he's tellin' us to keep our hands offen her," Travis said.

"It's not the same thing," Jerrod said. "I'm bettin' that slappin' her ain't exactly what you got in mind."

"No, what I got 'n mind is more of a poke than a slap," Travis said, and the others laughed.

"Hey, how much money are we goin' to get out of this?" Travis asked.

"I don't know," Jerrod said. "Corporal Jones, you know how to cipher, I've seen you do it. How much money will each one of us get?"

"How much money was you gettin' when you was in the army?" Jones asked.

"You know how much. Eleven dollars a month. We've sure talked about it enough."

"All right, say you was in the army for eleven years, and for that whole eleven years, you didn't spend anything, you didn't buy one beer, one razor, you didn't buy nothin'. Say you saved ever' cent you drawed across the pay table. That would be one thousand and five hundred dollars, and that's how much each one of us will be gettin' from this."

"Sumbitch!" Jerrod said. "With that much money I could have me a whore ever' night for . . . how many nights would that be?"

Jones took out a pencil and began to figure.

"How come you have to figure this, but didn't have to the other?" Dale asked.

"'Cause I'd already been thinkin' of the other," Jones said. "What kind of whore would you be gettin'? A fifty-cent whore or a two-dollar whore?"

"Hell, a two-dollar whore," Jerrod replied with a big smile.

"Ha!" Jones said. "You could have you a two-dollar whore ever' night for two years."

"Whooee! For two years?"

"For two years. Unless of course you wanted to eat or drink anything during that time."

"Well, what if I just had me a whore ever' night for a year? Then I could use the rest of my money for catin' and drinkin'."

Powell laughed. "And you wouldn' have to spend nothin' on hotels or boardin' houses, 'cause you'd just be sleepin' with a different whore ever' night."

"How many days is in one year?" Travis asked.

"Three hundred and sixty-five," Jones said.

"Well, there ain't no towns with three hundred and sixty-five whores, so, like as not, you'd have to sleep with the same one more 'n oncet."

"Yeah, and you know that some of them would be fifty-cent whores," Smith said.

From Mary Kate's position inside the way station she could hear the conversation of the men outside. Most of them she didn't know, though she did remember a few of them from when she lived on the fort with her father. She remembered Sergeant Casey and Corporal Jones. And she remembered Powell, because he had been a bugler. Shortly after she was taken, and when she recognized some of them, she entertained the hope that one of them might help her escape. But listening to them now, the way they were planning on spending the money, she was beginning to realize that she had only two hopes of escape. She would either have to be rescued, or she would have to escape herself. And seeing the way Ackerman used his men, like an army, deploying guards and such, she had very little hope of being rescued.

MacCallister, Colorado

At this very moment, Falcon was in the Boots and Saddles Saloon enjoying a game of cards with Dallas Frazier, owner of the local newspaper, the *MacCallister Eagle.* The other two players were Doc Satterfield and Pogue Willis. Pogue owned the wagon freight line.

"I swear, Falcon, the way you're going here, the town's going to have to put up another statue of you, standing right there beside your father," Pogue said. "I bet a dollar."

"I would hope not," Falcon said, sliding a dollar into the pot. "Anyhow, I could never stand anywhere but behind Pa. None of us could."

"He was quite a man, all right," Frazier said. "Who dealt this mess anyway?" He laid his cards facedown on the table.

"You did," Doc Satterfield said. "And I think you did a fine job. I raise a dollar."

"Sounds like Doc is trying to bluff his way into a pot," Pogue said. "I see your dollar and raise it one."

"I'm in," Falcon said.

"Call," Doc said.

"Call? You mean you really do have something?" Pogue asked.

Doc turned up three aces.

"I'll be damn," Pogue said. "You've got me beat."

"Me, too," Falcon said.

Chuckling, Doc began raking in the pot, when he saw young Jimmy Barnes coming into the saloon. Jimmy was wearing a Western Union cap and carrying an envelope in his hand. He looked around for a moment, then seeing the cardplayers, hurried over to the table.

"Mr. MacCallister, you have a telegram," he said.

Falcon picked up a fifty-cent piece from the stack of coins in front of him and handed it to Jimmy.

"Thank you, sir!" Jimmy said, smiling broadly.

Falcon opened the telegram, read it, then frowned.

"Bad news, Falcon?" Doc asked.

Falcon showed Frazier the telegram.

MEGAN'S SON IN LAW KILLED STOP HER DAUGHTER
TAKEN BY OUTLAWS STOP ASKING 20,000 FOR HER
SAFE RETURN STOP PLEASE COME STOP MATTHEW

"Megan? Isn't she your sister that married that English lord or duke or whatever he is?" Frazier asked.

"Yes."

"Wait a minute. She got married not too long ago, didn't she? You went to her wedding, I think."

"Yes, I did. Jimmy?"

"Yes, sir?" the Western Union delivery boy replied.

"Have the telegrapher send this reply for me. Taking next train."

"Yes, sir," Jimmy said.

Falcon stood up, and when he did, the others stood as well.

"Gentlemen, I hate to leave the game, especially when I'm losing. But I'm going to Montana."

CHAPTER TWELVE

"We didn't tell you in the telegram, but we know who killed Johnny, and who has Mary Kate," Morgan said when Falcon showed up at Brimstone Ranch.

"Who was it?" Falcon asked

"Boyd Ackerman. Have you ever heard of him?"

"Ackerman, yes, I have heard of him. I gave testimony for the prosecution when he was court-martialed for failure to go to Colonel Cahill's aid."

"Yes, that's the Ackerman we're talking about. But he's been quite busy since he left the army. Here's an article that ran in the *Helena Independent* a while ago," Matthew said. "Read this first, then you'll get an idea as to what we are dealing with."

The article had been cut from the newspaper and was only a small square. Falcon held it under the light to read.

> Boyd Ackerman is a former Major in the U.S. Army who was cashiered out a few years ago for dereliction of duty. Now he leads a group of former soldiers,

commanding them like a military unit.
They have robbed banks, held up
stagecoaches, and even rustled a few
cattle. But because there are so many of
them, and because they are so well
organized, no sheriff has been able to
deal with them. Authorities attribute at
least ten murders to Ackerman's Raiders,
and think there may well be many more.

"Ackerman's Raiders?" Falcon asked, looking up
after he finished the article.

"Yeah, the arrogant son of a bitch came up with
that name himself," Matthew said. "He's actually written a few letters to the newspapers. Would you like to
read one of them?"

"Yes."

Matthew handed his younger brother another
piece cut from the paper.

To The General Public:
    Never, at any time, was it my intention
to become an outlaw. I am a proud
graduate of the United States Military
Academy at West Point. I graduated with
honors, and because of my score was given
my choice of branches in which I could
serve. I chose the cavalry because I
wanted to serve my country.
    During my service, I participated in
several engagements with the Indians,
serving with intrepidity, but when I was
ordered on what would have been a
suicide mission for me, and for the men
under me, I refused to carry it out. Had I

done so another two hundred soldiers would have been slaughtered, to lie beside the men that Colonel Cahill so arrogantly wasted.

Because of that I was court-martialed and drummed out of the army, an institution that I had intended to serve until old age mandated retirement. I was unfairly treated and turned on by the army I so loved. Now, I have taken a new path. I have riding with me several superbly trained soldiers. These men are intensely loyal to me, and will do anything I ask of them. I call my command Ackerman's Raiders, and I believe that we are fully the equal to any army command of twice our strength. There is no sheriff's department, no U.S. Marshal and a cadre of deputies, nor a posse of civilians who would dare come after us. Be warned that should such a group attempt this foolish effort, they would do so at their own peril.

MAJOR BOYD ACKERMAN
Ackerman's Raiders,
Commander.

"That is the letter of an arrogant man," Falcon asked.

"And brutal. He has been terrorizing Montana and Wyoming for the last three years," Matthew said. "And, like he says in his letter, he has his own private army, which makes it very difficult for a sheriff with no more than one or two deputies to deal with him."

"I really don't know that much about him," Falcon

said. "As you recall, Edward, my testimony was more along the lines of, could a rescue operation have reached Cahill and if so, would it have made any difference? The more we know about him, the easier it will be to come up with a plan of operation to find him."

"What do you want to know about him?" Edward asked. It wasn't a question of curiosity; it was, rather, a question that promised some sort of response. "Specifically," he added. "Since I was his commanding officer, I can tell you anything you need to know."

"You are also the one who brought charges against him, aren't you?" Morgan asked.

"Yes."

"Then this isn't just a matter of trying to get money from you, is it? It's also revenge."

"Yes, I'm afraid it is."

"Good," Falcon said.

"Good? What a piquant thing to say. Why would his wish to extract revenge from me be a good thing?" Edward asked.

"Because it means he has his emotions tied up in this," Falcon said, explaining his response. "And when people have an emotional investment in something, they often make mistakes. And that's exactly what we need Ackerman to do."

"Oh, yes, I think I see what you are saying."

"Has Ackerman made contact with you since he took Mary Kate?"

"No. We have only the bill he left plastered on Johnny's corral gate," Edward said. He showed Falcon the poster.

"Have you posted an ad in the newspaper?"

"No," Edward said.

"We told him not to," Matthew said. "We thought we would wait for you, and see what you thought."

"Let's post something and see if we can smoke him out," Falcon said.

"What paper should we use?" Edward asked.

"Does Deer Lodge City have a newspaper?"

"Yes."

"Then I expect that is the paper he will be watching. Which means he probably isn't too far from here, right now."

"All right," Edward said. "What should we say?"

"We'll work on it a bit," Falcon said. "I'm sure we can come up with something."

"I know Jim Mills, editor of the *Deer Lodge Examiner*, quite well," Edward said. "We can meet with him today."

"As I understand it, so far we are the only ones who know that Ackerman and his men are the ones who did this. Is that correct?"

"Yes."

"Let's keep it this way. It is always good to have a piece of information that your enemy doesn't know you have. If Ackerman didn't leave his name on this note, then he didn't intend for us to know yet. And at this point he has no reason to be aware that we know who he is. We'll see if we can work that to our advantage."

"So, what's our first step?" Megan asked.

"First thing we do is go into town and put an ad in the paper just like he asked. Then, Edward, if you

would, I'd like you to put what you know about Ackerman on paper. Don't hold anything back, if he has
any particular skills or abilities, put that down. Don't
let your dislike of him, or your concern over Mary
Kate, color your perception."

"I'll do what I can," Edward said.

The *Deer Lodge Examiner* was the second newspaper
in Deer Lodge, the first being the *Weekly Independent*,
which moved to Helena. The *Examiner*'s office was a
long, narrow building with a big glass front, upon
which was painted, in black letters, outlined in red,
the name of the newspaper. A counter separated the
front of the building from the back, where sat the
type drawers, the composing tables, and the press.
Jim Mills, the owner, was wearing an ink-stained
apron when he stepped to the counter to greet
Edward and the MacCallisters.

"Yes, what can I do for you folks?" he asked, then
he saw Edward. "Colonel Hamilton," he said. "Have
you any news on your daughter?"

"No, nothing, I'm afraid," Edward said. He un-
folded the paper that had been left. "I didn't mention
this before, but this was left by the man who killed
Johnny and took Mary Kate. As you can see, he wants
us to respond by newspaper."

"This newspaper?" Mills asked.

"We are assuming it will be this newspaper," Falcon
said. "Since he knows Colonel Hamilton lives here."

"And you are?"

"Oh, I'm sorry, I thought you knew him," Edward

said. "You've met two of my brothers-in-law, Morgan and Matthew MacCallister. This is another brother-in-law, Falcon MacCallister."

Mills's eyes opened wide. "Falcon MacCallister?" he said. He smiled broadly and extended his hand. "I am very pleased to meet you, sir. I have heard much about you."

Falcon shook Mills's hand. "Good to meet you as well," he said.

"So, the killer wants a response by newspaper, does he? All right, what do we want to say?"

"First, we want you to print an article that says the sheriff still doesn't know who the killer is," Falcon said.

"Why in heaven's name should we do that?" Mills asked, confused by the request.

"He doesn't know, does he?"

"No, he doesn't, but do you really think that is information we should let the killer know?"

"We want to give him a real sense of security," Falcon said. "As long as he knows that we don't know who he is, he won't be quite as guarded. He may do something that would give us an advantage," Falcon said.

"Yes, yes, I think I see what you mean. All right, I'll write such an article. Now you said something about the killer wanting you to place an ad?"

"Yes."

"What do you want the ad to say?"

"I have it written out here," Edward said, handing a sheet of notebook paper to the editor.

*To the person who recently visited my son-in-law and
daughter:*

*You have me at a disadvantage, sir. You know
who I am but I don't know who you are. You have
something that I very much prize, and you have
proposed a price for dealing.*

*I am sure we can do business. Please do nothing
to lower the value of the product before our
negotiations can be conducted.*

I beg of you to contact me. You know how to reach me.

"Is this all there is? Do you not want to sign your
name?" Mills asked.

"No, I think not. I think the more we can keep this
business between just me and whoever did this, the
better our chances will be for a satisfactory solution."

"But, Colonel, I've already printed one article,
shortly after it happened. And of course there was the
funeral, so everyone knows about it."

"Yes, that can't be contained. They know of the
crime, but they don't know, nor do I want anyone to
know, of the ongoing negotiations. You have to understand, Jim, that what I want, the thing that is most
important to me in the world, is the safe return of my
daughter."

"Yes, I understand. All right, Colonel, I'll do what
I can to help you."

"You will have my eternal gratitude," Edward said.

Later that afternoon, Edward brought a piece of
paper to Falcon. "I've made as honest an appraisal
of Ackerman as I can," he said.

"Thank you, Edward," Falcon said, taking the paper.

Boyd Ackerman graduated from West Point with honors. He was a very good soldier, though a bit of a martinet who demanded strict discipline among the men who served under him. He is an excellent marksman and horseman. He understands tactics and strategy, and well knows the difference. If engaged in a shooting battle, he knows how to deploy his men for the best possible utilization, and would, I feel, be quite formidable.

On the negative side, he is overconfident to the point of arrogance, and rarely admits that he is wrong. This makes him somewhat less flexible, and, perhaps susceptible to innovative tactics used against him.

He has poor impulse control, limited tolerance for frustration, and an explosive temper. And on a personal level, though I have reason to justify this thought, other than my own feelings, I don't think he likes women. I think he tends to be intimidated by them.

"Very good, Edward, this will be helpful information to know," Falcon said.

"What do we do next?" Megan asked.

"Now, we wait for Ackerman to make the next move," Falcon said.

CHAPTER THIRTEEN

Colorado State Prison, Cañon City

Mo Fong and Harvey Hood were four years into their twenty-year prison sentence, and at the moment they were in the rock pit, breaking rocks. Some of the rocks were used to construct roadbed, but the primary purpose of breaking rocks was to keep the prisoners busy. They not only wanted to keep the prisoners busy, they wanted to keep them on the edge of exhaustion all the time. The reasoning for that was a belief that prisoners who were tired were prisoners who were easily controlled.

"I'll be damned!" Hood said. "Hey, Booker!" he called to the guard. "Come here, look at this! Damned if I don't think I've discovered gold."

"There ain't no gold here. Prisoners been breakin' rocks in this pit for five years now, there ain't been one ounce of gold found."

"Yeah? Well there's gold in Colorado, ain't they?"

Hood asked. "Ever' body knows that. And I just found some."

"What if you have? It sure ain't goin' to do you no good, bein' as you're in prison 'n all," Booker said.

"No, but you ain't in prison. You could take it into town 'n sell it. You can keep half of it, and maybe some tobacco and a few other things for me."

"And for me," Fong said. "Don't forget, me 'n you's partners."

"Look at it, Mo," Hood said. "You think that'll be enough for both of us?"

"Hell, yeah. I'll bet there's three ounces there, maybe more. Where was that rock, I'm goin' to start breakin' 'em there."

"Me, too!" one of the other prisoners said enthusiastically, moving over to where Hood had been working.

"All right, let me look at it," Booker said, curious now.

Hood walked over to him, holding the rock out. But just before he reached Booker, he dropped the rock and it started rolling down the hill.

"Damn! What did you drop it for?" Booker said. He turned his head to look at the rolling rock, and Fong looped the chain that was stretched between his hands around Booker's neck. He twisted it tight, and Booker dropped his rifle and put both hands up to try and resist the chain. Booker struggled, trying to draw a breath, then after a moment he went limp. Fong kept the chain around him.

"Get his rifle, Harvey," he said.

Hood moved over quickly to retrieve the rifle.

Not until he had it did Hood release the pressure on Booker's neck. He fell to the ground, dead.

"Get his keys, get his keys!" one of the other prisoners said.

Hood got the keys, unlocked his chains, then unlocked Fong's chains.

"Set us loose, set us loose!" one of the other three prisoners shouted.

Hood threw the key ring as far as he could throw it.

"Sorry, boys, but two can travel a lot faster, and without arousing as much suspicion as five. If you can find the keys, you can set yourself free."

"Come on!" one of the men shouted to the others. "Let's find those keys!"

Hood and Fong started in the opposite direction from the prison, moving quickly.

Five miles away from the rock pit where Hood and Fong made good their escape, sixteen-year-old Drew Tindol was working in the barn when his fifteen-year-old sister, Molly, came to get him.

"Mama says to wash up for dinner," Molly said. "But look at you. You're so dirty you won't be clean by suppertime."

Drew began pumping water into a basin. "And you think you are clean?"

"I'm always clean," Molly said. "I keep myself clean."

Suddenly Drew threw the basin of water at Molly. "Now you are a lot cleaner!" he said, laughing loudly.

"Oh! Oh! Drew, stop that!" Molly shouted, turning and running back into the house.

Molly was still complaining to her mother when Drew went inside.

"Drew, apologize to your sister," his mother demanded.

"I'm sorry, Molly. I was just funnin' you. I didn't mean nothin' by it. I tell you what, I'll let you ride Prince this afternoon."

"You will?" Molly asked, breaking into a smile.

"Sure. If you forgive me."

"I forgive you," Molly said.

"Good, here's your father. I'm glad this is all settled," Molly's mother said.

"There's a house," Fong said. "Damn, is that pork chops I smell?"

"Yeah, they must be cooking dinner about now."

They started toward the house, then saw a girl come from the house and walk toward the barn. Then they saw the boy throwing water on the girl.

"Ha! Did you see that?"

When the girl and the boy went back into the house, Fong and Hood started there as well, but stopped when they saw a man ride up, tie his horse off at the back porch, then go inside.

"I didn't see no gun on him, did you?" Hood asked.

"No. He wasn't wearin' a gun."

"Then let's go have us some pork chops."

Fong jacked a round into the chamber of the Winchester and the two ran quickly across the open space between the rocks where they had been and the house. Taking the back porch in one step, they burst through the door into the kitchen, Fong first.

The man was standing at a counter with his back to the door and when they burst in, he turned around quickly.

"Here, what is the meaning . . ." That was as far as he got before Fong pulled the trigger. The man went down as the mother and daughter screamed.

The boy reacted unexpectedly, grabbing a butcher knife and charging toward Fong before he could cock the rifle again. Hood picked up a chair and brought it down hard on the boy's head, dropping him to the floor. By now Fong had cocked his rifle, and he shot the boy. He fired a second shot into the head of the man and a second shot into the boy's head, making certain both were dead.

That left only the mother and daughter alive, and they were standing near the table, looking on with horror-struck faces.

"Damn, it's been a long time since I've et me a home-cooked meal," Hood said.

"Harvey, you know what else has been a long time?" Fong asked.

"What?"

Fong grabbed his crotch. "It's been a long time since either one of us have had us a woman."

"Yeah," Hood said. "Yeah, it has been, ain't it? You want the young 'n, or the mama? 'Cause it don't make no never-mind to me which 'n I get."

"Then I'll take the young 'n."

"No!" the mother screamed, but her scream was cut off by a hard blow to the side of her head.

Half an hour later, now wearing clothes other than the prison garb, Mo Fong and Harvey Hood rode away on the two horses they had found there. They also had eighteen dollars that they had taken from the sugar jar. Behind them, all four members of the Tindol family lay dead on the kitchen floor.

"Where we goin'?" Hood asked.

"North, out of this state," Fong replied. "By the time anyone discovers them, we'll be a long way from here."

Montana Territory

Mary Kate had been Ackerman's prisoner for a week. She had given up any idea of a hunger strike, or even of a hunger protest. She knew that she had to keep her strength up in order to take advantage of any opportunity that might present itself. And in order to do that, she had to eat.

Ackerman had made a point to get a newspaper every day, and at first Mary Kate thought that, perhaps, he was looking to see if an article had been printed about his crime. Was he that vain?

The answer to that question was . . . yes, he was that vain. But she soon realized that that was not why he was looking for the newspaper. He was looking for something specific, and evidently, today, he found it.

Killer Still Unknown

SHERIFF HAS NO NEW INFORMATION

Mary Kate Hamilton Still Missing

It has been over a week since the reprehensible murder of area rancher Jonathan McVey, and the disappearance of his wife, Mary Kate, who is also the daughter of Colonel Edward Hamilton.

The only clue available is the note that the killer or killers left at the scene of the crime in which there was left a demand for twenty thousand dollars to be paid for the safe return of the Colonel's daughter. The Colonel has been most distraught since the event, as has been the young woman's mother. Sheriff Tompkins has requested that anyone who might have some information to please visit him in his office.

The sheriff has stated that until such time as more information becomes available, that he can do nothing toward solving the crime, or apprehending the culprits.

It now appears that the only way to bring a happy ending to this case is for Colonel Hamilton to pay the twenty thousand dollars demanded by the scoundrel or scoundrels who abducted Mary Kate McVey. Colonel Hamilton has stated that he is willing to do so as the safe return of his daughter is the thing that is most paramount in his mind.

"Ah ha!" Ackerman said, showing the paper to Mary Kate. "I think perhaps we may be able to do some business with your father after all!"

"You mean because of this article?"

"This article, and the ad he placed in the paper," Ackerman said. "He wants to deal."

"Good. Then that means I can soon go home."

"Well, maybe not so soon."

"What do you mean? You said that my father wants to deal with you, didn't you?"

"Yes. But now that we know that the sheriff has no idea who did this, I see no need to rush things. It may be that I underestimated your value, my dear. If he is so quickly ready to part with twenty thousand dollars, then I don't think forty thousand dollars would be out of the question."

"Oh!" Mary Kate said. "How dare you do such a thing? My father is coming to you with an honest and honorable proposal, and you would betray him like that?"

"Betray?" Ackerman said with an angry snarl. "You dare talk to me about betrayal? What do you think your father did to me?" Ackerman shouted the last nine words.

"I don't know," Mary Kate admitted. "I didn't follow the court-martial that closely. I do know that my father agonized over it, and was very upset that it had come to that. I remember him telling my mother that he thought you were a good officer but that he had no choice."

"He had a choice," Ackerman said, spitting the

words out. "He could have seen that I was right. History proved that I was right, but reason seems to be a trait that your father lacks. Well, my dear, he has a choice now. He can either deal with me, or pay the consequences. And since it would be you who would ultimately be paying the consequences, I think he will deal." He thumped the paper with the back of his hand. "And his response tells me that."

"What are you going to do now?" Mary Kate asked.

"Now, my dear, I am going to open negotiations with your father."

Two days later Morgan returned from town with a copy of the *Deer Lodge Examiner*.

"It looks like we got our answer," he said.

> To the gentleman who recently contacted me through an ad in this paper:
> You have suggested that you are willing to do business with me. I welcome your open attitude to begin negotiations. Please understand that the price mentioned was merely a suggestion. Upon further contemplation, and in consideration of the value of the product I have that you hold so dear, I believe that the final sum may be much higher. I will contact you with further details by mail.

"I'm not sure this is what we want. Looks to me like he's trying to up the ante," Matthew said.

"It doesn't matter what the ante is," Falcon said.

"The bottom line is, he isn't going to get any money anyway, so it doesn't matter if he asks for a hundred thousand dollars. All we want to do is get him engaged in dialogue. As long as he is talking to us, he isn't doing anything else."

CHAPTER FOURTEEN

When Edward picked up his mail at the post office, two days later, Falcon was with him.

"This is odd. There is no return address on this letter," Edward said.

"Then I'm sure that's the letter we are looking for. Open it up and take a look," Falcon suggested.

Edward opened the envelope and removed the letter. He held it in such a way that both could read it at the same time.

Dear Colonel Hamilton:

I am glad to see that you are showing reason and common sense. Let me assure you that we both want what is best for your daughter. It is to my advantage to keep her safe so that the value not be diminished. And it is that, her value, that is the subject of this letter.

After careful consideration, I have decided to increase the price I am asking for her safe return,

to $40,000. I am sure that you agree with me that
your wonderful daughter is worth that amount.

Should you wish to communicate with me, please
do so by placing another ad in the newspaper.

You will forgive me if I do not sign this letter.

Falcon took the envelope over to the window and showed it to the postal clerk.

"Can you tell by looking at this, how this mail was delivered?" Falcon asked. "Did it come by train or stagecoach?"

Pleas Malcolm, the postal clerk, looked at the envelope. "Oh, neither, sir," he said. "As you can see, it has a Deer Lodge postmark. That means it was picked up at one of the mail drops right here in town."

"Do you know which drop?"

"Well, Walt Bizzel is out making his rounds now. It isn't likely that he will know where he got the letter, but it won't hurt to ask him."

They found Walt emptying a mailbox at the corner of Main and Montana.

"Mr. Bizzel," Edward said. "I wonder if we might have a word with you?"

"I don't mind a bit, Colonel, as long as you don't mind walking along with me. I have schedule to maintain, you know." Bizzel stuffed the handful of envelopes into his bag, then closed and locked the mailbox. He started toward the next corner at a brisk walk.

"We don't mind a bit," Edward said as they started walking along with him. He showed Bizzel the letter.

"I just picked this letter up at the post office. Mr. Malcolm said you might know where the letter was posted."

"Look, I handle more than a hundred letters a day, there's no way I would . . ." Bizzel stopped in mid-sentence when he saw the envelope Edward was showing him.

"Oh, yeah, I do remember where I got that one. I got that letter down at the Cottonwood box. I remember it because it didn't have a return address, which is pretty rare. And also I saw that it was addressed to you. I thought about it, because of your daughter being taken and all."

"The Cottonwood box?"

"Yes, it's the last mailbox at the north end of town."

"Thank you, Mr. Bizzel, you've been a big help," Edward said.

A few minutes later, Falcon and Edward were standing by the Cottonwood box at the north end of town.

"Where does this road go?"

"The next town is Washington Gulch. But I have to tell you, it isn't much of a town," Edward said.

There was a spirited discussion over what to say in the newspaper ad. Matthew and Megan wanted to suggest that forty thousand was too much, but that they would be open to negotiation. Falcon and Morgan wanted to give in to the demand.

"I just hate to give the son of a bitch what he is asking for," Matthew said.

"Yes," Megan agreed. "There is no way he should be rewarded."

"You don't understand," Falcon said. "We aren't going to give him anything. This is just a way of making him overconfident, and less cautious."

"I don't think we can make him any less cautious," Edward said. "Ackerman is one of the most cautious people I know. But he is arrogant, and that makes him prone to being overconfident. I agree with Falcon and Morgan. I think we should offer him what he has asked for."

"All right," Megan said. "Let's do the ad."

> This is Edward Hamilton, and I address
> this personal ad to the person with whom
> I have been in contact. If you can prove to
> me that the product I wish to buy is still in
> good condition, I am agreeable to your
> terms. Please provide me with that proof.

After Ackerman read the ad, he drummed his fingers on the table for a moment as he tried to decide how to prove to Edward that his daughter was still safe. Then he got an idea.

"Mrs. McVey, your father wants proof that you are still alive and unhurt. I think it would go a long way toward easing his concern about you. I am willing to give him this proof, but it will require your cooperation."

"What do you want me to do?" Mary Kate asked.

"I'm going to take you into Washington Gulch, where I will have your picture taken. I intend to send that picture, along with a letter from you, to your father. Are you amenable to that?"

"You are going to let me write to my father?"

"Yes. I intend to read it, of course, to make certain that you say nothing that can endanger this operation. But I think that, with your letter, and with a picture of you, it will help ease some of your mother and father's worry."

"Why, all of a sudden, are you concerned about my parents?"

"Because I want this transaction to go smoothly," Ackerman said. "The more smoothly it goes, the better it will be for all of us."

"All right. Take me into town and take my picture."

"Before we do this, I want your promise that you will do nothing to call attention to yourself. If I see that you are trying to, in any way, signal the photographer, I will kill the photographer. Do you understand that? I won't do anything to you, I need you alive to be able to make this operation work. But I don't need the photographer for anything but the picture. If you force me to do it, I will kill him, and his entire family. Do you want that on your head?"

"No, I don't. Of course not."

"Then I expect your fullest cooperation. Do I have your promise?"

"Yes," Mary Kate said quietly.

"Good girl."

Washington Gulch was little more than a flyblown speck, clinging to the side of a mountain. It was made up of whipsawed lumber shacks with unpainted, splitting wood turning gray, surviving by providing cowboys and miners with cafés, saloons, and bawdy houses.

The town, like so many other Western towns, had grown up with the promise of a railroad, but that promise never materialized. Then, when the Washington Gulch to Helmville Stage Line went out of business, Washington Gulch was barely hanging on.

As Ackerman rode into town with Mary Kate riding by his side, he had two riders in front and two behind, in case Mary Kate decided to make a break for it. Mary Kate sized up the town as they rode in, looking for any chance to escape.

"Do you see that mother and her two children over there, Mrs. McVey?" Ackerman asked, pointing to the little family that was walking down the boardwalk just in front of a mercantile.

"Yes, I see them."

"Quite a lovely family, don't you think?"

"Yes," Mary Kate replied, wondering where Ackerman was going with this.

"If you try and escape, I won't shoot you. But, I will kill that mother and her two children."

Mary Kate gasped. "You wouldn't dare do such a horrid thing!"

"I consider myself at war, Miss Hamilton. And when one is at war, one must put aside all human feelings in order to become the consummate warrior. Believe me, Miss Hamilton, I will kill that mother and the two little girls, and I won't give it a second thought."

"What kind of beast are you?"

"I am not a beast, I am a soldier."

"My father was a soldier, too, and he would never do anything like that."

"Your father was never a soldier. He was an experiment in international diplomacy. He exchanged his British title for a commission in the American army."

They stopped in front of a building that had a sign reading: RON DYSART, PHOTOGRAPHY.

"Smith, you and Waters go around back. Jerrod, you and Powell stay out here. Let no one else in the building until we come out," Ackerman said.

"Yes, sir."

"All right, Miss Hamilton. Let's have your picture taken."

Inside they were met by a woman who was wearing her hair tied up in a bun behind her head. She had a pair of glasses, but at the moment they were hanging from a cord around her neck.

"May I help you?"

"This is my daughter," Ackerman said. "I want a picture of her."

Mary Kate bristled at the suggestion that she was his daughter, but she said nothing about it, for fear that he might do harm to the woman.

"Wait here, I'll get Mr. Dysart," the woman said.

Dysart was a rather small man, very thin, with a prominent Adam's apple. He wore garters around the sleeves of his blue-striped shirt. He had a small, neatly trimmed mustache, his hair was very dark, combed straight back, and glistening from some sort of hair gel.

"My wife tells me you want a picture of your daughter," he said. He looked at Mary Kate, then held his hands up, making a frame with his thumbs and forefingers. "Oh, yes, what a lovely creature she is. She will be a great subject. But, are you sure you want her dressed in such a fashion? Suppose we let Mrs. Dysart show her some of the clothes we have here?"

"I want her photographed just as she is," Ackerman said.

"Oh, my, well, yes the customer is always right. Of course I will photograph her anyway you wish. Perhaps if she holds a bouquet of flowers. We have some beautiful flowers, made from silk. You can scarcely tell the difference between them and real flowers," Dysart said.

"She will be holding this newspaper," Ackerman said. "Can you take a photograph so that the date on the paper can be read?"

"What an odd request," Dysart said.

"Didn't you just say that the customer is always right?"

"Yes, but I am a professional, after all. And one would think that you would want to take advantage of my expertise. You do want the most beautiful picture I can compose, don't you?"

"I want a picture of this woman, holding this newspaper. And I want it clear enough that you can read the date on the paper. Now, can you do that, or not?"

"Yes, of course I can do that."

Mary Kate did not say a word, but let Dysart pose her, then give her the newspaper to hold. She told herself that seeing the picture would comfort her mother and father. Also Ackerman had warned her that if she said or did anything that would be disruptive, he would kill the photographer and his wife.

"Now, I'm going to put this little support behind your head," Dysart said. "If you will just lean your head back into it, it will help you keep a perfectly still pose."

Mary Kate did as asked, feeling the Y-shaped brace supporting her head.

"Now, remain perfectly still," Dysart said as he reached his hand down to the lens cover. He pulled the cover off. "Look at the water, look at the trees, look at the clover all filled with bees," he said in a singsong voice. He replaced the cover.

"You'll have this picture in a week," Dysart said.

"Wrong. I will have it before I leave this building," Ackerman said.

"Oh, but sir, I couldn't possibly do that. I have many other pictures waiting to be developed. It wouldn't be fair to put your picture ahead of all the others."

"How much are you going to charge for taking this picture?"

"That will be a dollar and a half."

"I will give you three dollars if you will develop the picture now," Ackerman said.

Dysart smiled. "Three dollars?"

"Yes."

"Very good, sir. If you and your lovely daughter will wait here, I'll have the picture for you within fifteen minutes."

"Do you have an envelope that we can mail the picture in?"

"Yes, sir, but it will cost you fifteen cents."

"I'll give you twenty-five cents if you will also furnish some paper and a pen."

"Nancy, provide the gentleman with a piece of paper and a pen," Dysart said.

The woman provided the paper, and Ackerman had Mary Kate write a letter to her parents.

"Remember, I am going to read it," Ackerman said.

Dear Mama and Papa—
I am all right. I hope someone took care of
Johnny. I hope you can do what it takes to get
me home again. I love you.

Mary Kate

When Mary Kate finished the letter, she showed it to Ackerman who read it, then nodded. "Yes," he said. "This will do."

A few minutes later Dysart came back into the room, holding the photograph. "Here it is, sir."

Ackerman took a quick look at it, then put it, Mary Kate's letter, and one that he had written into the big envelope. He paid Dysart, then left.

"What a lovely young woman," Dysart said to his wife after Ackerman left. "Do you suppose she is mute?"

CHAPTER FIFTEEN

Purgatory, Montana Territory

The town of Purgatory could not be found on any map. And whereas most towns would resent that omission, the residents of Purgatory did not take exception to it. In fact, they went to great lengths to see to it that their town wasn't put on any maps, for they valued their privacy. Purgatory was a town founded, and occupied, by outlaws.

As Fong and Hood rode into town, they saw very few people on the street, and those who were moved quickly and with purpose. No one lingered for conversation. They headed toward the saloon at the far end of town. Painted in red on the false front of the saloon were the words BLOODY BUCKET. Beside the word was a picture of a bucket, with streaks of red streaming down its sides.

"You think Moss is still here?" Hood asked as the two men dismounted in front of the saloon.

"As far as I know he is," Fong said. "Me 'n him discovered this place several years back. He decided he would stay here. It's safe here, there don't law ever come here . . ." Fong paused in midsentence to chuckle. "Maybe I ought to say that the law does come here, but they don't never leave. Anyhow, like I was sayin', it's safe here, but there ain't that much to do. I got bored and moved on. Better I should 'a stayed."

The two men went into the saloon, then stepped up to the bar and ordered a beer.

"Damn, that's good," Hood said. "How come, you think, they don't let us have beer in prison?"

"I don't know," Fong said. "I ain't ever been able to figure that out."

"How we goin' to make us a livin' while we're here?" Hood asked.

"Ever' now 'n then some of the boys here gets together and goes somewhere to pull a job. Then they come back here. I reckon we can do somethin' like that."

Fong turned around to look over the saloon's customers, then, seeing a couple of people he recognized, he smiled.

"Come on," he said to Hood. "Let me introduce you to some folks."

When Fong and Hood approached the table the two men looked up, expressions showing their irritation at being interrupted. Then they recognized Fong and both of them smiled.

"Fong, damn, where've you been for the past year?" one of the two men asked. He was short and clean shaven, with very dark hair. The other was tall, lanky, and with a drooping eye.

"In prison for some of the time," Fong said. "Dingus Burke and Bob Pell, meet my pard, Harvey Hood. Me 'n him busted out of prison a couple weeks back now."

"So you figured to come here and hide out, did you?"

"Yeah," Fong replied. "Onliest thing is, me 'n him's both near 'bout broke, and we're goin' to have to find some way to make some money."

"You'll find some money. They's always someone puttin' together a job of one kind or another, and they'll be lookin' for men."

"Is Moss still hanging around, or is he long gone?" Fong asked.

Burke laughed. "Moss is our town marshal now."

"Marshal?" Hood asked in surprise. He looked over at Fong. "I thought you told me there wasn't no law in this town."

Burke and Pell both laughed.

"It ain't the kind of law you're thinkin' about," Fong said. "This here law is only to keep peace in the town. It kind 'a settles things. Otherwise there would no doubt be a lot of killin's in town."

"There already is a lot of killin's in town," Pell said. "But as long as both parties is armed, there ain't much made of it."

"And merchants we have in town, the saloon, the café, the hotel, the goods store, they say they won't stay here unless there's some kind of law. And we need them to stay," Burke added. "Else, what's the purpose of havin' a town?"

"Are they outlaws, too?" Hood asked.

"Not actual outlaws. I mean, as far as I know, there ain't none of 'em actual wanted by the law or anything. But bein' here with all us sort of makes 'em outlaws," Burke replied.

"There's Moss now," Pell said.

Fong went over to talk to Moss.

"I'll be damned," Moss said, shaking Fong's hand. "I figured you was dead by now."

"Not yet," Fong said. "I see you ain't left, yet."

"I don't plan to. I got me a good thing goin' here."

"Yeah, I reckon so," Fong said. "I expect you purt' nigh run the town, don't you?"

"No, that would be Major Ackerman."

"Who?"

"Major Ackerman. You mean you ain't never heard of him?" Moss asked.

"I can't say as I have. Who is he?"

"He was a high-rankin' army officer oncet, and now he's got him a whole bunch of men that he calls Ackerman's Raiders. They're robbin' and such, and there can't nobody do nothin' to stop 'em. He spends a lot of time here in Purgatory between jobs, and when he's here, well because he's got his own private army so to speak, why, he is king of the roost."

"And there don't nobody complain?" Fong asked.

"No. Why would they? When Major Ackerman and his men are here, why they ain't no sheriff's posse, no United States Marshals posse, not even the United States Army would be able to come in here and take out as much as one person. We're as safe here as we would be inside a fort."

Fong smiled. "That's what I like."

Deer Lodge

The next day Edward picked up the envelope, which had again been dropped into the Cottonwood mailbox. Taking it back, they looked at the photograph.

"Look at the date on the newspaper," Matthew said. "It was yesterday."

"Yes, no doubt he had her hold the newspaper just to establish the date," Falcon said.

Megan read the letter from Mary Kate. "She doesn't say much."

"I'm sure she said just what Ackerman told her to say," Falcon said.

"I see that Ackerman also included a letter," Edward said.

"What does he have to say?" Megan asked.

Colonel Hamilton,

As you can clearly see by the enclosed photograph, your daughter is alive and well. I am sure we both want to keep her that way. As an act of good faith, I want you to put one thousand dollars in a bag and leave it 30 paces south of water tank number five on the railroad track that runs from Deer Lodge City to Helena. Mark the location by making a triangle of three rocks. If we are able to make this exchange without difficulty, then we can set up our next step.

Oh, and a warning. If the money isn't there, then I intend to leave one of Mary Kate's hands there. And in all future communications with you, I will include one of her body parts. I think, to prevent

*undue pain from being inflicted on this young
woman, that you had better cooperate with me.*

*And as an article of good faith on my side, the
one thousand dollars that you leave will be counted
as part of your final settlement.*

"It's not by chance that he has chosen that particular water tank," Edward said. "I know that track well.
Right through there, there is an open area for at least
three miles in all directions. I would be impossible to
keep an eye on it without being seen."

"Look at this," Ackerman said, pointing to the photograph. "There is a name here. Dysart. This must be
the name of the photographer's studio. Do either of
you recognize it?" he asked Megan and Edward.

"It's not in Deer Lodge, I know that," Edward said.

"No, but I'll bet your newspaper friend knows
where it is," Falcon said.

"It's in Washington Gulch," Mills said. "Ron Dysart
is his name. He has advertised his shop in my paper.
My paper is quite widely read in Washington Gulch,
since they have no paper of their own."

After they left the newspaper office, it was decided that Matthew, Morgan, and Megan would go
with Edward to leave the one thousand dollars, while
Falcon would go to Washington Gulch to talk to
Ron Dysart.

* * *

"Oh, yes, of course I recognize this photograph. I took it only yesterday. Such a lovely young girl. She was a mute, poor thing."

"Mute?"

"Yes, sir, why she didn't say one word the entire time she was here."

"Do you know where they went after they left here?"

"No, I can't say as I do. But . . . there was one thing. I didn't think anything about it at the time, and it may be nothing. Still, it is a little strange."

"What is it?"

"Well, Nancy found it when she was cleaning up this morning, and it had to come from either this young lady or her father . . ."

"Her father?" Falcon asked.

"Yes. It was her father who brought her in for the photograph."

"Did he tell you he was her father?"

"Oh, he did indeed. Is there some reason I should doubt it?"

"It's not important," Falcon said. "What is it that you wanted to show me?"

"Oh, yes. Just a minute. We started to throw it away with the trash but I found it so strange that I held on to it. I'll get it for you."

Dysart left Falcon standing in the front room for a moment, then returned holding a torn piece of paper.

"As you can see it is torn, so you can't read much of it. But it appears to be part of a flyer for the WG and H stagecoach line. See, you can see the letters,

WG and H, and just the back part of the drawing of a stagecoach."

"WG and H?"

"Yes, and that is why I found it interesting. WG and H is the Washington Gulch and Helmville stagecoach line. Or rather it was. The WG and H has been out of business for, oh, at least two years now, maybe more. I know we certainly didn't have any of their flyers around. It wasn't here when Nancy cleaned the place yesterday morning. And the only customers we had who actually came into the shop yesterday were this young lady and her fath . . . that is, the man with her, who told me that he was her father."

"May I have this?"

"Yes, I don't see why not. Look here, what is this all about?"

"Do you read the *Deer Lodge Examiner*?" Falcon asked.

"Yes, it's the only newspaper that is readily available."

"You may have read that someone abducted the daughter of Colonel Hamilton."

"Yes, what an awful thing to have happen."

Falcon pointed to the picture. "This is his daughter, Mary Kate Hamilton McVey. The man who brought her in for her photograph yesterday was her abductor, and the one who murdered Mary Kate's husband."

"Oh, Lord help me," Dysart said, lifting his hand to his mouth. "And he was here, in this very building. I'm so sorry. I didn't know, I had no way of knowing.

And of course, the young lady said nothing. Why, he could have murdered my wife and me."

"You can thank that young woman for not saying anything. If she had said something there is no doubt but that Ackerman would have killed you."

"Ackerman? You mean the one they call Major Ackerman?"

"Yes."

Dysart staggered back and sat heavily in the chair. "To think, he was right here. I can see, now, why the young lady didn't speak."

"Oh, but she did speak," Falcon said.

"What? What do you mean?"

"I'm sure that she was the one who brought this and somehow managed to leave it behind. And thanks to you, we now have our first lead."

As Falcon was leaving town he saw, sitting up against the blacksmith building, an old stagecoach, covered with dirt, and with the paint peeling. Under the mantle of dirt he saw the letters WG and H, and he turned Lightning toward the building. A shirtless black man, his muscles rippling and his sweat-covered chest and arms glistening in the sunshine, was at the forge and anvil, holding a piece of metal in the fire, then, when it was glowing red, putting it on the anvil and hitting it, causing the sparks to fly.

Falcon dismounted and watched the blacksmith for another moment until, finally, he put the piece of iron in a tub of water to cool. On the wall behind the blacksmith, Falcon saw a poster with a drawing of a black man in the pose of a prizefighter. The print beside the picture read: Fighting July 4th, 1876, Mike Taylor.

"Would you be Mr. Taylor?" Falcon asked.

"Yes, sir," Taylor said.

"How did you do in that fight?" Falcon asked, pointing to the poster.

Taylor smiled. "I won that fight by a knockout. Truth to tell you, sir, I wouldn't have that poster up here if I had lost."

Falcon laughed. "I can't say that I would blame you." Falcon pointed to the coach. "I wonder if I could ask you about that coach."

"Yes, sir, what do you want to know about it?"

"What's it doing here?"

"Mr. Montgomery, he's the man owns this black-smith shop, was doin' business with the WG and H stagecoach line. We shoed their horses, put the iron tires on their wheels, did all sorts of things and, next thing you know, why the WG and H owed Mr. Montgomery a lot of money and didn't have enough to pay what they owed. So Mr. Montgomery, he took the coach and said he would hold it until they paid their bill." Taylor chuckled. "Well sir, they ain't paid their bill yet, and they ain't likely to, seein' as they ain't in business no more."

"Where was their depot?"

"They didn't have no depot here in town. The coach picked up folks at the Morning Star Hotel, but the actual office was in a buildin' about halfway between here and Helmville."

"What's in that building now?" Falcon asked.

"Oh, sir, why there ain't nothin' in it now. The whole stage line went broke an' all the folks that was with it just packed up 'n moved on to somewhere else."

"I see."

"Sir, if you don't mind my askin', I mean I know it's none of my business an' all, but just why is it you're so interested in the WG and H?"

"Before I answer that question, let me ask you one more." Falcon showed Taylor the triangular piece of paper that had been torn off the corner of a larger sheet.

"Would this be something that the WG and H would have?"

Taylor looked at it and nodded. "Yes, sir, this piece of paper come from the way station. I know that for a fact."

"How do you know that?"

"I was out there a whole bunch of times, doin' first one thing and another for Mr. Peabody. He's the one that owned the stagecoach line. And I seen this very poster a whole lot of times."

"How do you know it was this same poster?"

"You see the G here, in WG? How it's got this cut through it?"

Falcon looked closer at the piece of paper he was holding, and saw the cut that Taylor was talking about. He either hadn't noticed before, or he had thought it had been part of the tear in removing it from the rest of the poster.

"Yes, I see it."

"I put that cut there," Taylor said with a broad smile. "And I won half a dollar by doin' it."

"What do you mean?"

Taylor reached down to his boot, then pulled out a knife. "Watch this," he said. He turned toward one wall of the shop. "Do you see that calendar?"

"Yes."

"I'll show you today's date."

Taylor threw the knife and it whizzed through the air, then stuck through the calendar, into the wall behind it. The handle of the knife quivered for a second.

"That's pretty good," Falcon said.

"Mr. Peabody, he bet me I couldn't hit the G by throwin' the knife. I did, and I won half a dollar. Now, you said if I answered another question for you, you'd tell me what this is all about. I know it ain't none of my business, but a man does get curious."

"A few days ago some men killed a rancher by the name of Johnny McVey, back in Deer Lodge," Falcon said. "And after they killed him, they took his wife. His wife happens to be my niece, and I'm looking for her."

"And you think this here piece of paper might have somethin' to do with it?"

"I think it might help me find her, yes. And I'm very appreciative to you for your help."

"Yes, sir, well, I don't know as I was all that much of a help, but I'm right proud if I could do anything for you."

"Thanks again," Falcon said, walking back out to mount Lightning.

CHAPTER SIXTEEN

"I have a feeling we need to be moving on," Ackerman said. "We have been here too long."

"Where are we going, Major?" Casey asked.

"The first thing we are going to do is pick up the money they left at the water tower."

"How do we know it will be there?"

"It will be there. I'm sure Colonel Hamilton doesn't want to find his daughter's severed hand."

Mary Kate gasped.

"And it's such a lovely hand, too," Ackerman said, smiling.

Mary Kate did not think she had ever seen such evil as there was in that mirthless smile.

"Then where?" Casey asked.

"Purgatory."

Casey smiled. "Good. The men will appreciate that."

"Sergeant, I don't make decisions based upon what the men will appreciate," Ackerman said. "I make decisions based upon what I think is the best move at the moment."

"Yes, sir," Casey said, the smile gone.

Leaving the way station, Ackerman led his men toward the water tank where he expected the one thousand dollars to be left. Before actually approaching the tank, however, he dispatched riders to all cardinal points around the tank. It took an hour for them to return. All four reported that the coast was clear.

Half an hour later, at exactly thirty paces south of the water tank, Ackerman saw three rocks arranged as a triangle. Buried under the rocks was a canvas bag, and inside the bag was a bound packet of ten-dollar bills. It took but a moment to count them and ascertain that the amount stipulated had been left.

"Well, I'm beginning to believe this is all going to turn out well for you and for me," Ackerman said to Mary Kate.

Remounting, he resumed the march, his riders following behind in precise military position.

After leaving the blacksmith shop, Falcon debated whether to return to Brimstone and wait on the others before going to the way station or to go there himself. Every moment he waited was one moment longer in the ordeal that Mary Kate was having to go through. He thought of his conversation with her on the night before she was married.

"Still, if I ever got into trouble, and needed a knight in shining armor, riding a white horse, to come rescue me, promise me that you will do it," she had said.

Falcon had laughed it off. "Darlin', I'm not a knight, I don't have armor, in fact I don't even think I would fit into one of those suits of armor out in the hall. And Lightning is black, not white."

"But promise me if I ever need you, that you will come rescue me."

Falcon had put his hand on Mary Kate's cheek and she reached up to pull his hands over to her lips to kiss.

"Of course, I promise," he had said.

Falcon had made his niece that promise, and he intended to keep it. But could he go up against Ackerman's army, alone? If he failed, it would make the situation even worse for Mary Kate. No, he had no choice. He was going to have to return to Brimstone and tell the others what he had learned.

Frustrated that he was this close, but unable to do anything about it, Falcon turned his horse south, for Brimstone.

"Yes, I know exactly where the way station is," Edward said.

"I am convinced that Mary Kate is there," Falcon said.

"Then let's go get her!" Megan said.

"We can't just ride up there," Falcon said. "If Ackerman is as military as everyone is saying he is, he isn't going to bivouac anywhere without posting guards. And I have a feeling these guards won't be shouting 'Who goes there?' I expect they'll shoot first, and ask questions later."

"I think you're right," Edward said.

"All right, we need some traveling rations," Falcon

said. "Jerky, hardtack, bacon, beans, coffee. I expect we'll have to go into town for that."

"No, we won't," Morgan said. "Matthew and I stocked up on that sort of thing before we even came down here. We figured we might be going out for an extended period of time."

"Smart move," Falcon said. "All right, I suggest we leave now, and we'll reach the place after dark. More 'n likely, we'll have to deal with whatever sentry he has posted, but the main body would be asleep."

"Good idea," Matthew agreed.

"Then let's saddle up and get on the way," Falcon suggested.

It was dark, and as they approached the way station they could see it in the moonlight. Dismounting, they ground-tied their horses, then moved a little closer to examine the building.

"There are lights," Megan said quietly.

"Maybe everyone inside is asleep," Matthew suggested.

"No, it isn't that late. Someone would be awake," Falcon replied.

"Do you think it's empty?" Edward asked.

"Maybe they were never here in the first place," Morgan said.

"They may not be here now, but I know they were here," Falcon said. "I'm convinced that Mary Kate left that corner of the poster as a message. And if we don't follow up on it . . . we are doing her a disservice."

"What now? Should we continue to advance?" Morgan asked.

"Not all of us. I'll go on by myself, there's less chance of being discovered. The rest of you stay here."

"What if they are there, and you are discovered?" Megan asked.

"No, that might endanger Mary Kate. Just stay put until you see what is happening and you figure out what you can do."

Pulling his gun and bending over in a crouch, Falcon moved quickly toward the way station, staying behind bushes and rocks when he could, and using shadow when he couldn't. After a couple of minutes, he made it all the way to the building. He could smell the droppings of horses from the overhang, but there were no horses there.

The fact that there were no horses but that their droppings were fresh enough that he could still smell them convinced him that there had, indeed, been people here, and very recently. But the horses were gone, and that made him reasonably certain that nobody was here now.

Nevertheless, he moved with extreme caution all the way around the building, listening for any sound of life. When he got to the front of the building, he saw that the door was standing wide open. He doubted, seriously, if the door would be standing open if there was anyone inside, but still, he moved cautiously.

Falcon slipped in through the door as quietly as he could. Suddenly he heard a loud flopping, fluttering sound, and he swung around with his pistol up and cocked!

Two birds flew by him, through the door, then out

into the night, and Falcon smiled. If birds were in here, no people were in here. He struck a match and in the flare of the flame made a quick perusal. He saw nobody here, but he did see a candle, which he lit. Then, with the lit candle, he stepped out on the side of the house nearest where he had left his siblings and waved the candle back and forth.

"I'm sure that means it's clear to come in," Morgan said.

"Unless it's Ackerman and he's trying to lure us in," Matthew suggested.

"It's Falcon," Megan said.

"How can you be so sure?"

"It's Falcon," Megan said again, and she started toward the building.

"Wait, if we are going to go down there, we may as well take the horses with us," Edward suggested.

"I'll bring Lightning," Morgan offered.

Half an hour later, Falcon was sitting on the edge of the porch, eating peaches from a can. The moon cast a silver rim around Rattlesnake Mountains. High overhead, the black-velvet sky was filled with stars that ranged in magnitude from pulsating white, all the way down to a barely perceptible blue dust.

Falcon had taken his supper with the others inside the building, then he came outside to eat his peaches and get a breath of fresh air. They had not yet decided what their next move might be, but they had decided that they would spend the night here and would make further plans before everyone bedded down.

Falcon heard someone walking across the porch behind him. Without turning around, he spoke.

"Hello, Megan."

"That's very good," Megan said. "How did you know it was me?"

"Your steps are lighter and quicker than the others," Falcon said. He held out his can. "Would you like the rest of my peaches?"

"Why, how nice of you to share," Megan replied, sitting on the porch beside him.

"I have sort of a weakness for canned peaches," Falcon admitted. "I almost always have three or four cans in my saddlebags." He chuckled. "I'm not sure my horse appreciates my habit."

Megan pulled a spoon from her shirt pocket and began eating.

"They are very good," she said as she took the first bite.

"Don't drink the juice," Falcon said.

"Why not?"

"Something about peach juice left in a can. It's bad for you."

Megan smiled. "If you want the juice, Falcon, just ask for it. They're your peaches, after all."

"I want the juice," Falcon said.

"Yeah, that's what I thought." She handed the can back to him, and Falcon turned it up to drain the rest of the juice.

"Hey, you two, come in here," Morgan called. "We found something."

When Falcon and Megan went back inside, they saw a wedding ring lying on the ticket counter.

"Mary Kate's ring!" Megan said, moving quickly to pick it up. She looked inside. "Yes! Here's her initials, MKM."

"Bless her heart, she's doing everything she can to help us," Matthew said.

"Yes, she is," Falcon said. "And I feel really good about our chances of finding her. This girl is a fighter."

"I wish there had been some way she could have let us know where they went," Morgan said.

"Chances are she didn't even know where they were going," Falcon said.

"But with that many horses traveling together, it should be easy enough to track them."

Ackerman and his men had bivouacked the night before at the foot of Bray's Butte. They had gotten under way just after sunrise this morning and had been on the trail for nearly an hour when Les Waters, who was riding point, came galloping back. Ackerman held up his hand, and the column stopped.

"What is it, Waters?" Ackerman asked.

"I found us a resupply point, Major," Waters said. "No more 'n a mile ahead."

"Personnel at the target?"

"Looks like just two, a man and his wife."

"Very good. Return to the point; keep the target under observation until we arrive. Make certain there are no more people there than the two you have reported."

"Yes, sir," Waters said. Turning his horse, he galloped back up the trail.

"Men, we are about to engage," Ackerman said to the column. "I believe there will only be one man and one woman at our objective. We will take care of them, quickly, then resupply ourselves from whatever they have in their personal larder. Be vigilant as we approach."

"What does he mean when he says you will take care of them quickly?" Mary Kate asked Casey.

"That's none of your concern, missy," Casey said. "Your only concern is to stay with us. And if there is any shooting, stay as close to me as you can."

"Shooting? Why would there be shooting?"

"Stay close," Casey said without responding directly to Mary Kate's question.

"Sergeant Casey!" Ackerman called back.

"Yes, sir?"

"Bring the column forward at a trot."

"Yes, sir," Casey replied. "Column, at a trot, forward, ho!"

The column of two broke into a trot and caught up with Waters within a few minutes.

"Have you maintained constant observation?" Ackerman asked.

"Yes, sir. Still only two people. The man is over there, working on the corral fence, do you see? The woman is still in the . . . no, there she goes, sir. She's got a bucket and she's headed for the barn. Looks to me like she's goin' to do her mornin' milkin'."

"Sergeant Casey, we'll advance on the house in platoon front position," Ackerman said.

"Troop!" Casey called. "Form front right!"

All the horses in Ackerman's Raiders moved in line, side by side, stretched out ten wide.

"Bugler, sound the charge!" Ackerman called.

Powell played the charge and twelve horses thundered across the ground headed for the house. There were twelve horses in the attack, because Mary Kate had no choice. Casey was holding her reins, and she was holding on to the saddle horn.

Upon hearing the sound of galloping horses, and the bugle call of "Charge," Clyde Byrd who was working on his corral fence turned to see what was happening. At first he was so flabbergasted at seeing what appeared to be a cavalry charge that he had no fear. He had only curiosity. He started toward them, wondering what they were doing.

Byrd's confusion was short-lived, however. He saw every rider but one draw their pistols. Then he was shocked to see that the pistols were all pointed at him.

"Here! What are you . . . ?"

Several guns barked at the same time, and Byrd went down with at least three bullets in his body.

Emma Byrd came running out of the barn. "Clyde! Clyde!"

"Shoot the woman!" Ackerman shouted.

"No! No!" Mary Kate screamed. "Run, run!"

Again several guns roared, and Emma went down under the fusillade.

The charge halted, and the riders milled around in the yard between the small house and the barn.

"Troop, recover!" Ackerman called.

Again the riders formed into a column of twos.

"Prepare to dismount . . . dismount!"

As one, the riders dismounted.

"Sergeant, foragers for eggs, meat, flour, coffee."

Mary Kate dismounted and hurried over to look at the man who had been shot. It took little more than a glance to see that he was dead. She ran to the woman next, and she was still gasping for breath. Mary Kate took her hand, and the woman looked up at her with a pained and confused expression on her face.

"Why?" she asked.

"Oh, I'm sorry," Mary Kate said as tears streamed down her face. "I'm sorry, I'm so sorry."

The woman took a few more gasping breaths, then she stopped breathing, her mouth and eyes still open.

"How could you do this?" Mary Kate shouted. "How could you? You were an army officer! Doesn't that mean anything to you?"

"Mary Kate, do you think we never killed Indian squaws? And children, too," Ackerman said. "Why would this be any different? Ask your father, and he will tell you. In any army the mission is paramount. Casualties are secondary."

"What possible mission would require you to kill an innocent man and woman?"

"Why, you are the mission, of course," Ackerman said easily. "The mission is to hold you captive until such time as your father pays the ransom for your release." He laughed. "So, since you are the mission, you might say that you are responsible for the death of these two people."

"Ya hoo! Ham, boys! They have six big smoked hams!" Jerrod shouted.

"And bacon!" Smith added.

"I am not responsible," Mary Kate said, shaking her head and clenching her fists. "I am not responsible."

"Of course you are. Oh, but don't blame yourself. As I said, the exigencies of the mission required quick and positive action."

"You are a beast," Mary Kate said.

"General Butler was called a beast, my dear. And General Sherman was called a butcher. It is part of war."

"War? This is no war!"

"Oh, but it is," Ackerman said. "It is a war between your father and me."

CHAPTER SEVENTEEN

Falcon and the others spent the night at the way station, then started out the next morning. By mutual agreement, Falcon was leading them because he was the best tracker. In truth, though, this trail was so obvious that any one of the five of them could have followed it. There were many hoofprints, and the trail was liberally strewn with horse apples. Falcon estimated that there could be as many as a dozen horses.

"Here's Ackerman's first mistake," Falcon said. "He's keeping them in a military formation, column of twos. It not only makes it easier to track him, it also identifies him. Who else but Ackerman is going to go across country in such a precise formation?"

They reached a ranch house at midmorning.

"Let's stop here so I can use the privy," Megan suggested.

"There you go," Morgan teased. "Wanting special treatment 'cause you're a woman. Ha, can't stand up and pee against a tree like we can, can you? It's not too late for you to turn around and go back, you know."

"In a pig's eye I'll go back," Megan said.

"Ahh, he was just teasing you," Falcon said. "We'll water the horses and find out if they've seen anything."

When they arrived and tied their horses off at the hitching rail, they could hear the cow bawling in the barn.

"Damn, I wonder why they haven't milked the cow yet?" Falcon said. "That cow sounds awful anxious." He cupped his hands around his mouth. "Hello the house! Anyone home?"

"Falcon, there's something wrong here," Matthew said. "I don't like it."

"Yeah, it is a little strange," Falcon said.

"Let me know what you find out," Megan said as she started toward the privy. "And tell them for crying out loud to milk their damn cow. It's cruel to let it go this late."

The cow bawled again, and Falcon looked toward the barn. "I don't know who lives here," he said. "But it looks like they keep the place up really well. And anyone who keeps a place up this well wouldn't let a cow go this long without being milked." He started toward the back.

"Where are you going?" Edward asked.

"Something's not right, here. I'm going to have a look around." Falcon pulled his pistol as he started toward the barn. When he got to the back of the house he heard the sound of a hundred or more buzzing flies. The sound stopped him cold. He had heard buzzing flies before and he knew when they buzzed with this kind of intensity, there was a reason.

Falcon moved slowly toward the barn, then he saw her, lying on the ground just in front of the barn. He ran to her, but she was covered by so many black flies that it almost looked as if she were moving. He put his pistol away and shook his head.

"What have you found?" Edward asked coming up then. "Oh, my," he said when he saw the woman's body.

"It takes one evil son of a bitch to do something like this," Falcon said.

"It does indeed. And to think that monster has my daughter."

"Falcon, maybe you'd better come over here!" Matthew called alongside the corral fence.

"What is it?"

"Here," Matthew said, pointing.

Falcon saw a man was lying on his back with at least three bullet holes in him. A hammer was still grasped in one hand, and a little pile of nails lay beside his other hand.

"I don't think there's any doubt but that they came through here," Matthew said. "But why, in God's name, did they have to kill these people?"

"Resupply," Edward said.

"What?"

"They have Mary Kate with them. They can't very well go into a store and obtain provisions right now, so they are having to survive by what they can acquire from the land. I expect that if we examine the larder we will find their stores depleted."

Morgan went into the pantry, then came back a moment later.

"There's flour and cornmeal scattered all over the floor in there," he said. "The coffee bin is empty."

"I expect their smokehouse has been raided as well," Matthew said.

"What are we going to do, now?" Megan asked.

"We're going to bury them," Falcon said.

"Just like that?" Edward asked. "Don't you think we should notify the authorities?"

"Why?" Falcon asked. "They would still be dead, and we know who did it. We can't just leave them here. Megan, you milk the cow. Morgan, you and Matthew see if you can find something to use as a shroud for them. If necessary, we'll wrap them up together. I'll start digging."

"I'll help," Edward said.

They found a couple of spades in the barn, then Falcon pointed to a tree. "I expect that would be a good place to bury them," he said. As they got closer they saw a small grave marker. "It looks like it's been used before," Falcon said.

LYMON BYRD

infant son of
CLYDE *and* EMMA BYRD

"At least we know who they are, now," Falcon said as he turned the first spade full of dirt.

Matthew found some boards and a saw in the barn and he made two grave markers, rounding off the top and making a point at the bottom so they could be driven into the ground. He painted their names on the markers, then took them out to where Falcon and Edward were digging.

It took about an hour to dig both graves with Matthew and Morgan spelling them. Both Clyde and Emma Byrd were wrapped in individual shrouds and lying alongside the open graves.

"Shouldn't we say something before we just dump them in?" Morgan asked.

"I've buried soldiers with an Anglican prayer," Edward said. "It's very short; I can say it if you'd like."

"All right," Falcon said.

The others bowed their heads as Edward intoned the prayer. "I know that my redeemer liveth, and that he shall stand at the latter day upon the earth; and though after skin worms destroy these bodies, yet in their flesh shall they see God. Amen."

"Amen," the others said.

"All right, we've done all we can do here," Falcon said. "I think we had better get started. I don't want them to get too far ahead of us."

It was late afternoon when they approached the little town. From this perspective, and at this distance, the settlement looked little more inviting than any other group of the brown hummocks and hills they had encountered for most of the day. They stopped on a ridge and looked down at the town as Falcon removed his canteen from the saddle pommel. He took a swallow, recorked the canteen, then put it back.

"What do you think?" Morgan asked. "You think they're there?"

"They could be. This looks like it's far enough out of the way that the people in the town may not have heard of them. And even if they aren't there, it seems unlikely that the kind of men he's got riding with him are going to pass up a chance to stop at a saloon."

"So you think we should go down?" Edward asked.

"Yeah, I do." Slapping his legs against the side of his horse, Falcon headed the animal down the long slope of the ridge, wondering what town this was.

A small sign just on the edge of town answered the question for him.

LINCOLN
Population 246

If You Lived Here,
You Would Be Home Now!

The weathered board and faded letters of the sign indicated that it had been there for some time, the funny little saying perhaps put there when there was still some hope and pride in the town. The truth is, Falcon doubted that there were 246 residents in the town today, or that there were even half that many.

In addition to the false-fronted shanties that lined each side of the street, there were a few sod buildings, and even some tents, straggling along for maybe one hundred yards or so. Then, just as abruptly as the town started, it quit, and the prairie began again.

Falcon had an affinity for such towns; he had been in hundreds of them over the last several years. He knew that in the spring the street would be a muddy mire, worked by the horses' hooves and mixed with their droppings to become a stinking, sucking, pool of ooze. In the winter it would be frozen solid. It was summer now, and the road was baked as hard as rock.

The buildings were weather-beaten and some were

barely standing. The painted signs on front of the buildings were mostly faded and hard to read. A couple of men were pitching horseshoes in a pit right next to the blacksmith shop. In front of the apothecary two men with white hair and white beards were sitting in chairs that were tipped back against the wall. They looked over the five riders who came into town, but, it seemed to Falcon, with very little curiosity.

"There's a café there," Falcon said, pointing to a building that said: THE BULLDOG CAFÉ. Morgan, why don't you and Matthew take Megan in there and have dinner?"

"Aren't you going to eat?" Megan asked.

"I will if the saloon has food. I'm going to see what I can find out."

"We'll all go," Matthew suggested.

"No," Falcon replied. "First of all, we're not taking Megan into a saloon. And secondly, how will we find out anything if all of us barge in there? Edward, I do want you to come with me, though."

"Why him and not me?" Matthew asked.

"If any of Ackerman's men are in the saloon, Edward might recognize them," Falcon said. "I doubt that you would."

"He is right, Matthew," Morgan said. "Falcon, are we going to spend the night here?"

"We may as well."

"Then I'll get us some rooms at the hotel."

"Good idea."

Although the town was quite small, it had three saloons. Marvin Boyle and Les Waters were in the Ace

High Saloon, Ackerman having sent two of his men into town to have a look around.

Because the money under the water tank had been in cash, Ackerman had already given the men their share, which came to eighty dollars apiece. Boyle and Waters had eaten a meal in the café and were now enjoying a whiskey.

"We're supposed to be lookin' around town," Waters said.

Boyle laughed. "We are lookin' around," he said. "I'm lookin' at that woman, and I'm lookin' at that woman, and I'm lookin' at that one." He pointed to each woman in turn.

"Hey, what do you say we get us a woman while we're here?" Waters suggested. "The major don't need to know."

"Yeah, good idea," Boyle said. "But before we do, let's check out the other saloons first, see which one has the best-lookin' whores. I'll go over to the Red Bull while you check out the Silver Bell. We'll meet back here, then decide where to go."

"What if what me 'n you think is good lookin' is different?" Waters asked.

"You think that little ole' gal we got with us is good lookin'?" Boyle asked.

"I don't think about it one way or another. Not with what the major's sayin' about we can't touch her 'n all."

"Yeah, but, do you think she's good lookin'?"

"Well, yeah, she's good lookin'. But I'm tellin' you right now we ain't goin' to find nobody that looks like her in no saloon."

"No, we ain't, and that ain't the point. But you said

what if we think good lookin' is different. To me, this proves that we both will think the same thing."

"Yeah," Waters said with a giggle. "Yeah, you're right. Oh . . . and don't forget, we got enough money to buy us the best-lookin' whore we can find."

"All right, let's go find us one," Boyle said. The two men left the Ace High.

CHAPTER EIGHTEEN

As Boyle and Waters were making their plans over at the Ace High, Falcon and Edward were dismounting in front of the Red Bull Saloon.

"I'm going in first," Falcon said. "You wait just outside the door until I call you."

"Why?"

"Because, over the years I've developed a way of entering saloons that seems to work for me," Falcon said without any further explanation.

Falcon pushed open the batwing doors and went inside. As always when he entered a strange saloon, he checked the place out. To one unfamiliar with what he was doing, his glance appeared to be little more than idle curiosity. But it was a studied surveillance. Who was armed? What type guns were they carrying? How were they wearing them? Was there anyone here he knew? More important, was there anyone here who would know him, and who might take this opportunity to settle some old score, real or imagined, for himself or a friend? He was pretty sure that, this far from his normal territory, and especially in a town this small and this remote, he wasn't likely to see anyone. But it was always better to be cautious.

It appeared that the only ones in the saloon were people of the town and the nearby cowboys. Only a couple of them were armed, and it looked as if they were wearing their pistols only as an afterthought. Falcon doubted they had ever done anything with them except, perhaps, plunk away at a few snakes. The bartender stood on the other side of the bar managing his guests by pouring a drink here, refilling a beer mug there, doing so with all the dexterity of an orchestra director. Behind him was a glass shelf, filled with bottles, in front of a mirror, the reflection in the mirror doubling the number of bottles.

"All right, Edward, come on in," Falcon called quietly.

Edward came inside, then the two of them stepped up to the bar.

Seeing them, the bartender moved down toward him.

"Whiskey," Falcon said.

"Would you have Scotch?" Edward asked.

"Old Overholt," the bartender said.

"Then I'll have a beer."

The barman drew a beer for Edward and pulled the cork on a bottle of whiskey for Falcon.

"You two boys are new in town," the bartender said. It wasn't a question, it was a declaration.

"We're not in town," Falcon said. "We're just passing through."

Edward raised his beer to take a drink, then he paused. "Falcon," he said quietly. "The man just coming in, standing at the door."

"You know him?"

"Yes. That's Private Marvin Boyle. Or at least, it was Private Marvin Boyle. He is one of the three men I charged with murder. I'm sure he is with Ackerman."

"Pull your hat down and don't look around," Falcon said.

But Falcon's suggestion was too late. Boyle had seen and recognized Edward.

"You son of bitch!" Boyle shouted. He pointed toward the bar. "Turn around!"

Falcon turned toward Boyle. "You're making a mistake."

"Stay out of this, or I'll kill you, too," Boyle said.

"No, we don't have to . . . ," Falcon shouted, but his shout did nothing to dissuade Boyle from his intention.

Boyle drew his pistol, and Falcon waited until the last minute before he drew his own. Boyle had his pistol up and aimed when Falcon drew and fired in one, lightning-fast, fluid movement. His bullet caught Boyle in the chest, and Boyle dropped his unfired pistol and clamped his hands over the hole in his chest. He looked down with a quizzical expression on his face as the blood spilled through his fingers.

"Son of a bitch," he said in surprise. "You've kilt me."

Boyle collapsed to the floor and Falcon stood there for a moment longer, holding the still smoking pistol.

"Do you see anyone else in here that you know?" Falcon asked quietly, as Edward took a quick look around before he responded.

"No," he said.

"Damn. I didn't want to kill him. He could have led us back to Ackerman."

"You obviously had no choice," Edward replied.

"I think you should go on down to the café and join the others," Falcon said. "I expect I had better stay here until the town marshal arrives to check up on this."

"All right," Edward said. "Will you be coming down as soon as you are finished with the marshal?"

"Yes, I may as well. After this, I don't expect I'll be getting much information in here, tonight."

The marshal and a deputy arrived less than a minute after Edward left. No one had to summon him; the town was so small that the gunshot was heard from one end to the other. He paused for a moment and looked down at the body. Boyle's gun was still clutched in his hand.

The marshal took off his hat and ran his hand through his thinning hair, then he put it back on and looked up to address everyone who was in the saloon.

"Who did this?"

"I did, Marshal," Falcon said.

"Why did you shoot him?"

"Hell, Marshal, he didn't have no . . . ," the bartender started, but the marshal held his hand out to stop him.

"I asked him, not you."

"I didn't want to shoot him," Falcon said. "I wanted to talk to him. But since he was about to shoot me, I had no choice."

"Do you know him?"

"No."

"You don't know him, but you wanted to talk to him. He didn't want to talk to you, so he tried to shoot you. Is that about it?" the marshal asked cynically.

"Yeah, that's about it," Falcon said.

"What's your name?"

"MacCallister. Falcon MacCallister."

There were a few gasps from the other customers in the saloon, and the marshal's eyes opened wide.

"Well, that changes things," the marshal said. "More 'n likely he was just tryin' to make a name for himself."

"I expect that's it."

"Wow," the bartender said. "I'm goin' to put up a sign that says Falcon MacCallister kilt a man in here! That'll for sure bring in business."

Falcon drained the rest of his whiskey, then swiped the back of his hand across his mouth. "Will you be needing me for anything else, Marshal?"

"No, I don't reckon I will. I can get all the information I need from these folks, that is, from the ones that seen it."

"I seen it, Marshal!" someone shouted, and his shout was echoed by several others.

Falcon left the saloon as the witnesses were crowding around the marshal. He walked, quickly, down to Annie's Café, and when he stepped inside he saw the others sitting around a table in the back of the room. He started toward them, picking up a chair from an empty table so he could join the others.

"We must be very close," Falcon said. "I'm sure the man I killed was one of Ackerman's Raiders."

"I'm absolutely positive he was one of the Raiders," Edward said. "He was one of the first three people that Ackerman turned out of the guardhouse, shortly after he was cashiered from the service."

"And that being the case, I don't think Ackerman

would have let him come into town if they weren't real close by."

"I think you are right," Edward said. "What did you tell the marshal when he got there?"

"I didn't have to tell him much," Falcon said. "The marshal thinks that I was Boyle's target."

"But I'm the one he yelled at," Edward said.

"You know that, and I know that, but nobody else does. And if you recall, Boyle didn't say your name."

"That's right, he didn't say it, did he?"

"Which is a good thing," Falcon said. "If there was another one of Ackerman's men in the saloon, we don't need him to know you were here."

"Yes, I suppose that could complicate things," Edward said.

"Which is why I've been thinking about this, and I think that you should return to Brimstone. You, too, Megan."

Megan shook her head. "Oh, no, Falcon, we have already been through this. As long as Mary Kate is in danger, I'm going to be a part of this. There is no way I'm going back home."

"Think about it for a minute, Megan," Falcon said. "If they find out that you and Edward are looking for them, instead of waiting at the ranch for further instructions, don't you think that might put Mary Kate in even more danger?"

"Falcon has a point, Megan," Morgan said. "If you don't think Ackerman isn't capable of killing Mary Kate on the slightest pretext, just think of those poor people we buried back there. He killed Clyde and Emma Byrd for no other reason than that he wanted to steal from their pantry."

"Don't make me do this, Falcon. Edward. Don't you see? I can't just sit back there and do nothing," Megan complained. "I am telling you, I would go stark, raving mad."

"It isn't like you won't be doing anything," Falcon said. "You will be establishing a cover for the rest of us. I mean if they think you are back there waiting to negotiate with them, they are less likely to think that anyone is coming after them. And if they don't think anyone is after them, then they might be a little less cautious. That might give us a slight edge and, right now, we need every edge we can get."

"I think Falcon is right," Edward said. "I am convinced that Boyle recognized me back there in the saloon. And if he recognized me, the others would recognize you as well."

"All right then, you go home, Edward. I can understand that they might recognize you. You were their commanding officer. But how would they recognize me? I wasn't in the army."

"My dear, you said it yourself. I was their commanding officer, and you were the colonel's lady. You were not only the colonel's lady, you were the prettiest woman on the entire post. Anyone who served at Fort Ellis would know you in an instant."

"He's right, Megan," Matthew said.

"I agree," Morgan said.

"Is that how it is?" Megan asked in a pained voice. "All four of you are against me?"

Falcon reached across to take his sister's hand. "We aren't against you, Megan. We are just trying to do what is best for Mary Kate. And I know that's what you want, too."

"Yes, of course, you know it is."

"Then, please, go back home. That is absolutely the best thing you can do for her."

"All right," Megan agreed reluctantly.

"Falcon, do us a favor, will you?" Edward asked. "As soon as you have found her, and have her safely in your hands, send us a telegram. Please let us know."

"I promise you, I'll do that," Falcon said.

At that very moment, ten miles out of town, Waters was giving a report to Ackerman as to what happened to Boyle.

"I didn't actually see it," Waters said.

"How is it that you didn't see it?" Ackerman asked. "I sent the two of you in town together."

"Yes, sir, and we was just lookin' around town just like you said to see if we could find out anything. But Boyle, he said maybe we should split up so as to see more. He went to one saloon and I went to another. I heard the shot, and since it come from the saloon Boyle had went to, I went over to ask 'im what happened. Onliest thing, I didn't get to ask him nothin', 'cause he was the one that was shot. I was listenin' to the others, and it turns out Boyle was tryin' to kill someone named Falcon MacCallister. Only MacCallister kilt him instead."

"Falcon MacCallister? Are you sure? What's he doing up here? I thought he stayed down in Colorado, most of the time," Ackerman said.

"Well, they said it was Falcon MacCallister," Waters said. "I ain't never seen him before, but I've heard of him. The fella they was pointin' out was a big man with shoulders as broad as an axe handle."

"Yes, that sounds like him."

"Do you know this feller, Falcon MacCallister?" Waters asked.

"Yes, I know him."

"No, I mean do you actually know him? Like face-to-face talkin' and such?"

"He testified against me at my court-martial," Ackerman said. "I don't know what he's doing around here, but I would dearly like to see the son of a bitch killed."

"It's goin' to be hard to do. Ever' one that saw it said Boyle drew first and already had his gun out before MacCallister drew his gun and shot him."

"I'll get around to him sooner or later," Ackerman said. "For now, the most important thing is to get the money from Hamilton."

Mary Kate overheard the conversation, and, for the first time since she had been taken by Ackerman and his men, she felt a surge of hope. She thought of her uncle Falcon on a white horse, wearing shining armor, and she smiled, though she managed to hide it from the others. She didn't even mind when it started to rain. Ackerman gave her a poncho, and she crawled up under an overhanging rock, which kept most of the rain away from her. As was usual, Ackerman kept a guard on her, and because the guards changed every two hours, there was little chance of one of them going to sleep, which meant she had no opportunity to escape.

* * *

Back in Lincoln, the rain that had started just before sundown continued into the night. In the distance, lightning flashed and thunder roared and the rain beat down heavily upon the roof of the hotel, then cascaded down off the eaves before drumming onto the porch overhang, below.

Falcon stood at the window of his hotel room, looking down on the street of the town. There were few people outside, and when someone did go outside, they would dart quickly through the rain until they found a welcome door to slip through. The town was dark, the rain having extinguished all outside lamps, and those that were inside provided only the dullest glimmers in the shroud of night.

The room behind Falcon glowed with a soft, golden light, for he had lit the lantern and it was burning very low. He thought of Mary Kate outside in this weather and hoped that she had found a dry place.

CHAPTER NINETEEN

The rain stopped around one o'clock in the morning, but the combination of the overhanging rock and poncho did a reasonable job of keeping Mary Kate dry. And, because the sun came out shining the next day, the residual dampness dried rather quickly.

"Major, are we going on to Purgatory today?" Casey asked.

"Yes," Ackerman replied. "And our luck couldn't be better. I have no doubt but that last night's rain washed away all our tracks. If anyone actually is following us, they'll have a hard time."

"Do you think someone is following us?"

"I think Falcon MacCallister may be following us. I told you that he testified against me in the trial. And it turns out that he's Hamilton's brother-in-law. No sir, I don't believe it was just a coincidence that Boyle encountered him back in town."

"Hell, Major, if he is followin' us, why don't we let

him catch us? They's just one of him. What could he do against all of us?"

"Don't underestimate Falcon MacCallister. After his testimony in my trial, I sort of made it a point to find out all I could about him. He is a most formidable adversary. And while he couldn't take us all, he is quite capable of getting two or three of us. I don't want to lose anyone to him, especially myself."

"Yes, sir, I guess I see what you mean."

"It isn't fear, Sergeant Casey. It is merely a reasonable assessment of loss and gain. No battle should ever be fought without a reasonable consideration of anticipated losses. That is something I learned at West Point, and it has served me well for many years."

"Yes, sir," Casey said.

Ackerman smiled. "Battles are also won by taking advantage of situation and terrain. And in this case, situation and terrain tell me that, with our tracks washed away by the rain, even someone as good as Falcon MacCallister will not be able to track us. The best he can do is guess as to where we might go. And I would be willing to bet you any amount of money that he has never even heard of Purgatory. By intention, very few have ever heard of the place. That is the tactical advantage of going to Purgatory."

Mary Kate now knew that her uncle Falcon was following, and she felt a drop in her spirits when she heard Ackerman say that all the tracks had been washed away. How would he be able to follow, if there were no tracks?

She wished she had been wearing a dress when they captured her. If she had on a dress, she could tear off little strips of it to leave as a marker. But she couldn't as easily tear off strips of the denim trousers she was wearing, and even if she could, how would he know it was her? She had to find some way to leave a sign for him.

But, realistically, she knew that even if she had been wearing a dress she couldn't drop pieces of it without being seen. She was, after all, riding in the very first row, alongside Sergeant Casey.

They had been riding for about an hour when Ackerman, as a true cavalry officer, ordered everyone to dismount and walk their horses.

"Major, before we remount, I need a moment of privacy," Mary Kate said.

"Just a moment, let me find a place for you," Ackerman replied. He walked around for a bit, then came back. "You can go over there, behind those rocks. I don't think you'll try and get away, there is about a two-hundred-foot drop-off behind you."

"Thank you."

Mary Kate went behind the rocks, then looked around and saw that it was, indeed, a long drop-off behind her. Using a stick, she scratched into the dirt: PURGATORY MARY KATE. But the message was off the main path, so she knew that the chances of Falcon seeing it were very remote . . . unless she could improve the odds somewhat.

Then she got an idea. She broke two small pieces off the end of the stick so that she had a longer piece, and two smaller pieces.

"Hurry up, or I'll send someone back there after you!" Ackerman called.

"I'm coming," Mary Kate replied, hurrying back out, holding the sticks in her hand. Everyone else had already mounted by the time she got back to the trail. Mary Kate started limping.

"Wait just a moment," she said. "I've got a rock in my shoe."

"Well, hurry up," Ackerman ordered.

Mary Kate sat down and pulled off her right boot, and made a show of dumping it. Then she adjusted her sock and reached down for her boot. As she did so, she laid the sticks on the ground, and with the two smaller pieces made an arrow. The arrow was pointing back to the rocks where she had just been.

"All right," she said, remounting. "I'm ready to go."

"Forward, ho!" Ackerman shouted, and the body of men, in a column of twos, started out.

Mary Kate held her breath until she was sure that the last two men had passed her arrow. Nobody called out. Now she had only three worries remaining. She had to pray that Hugh Smith, who was the man riding trail, didn't see it, that there not be another rain to wash out what she had written in the dirt, and that her uncle Falcon would see the arrow and make the connection.

Back in Lincoln, Falcon, Morgan, and Matthew were standing in front of the hotel, as Megan and Edward were preparing to return to Brimstone.

"I wish you would change your mind and let us come with you," Megan said.

"Megan, we've been through all that. If you would just think about it, you would know I am right," Falcon said.

Megan sighed and put her hand on Falcon's shoulder. "I know you are right," she said. "Please find her for me, Falcon. I don't know what I would do if anything happened to her."

Falcon kissed his sister on the forehead. "We'll find her," he said. "I promise you, we'll find her, and we'll bring her home safe and sound."

"That's quite a promise you made, little brother," Matthew said as they watched Megan and Edward ride away.

"Yeah," Falcon said.

"Do you think you can keep it?"

"Yeah," Falcon said again, but without elaboration. He untied Lightning, then swung into the saddle. "Let's go."

As Ackerman's Raiders rode into the town of Purgatory, Mary Kate saw a building with a sign in front that said TOWN MARSHAL.

This was the first town they had actually passed through since she had been taken, and seeing the marshal's office gave Mary Kate a surge of hope. Suddenly she slid down from the horse and ran toward the building.

"Here, where are you going?" Casey called after her.

"Let her go, Sergeant," Ackerman said. "She needs to learn."

"Marshal, Marshal, help me!" Mary Kate called as she ran toward the building. She pushed the door open and dashed inside, where a man wearing a badge on his shirt was sitting behind the desk, drinking whiskey from a bottle. "Help me!" she said desperately.

"Here, here, now!" the marshal said. "What's the meaning of this? What are you doing, running in here like a crazy woman?"

"Those men out front!" Mary Kate said, pointing behind her. "They killed my husband and they've taken me. They're holding me for ransom!"

Ackerman stepped into the Marshal's office then.

"Hello, Moss," Ackerman said. "How are you doing?"

"Oh, pretty good, Major. How are you?"

"What?" Mary Kate said. "Marshal, didn't you hear what I just said?" She pointed to Ackerman. "This man killed my husband and has taken me prisoner! He is holding me for ransom!"

Ackerman took out two twenty-dollar bills and handed them to Moss. "Think you can take care of her for me, for a while?"

"Oh, I think I can," Moss said. Standing, he reached over to grab hold of Mary Kate's arm.

"Are you crazy? What is going on here? You're supposed to be the law!"

"Well, girly, the other towns have their law, and Purgatory has its law," Marshal Moss said. "Come along now, and don't give me any trouble."

"What are you doing?"

"What does it look like I'm doing? I'm putting you in jail for disturbing the peace."

"What? What kind of marshal are you? What kind of town is this?"

"It's my kind of town," Ackerman said. "Now you behave yourself. I have to keep you in good shape if I'm going to get any money from your father."

"No!" Mary Kate screamed. "Help me, somebody! Somebody please help me!"

Quickly, and without any prior warning, Ackerman crossed over to her and slapped her hard in the face. Mary Kate felt her eye swelling almost instantly.

"There is no sense in yelling," Ackerman said, his voice amazingly calm. "There is no one in this town who will lift so much as a finger to help you. This is my town, do you understand? This town belongs to me."

Mary Kate held her hand to the side of her face, and though her eyes welled with tears, she made a concerted effort to keep from crying.

"Come along, now, missy," Moss said, leading her to an open cell, back in the corner of the jail. "This is the ladies' cell back here; it's where we put the whores when they act up," he said. "It's a little nicer than the other cells, and you have some privacy here, if you know what I mean."

Moss pushed her inside; it required only a gentle push because she cooperated, then he closed the cell door and locked it.

"Ha!" Moss laughed. "I'll just bet you ain't never been in jail before, have you, girly?"

"No," Mary Kate replied, her voice so low as to barely be heard.

"No, ma'am, I didn't think so. I can tell by lookin'

at a woman whether she's a decent woman or a whore. Soon as I saw you, I seen that you wasn't no whore."

"I'll have someone bring some lunch for her," Ackerman said as he left.

Ackerman remounted, then the group started riding again. A mongrel dog came running from behind one of the buildings yapping and snapping at the heels of Casey's horse. The horse grew skittish and began kicking at the dog, prancing away from it, and Casey had to fight to keep the animal under control.

"I aim to shoot me a dog here!" Casey said, pulling his pistol.

"You shoot that dog, and I'll shoot you," a man standing on the boardwalk said. He was holding a rifle, and he raised it to his shoulder and aimed it at Casey.

"Then call your damn dog off!" Casey said.

"He ain't my dog. He ain't nobody's dog. But you ain't goin' to shoot him, neither."

By then the issue had resolved itself as the dog went running away, barking and yelping all the while.

"Detail, halt!" Ackerman said. "Make certain that either I, Sergeant Casey, or Corporal Jones know where you are at all times. Other than that, you are free to go wherever you wish. Dismissed!"

"Ya hoo!" the men shouted.

Some of the men rode directly to the nearest hitching rail; several others rode on down the street, looking for greener grass. It was obvious that they had all been here many times, not only because they knew the town so well, but also because those few who were on the street called out to them, including a couple of scantily clad women who were on the second-floor balcony of the House of Pleasure, leaning over the rail to show a goodly amount of cleavage.

Ackerman tied his horse off at the rail in front of the Bloody Bucket Saloon. He heard a woman's short, sharp exclamation, followed by loud boisterous laughter from several men.

"That wasn't funny!" a woman's voice said. Her protest was met with by more laughter.

Ackerman went into the saloon and stepped up to the bar.

There was a man standing behind the bar with his arms folded across his chest. He was nearly bald but had narrow sideburns that flared out into a beard, though the chin and above his lip were clean shaven. This was Hodge Dempster, owner of the saloon.

"Major Ackerman," Dempster said, greeting him. "It's good to see you again. Are your men all with you?"

"They are indeed."

"Good, good, all the business folks in town will be happy to know that. Your boys are big spenders, and we all appreciate that."

Ackerman put a coin on the bar with a snapping sound. "Will this get me a drink?" he asked.

"Yes, sir," the bartender said, starting toward him.

"No, it won't," Dempster said. "At least-wise not the first one. The first drink is on the house. You and your men are some of the best customers our town has."

"That's very nice of you to say so," Ackerman replied.

Ackerman looked at his reflection in the mirror behind the bar, and he hated what he was seeing. He had always made a point to keep his uniforms spotlessly clean, and he wore them with pride. The clothes he was wearing now, denim trousers and a white shirt, were nothing like the dash of his spotless uniforms.

It had been at least a week, maybe longer, since these clothes had been cleaned . . . or even since the last time he had taken them off. He knew that both he and the clothes he was wearing reeked of every odor imaginable, but he considered himself on campaign, so he not only tolerated it, he had almost gotten used to the smell, at least enough that he could tolerate himself. And that took a lot of toleration, because there were so many layers of dirt and filth on his skin that he couldn't even see his skin.

The bartender poured a shot of whiskey for Ackerman, then started to walk away.

"Leave the bottle," Ackerman called out to him.

"Sure thing," the bartender said.

"How much is the bottle?" Ackerman asked.

"Six dollars," the bartender replied.

"Six dollars?" Ackerman shook his head, then looked up at Dempster. "You do realize, don't you, that that is twice as much as it is anywhere else? I can afford it, but I am sure there are many here who can't. Do they never complain?"

"Where else are my customers going to get whiskey?" Dempster replied. "There are two other saloons in town, the Pig Palace and the Rattlesnake Den, and we all charge the same. Like I say, it isn't likely that none of our customers are goin' to be buyin' in Helena, or Deer Lodge, or Bozeman now, is it?"

Ackerman laughed. "You've got a point there," he said. "I might even be talked into buying into this business, if you're willing to sell part of it."

"Now why would I want to do that? I've got a license to steal," Dempster said, then he laughed out loud. "A license to steal in Purgatory. I like that."

"Real clever." Ackerman poured himself a drink, which he tossed down fast, feeling the raw burn of it going down his throat. Then he poured a second glass, this time to sip.

CHAPTER TWENTY

Mo Fong and Harvey Hood had been sitting at a table in the back of the saloon when Ackerman came in. They watched the deference everyone paid to him, then Fong leaned over to speak to one of the other saloon patrons.

"Who is that fella there, that ever' body is cottonin' up to?"

"That's Major Ackerman."

"Major? You mean he's in the army? He ain't in uniform. And what's he doin' here?"

"You mean you ain't never heard of Major Ackerman?"

Fong shook his head. "Nope, I can't say as I have."

"Well, he used to be in the army, see, only he got out. But now he has him a bunch of men that ride with him and they get by with purt' nigh anythin' they want. They hold up stagecoaches, they rob banks, and there ain't nothin' no sheriff or anyone can do to 'em, 'cause there's too many of 'em. And, they say he treats 'em just like they was still in the army. When they ride somewhere, they always ride in formation. And they have to call him major, and yes, sir and no, sir, and all that, just like they was really in the army. But it's 'cause they're like an army that they can fight off just about anyone that might be dumb enough to want to come after 'em. I heard tell that last year, after they held up a bank up in Clendennin that the sheriff got up a posse of twenty men. Most of 'em had money in the bank, so it was their own money that was stole, you see.

"Well sir, that sheriff and his twenty-man posse tracked down Ackerman and his men and cornered 'em in a gulch in the Belt Mountains. And when all the shootin' was over, not a one of Ackerman's men had so much as a scratch, but only three men of the posse made it back alive. The sheriff and seventeen of the posse was left lyin' there dead."

"Yeah, but with that many men, it ain't likely there's much money in ridin' with him, is it? I mean it has to be divided up into too many shares."

"Oh, I wouldn't say that. Seems like ever' time they come into town, they got more money than just about anyone else."

"Is that a fact?"

"Yeah, it sure is. I asked him oncet could I join, only he said no on account of I wasn't never in the army."

The man they were talking to finished his beer, then stood up. "I'd better be goin'. All I do when I'm in here is spend money, and I ain't got that much left to spend"

Fong watched him leave. "Did you hear what that fella said about ever' one that rides with Ackerman has a lot of money to spend?" he asked Hood. "And how he only wants you if you was ever in the army? Me 'n you was in the army before we deserted."

"Yeah. I also heard how they are treated like they're still in the army, yes, sir, and no, sir, and all that. That's how come me 'n you deserted in the first place."

"The only money we've made since we come here is what little we've got from muckin' out the stalls over at the stable, and cleanin' out the spittoons and moppin' the floor here. And the only pay we get for that is food. Hell, we ain't much better off now than when we was in prison."

"Yeah, but you said we was goin' to go out and pull us a job somewhere real soon."

"I said that, but wouldn't it be better if we could ride with Ackerman? We'd make a lot more money, and there wouldn't be no danger of us gettin' caught."

"Yeah, I guess it would. Do you think he'd let us ride with 'im?"

"It won't hurt none to ask," Fong answered.

Ackerman saw a bar girl he knew, and he motioned to her. She looked away as if she didn't see him, but he knew that she had.

"Bart," Ackerman called to the bartender.

"Yes, sir, Major?"

"Tell Peggy that I want to see her."

The bartender nodded, then went down to the other end of the bar. "Peggy, Major Ackerman wants to see you."

"Please, Bart," Peggy said. "Don't make me go to bed with him. He . . . he," she paused in midsentence, remembering that Ackerman had warned her not to say anything about his sexual habits.

"He what?"

"Look at how dirty he is," she finally said.

Bart laughed. "You know what a highfalutin dresser he is. He ain't about to ask anyone to go to bed with him lookin' like he docs now. Anyhow, that's not what he wants. He just wants to see you about somethin'."

Peggy nodded, then walked down to Ackerman and forced a smile. "I haven't seen you in a while," she said.

"No, I've been keeping busy." Ackerman took a ten-dollar bill from his billfold and gave it to her. "I want you to do me a favor."

Peggy looked at the money. That was as much as she made in three good days. She didn't know what Ackerman wanted, but she screwed up her courage and gritted her teeth. If he wanted to slap her around for ten dollars, she would let him.

"All right, honey," Peggy said, trying to keep the fear out of her voice. "What do you want me to do?"

"I've got a woman locked up over in the jail," Ackerman said. "I want you to go across the street to Annie's Café and get something for her supper. You can keep the change."

Now the smile on Peggy's face was genuine. Even with everything costing more in Purgatory than anywhere else, the most expensive meal at Annie's was still only two dollars. That would leave her eight dollars.

"All right, yes, I'd be glad to," Peggy said, and

taking the money, she hurried out of the saloon before Ackerman could ask anything else of her. The street was still relatively empty and the saloons quiet, but that was normal. Purgatory didn't come alive until after dark.

Fong watched Ackerman say a few words to the bar girl, then he saw her leave.

"If we're goin' to ask, this would be about as good a time as any," Fong said. "Come on. And remember, it's just like bein' in the army. Yes, sir, no, sir, and all that."

"All right," Hood said.

The two men walked up to the bar, just as Ackerman turned to pour himself another drink.

"Mist . . . uh, that is, Major Ackerman. My name is Mo Fong. This here is my friend, Harvey Hood. I was wonderin' if maybe we could talk to you? Uh, I mean sir."

"What do you want to talk about?" Ackerman asked.

"Well, sir, me'n Harvey here, we used to be in the army. An' when we heard that you was runnin' a bunch of men like an army, and you was holdin' up stagecoaches an' banks an' the like an' there couldn' nobody do nothin' to you, why, we got to wonderin' if maybe you could use another couple of good men."

"Good men, are you?" Ackerman asked. He poured himself another drink, but he didn't offer one to Fong or Hood.

"Yes, sir, we're good men. We can ride and shoot real good."

"Do you know why no sheriff's posse can touch us?" Ackerman asked.

"Yes, sir, I know," Hood said. "It's 'cause they's too many of you."

"That is not the reason."

"I know the reason, Major," Fong said.

"What is the reason, Mr. Fong?"

"Because you are a good commander, and your men know how to take orders. And that is somethin' that me 'n Hood is just real particular good at."

"You can take orders, can you?"

"Yes, sir, we can."

"Bart?" Ackerman called to the bartender.

"Yes, sir, Major?"

"Bring two more glasses for Privates Fong and Hood."

"Thank you, Major!" Fong said.

"How much money do you have right now?" Ackerman asked.

The smile left Fong's face. "Oh, Major, if, uh, me 'n Hood have to pay to join up with you, you're goin' to have to wait 'til we do another job. I only got a dollar and twenty cents."

"And I ain't even got a whole dollar," Hood said.

"How are you eating?"

"Mr. Dempster, he feeds us free for workin' about the place here."

Ackerman reached into his pocket, removed his billfold, and took out two ten-dollar bills. He gave one to Fong and one to Hood.

"Here is a little advance for you," he said.

"Thank you!" Fong said enthusiastically. Hood added his thanks as well.

"Bart?" Ackerman called.

"Yes, sir?"

"Get me a pencil and a piece of paper."

The bartender reached under the bar and came up with a sheet of paper and a pencil, then slid it across to Ackerman, who wrote:

> *Privates Mo Fong and Harvey Hood have been inducted into Ackerman's Raiders.*

"Find Sergeant Casey and give this to him."

"Uh, where will we find him, sir?" Fong asked.

Ackerman smiled. "He is in town somewhere, but I have no idea where. Finding him will be your first assignment."

"Yes, sir," Fong said. "Come on, Harvey. Let's go find Sergeant Casey."

Ten miles south of Purgatory, Falcon, Morgan, and Matthew were still following the trail when Falcon saw something strange on the ground. "Wait a minute," he said, holding his hand up to stop his two brothers. He stared at the ground. "This can't be an accident."

"What is it? What have you seen?"

"Look at this stick on the ground. With the two pieces, it's forming an arrow."

When Falcon dismounted, the other two did as well.

"No, it has to be an accident," Morgan said. "I mean the sticks were broken and just fell this way."

"Huh, uh. It's too perfect," Falcon said. "Somehow Mary Kate was able to leave this for us."

"Well look at it, at the way it's pointing," Morgan said. "What's it pointing to? There's nothing that way but the edge of the trail."

"Maybe it is real, but it wasn't left by Mary Kate," Matthew suggested. "Have you thought about that?"

"Well if Mary Kate didn't leave it, who did?" Falcon asked.

"Maybe Ackerman. Maybe he's trying to throw us off the trail."

"Well, pointing to a two-hundred-foot drop-off isn't going to throw us off the trail. You can only go about fifty more feet in that direction," Morgan said. "No, I still think it's just a coincidence that the sticks fell in that position."

"Like you said, Morgan, you can only go fifty more feet in that direction, so how much time will it take to check it out?"

Morgan nodded. "Yes, you have a point there. We may as well check it out. Maybe she did leave it there, maybe there's something at the bottom of the hill."

"Or, maybe if we go there we can see something over on the next mountain," Falcon suggested.

Ground-tethering their horses, the three men walked over to the edge and looked to the south. There was nothing but another mountain, about a mile across the divide from them.

"Do you see anything over there? A cabin? A mine? A cave, maybe?" Falcon asked.

"I don't see a damn thing, little brother, except trees and rocks," Matthew said.

"I guess Morgan is right. Maybe it isn't anything but a fluke."

"No, you're right, Falcon. It's not a fluke," Morgan said. "Come look at this."

Falcon and Matthew walked over to see what Morgan was pointing to. There, scratched in the dirt on the ground were the words: PURGATORY MARY KATE.

"Purgatory?" Matthew said, scratching his head. "What do you think that means?"

"Other than halfway to hell, I don't have any idea what it means," Falcon said. "But it has to mean something, or Mary Kate wouldn't have taken the risk she did of leaving the message for us."

CHAPTER TWENTY-ONE

Annie, who ran Annie's café, was a friend of Peggy's and had, at one time, been on the line just like Peggy was now. But Annie had gotten old, and fat, so the time came when no man, no matter how desperate he was for female companionship, would have anything to do with her. However, she had seen that coming and had prepared for it. She took what money she had managed to save and started a café. Ironically, she was now making more money from the café than she had ever made when she was "in the profession."

"Hello, Peggy," Annie greeted when Peggy went into the café. "Are you going to eat with me tonight?"

"Yes," Peggy said. "No," she corrected.

"Well, which is it? Yes, or no?"

"Major Ackerman is in town," Peggy said.

"Yes, I know. That's some of his boys back there," Annie said, pointing to a table where four men were sitting, eating, laughing, and talking.

"Yes, well, he brought a woman with him."

"Really? Major Ackerman has a woman friend, and she's actually riding with him?"

Peggy shook her head. "No, I don't think it's like that," she said. "Ackerman told me that he has her locked up in jail."

"What? He brought a woman with him, and now he has her locked up in jail? What for?"

"I don't know. But he wants me to take supper to her. What have you got that I can take with me? I need something I can put in a basket."

"Fried chicken, biscuits, mashed potatoes, gravy. Oh, and I made blueberry pie today, it's just real good."

Peggy smiled. "You know what, that sounds so good that I think I'll have it as well. I tell you what, put together two meals. I'll eat my supper with her and find out what this is all about."

"Oh, that's a good idea. Tell me when you find out, will you? I'm curious as all get out as to why he would bring a woman with him. And especially why he would put her in jail."

"All right."

"Hey, Peggy, you goin' to be available later tonight?" Powell called to her from the table where Ackerman's men were sitting, having their supper.

"I'm always available for you, honey," Peggy replied with a broad smile.

"My, oh, my, Zeke, I do believe that gal is in love with you," Baker said.

"Oh, I am in love with him," Peggy said. "I'm in love with any of you, as long as you got money."

"Ha! Do you hear that? She loves all of us!" Jerrod said, and the men laughed.

In truth, Peggy would rather be with Powell, or with any of Ackerman's men, than with Ackerman. She didn't understand someone like Ackerman. His men rarely bathed, rarely changed clothes, were rough talkers and heavy drinkers. Ackerman was always so precise with his personal appearance, but where none of his men had ever hurt her, Ackerman beat her the last time he was with her. She hadn't done anything to anger him, there was no reason for it, he just seemed to enjoy beating her. Afterward, he didn't apologize, but he did pay her double what her normal fee was.

"Here's your supper, honey," Annie said then, handing Peggy a basket that was covered by a red and white checkered cloth. "Just bring the plates and silverware and glasses back when you're finished. I've included a mason jar of tea for you to drink."

"Tea," Peggy said, making a face.

Annie laughed. "Oh, heavens, I forgot. You girls drink tea all day long, don't you?"

"Well, we couldn't very well drink whiskey every time a man buys us a drink now, could we?" Peggy replied.

"Well, working at the House of Pleasure, we never really had to do that. When a man came there, he came for one reason only. But if you'll wait just a minute, and I'll get lemonade for you."

"Thank you, I would appreciate that."

Annie replaced the tea with lemonade, and Peggy went down the street to the marshal's office and jail.

"Hello, Marshal Moss," Peggy said when she stepped into the office.

"What have you got there?" Moss asked.

"Major Ackerman asked me to bring supper to your prisoner. He said you have a woman in jail. Or was he just fooling me?"

Moss laughed. "No, no, he was tellin' you the truth. I sure as hell do have a woman in jail. And Major Ackerman told me he would be sending a meal over to her. Come on, and I'll take you back to her."

"Thanks."

Peggy followed Moss back to the cell that was reserved for women, though rarely used. Peggy saw a young woman lying on the bed with her hands laced behind her head as she stared up at the ceiling. Peggy was surprised at the way she was dressed. She was wearing denim trousers and a man's shirt. Peggy had thought that the woman might be another prostitute, but this woman didn't look like one at all. She was very pretty, but those certainly weren't the clothes of someone on the line, and she didn't have one bit of makeup on.

"Here's your supper, girly," Moss said as he opened the cell door. He looked over at Peggy. "Go on, take it to her," he said.

Peggy stepped into the cell, then Moss closed the door behind her and locked it.

"Here, what are you doing, Moss?" Peggy asked.

"I'm goin' to go check out the saloons," Moss said.

"I can't leave you with my prisoner, I don't know but what bein' another woman and all, you might let her out. I'll let you out when I come back."

Peggy said nothing until he left.

"Ha! What the old fool doesn't realize is, I'd just as soon stay here as go back," she said. She smiled at Mary Kate. "My name's Peggy, honey. What's yours?"

"Mary Kate Ham . . . that is, Mary Kate McVey."

"Well, Mary Kate McVey, I've brought supper for us," Peggy said. "If you don't mind, I'll eat with you. We've got fried chicken, biscuits, mashed potatoes, gravy, and blueberry pie. How does that sound to you?"

"Oh, it sounds very good," Mary Kate said as she sat up. "I've had nothing but camp food for almost two weeks now."

"Tell me, Mary Kate, though it's none of my business, but why are you in jail?"

"I was sort of hoping maybe you could tell me that," Mary Kate replied.

Peggy frowned. "Well, how would I know that?"

"You haven't heard of me, have you?"

Peggy had both plates out of the basket and she handed Mary Kate a knife and fork.

"No, I can't say as I have. Should I have heard of you?"

"I know that my name has been in all the papers for the last two weeks."

"Oh, well, that explains it. We don't have a local paper, and no papers ever come in here . . . at least; not more than one or two a month. And then it's likely to be only one paper for the whole town. We have no railroad. We have no stagecoach service. We don't even get mail in this town."

"You don't even get mail here?"

"No."

"What kind of town is this, that you get no mail?"

"You mean you really don't know?"

"No. Actually, I've never heard of Purgatory, and I've lived in Montana for at least ten years."

"That's because nobody who lives here wants anyone to know about this town. We aren't on anyone's map, and that's by design," Peggy explained.

"What a strange way for a town to be. I don't understand."

"Purgatory is what they call an outlaw town."

"An outlaw town?"

"Yes. And the town is well named, for if ever there was an earthly portal to hell, it would be Purgatory. Every robber, thief, murderer, and derelict in the country has been here at one time or another."

"And Marshal Moss does nothing about it?" Mary Kate asked.

Peggy laughed. "Honey, Moss is as big an outlaw as any of them. He's hired by the town just to sort of keep an eye on things within the town. Anything that somebody does outside of Purgatory is fine. You can come here and not worry about the law comin' after you. But there is a law, or more like a code of the outlaw, which sort of governs what happens here. Don't rob from each other while you are in town, don't kill someone unless the person you kill is armed. Just about everything else is wide open. Like my profession."

"Your profession?"

Peggy laughed. "Honey, don't tell me you don't know what my profession is."

Mary Kate shook her head. "I don't have any idea."

"Well, let me put it this way. I'm not a school-teacher." Peggy laughed out loud. "Look at me, honey. Look at how I am dressed. Look at the paint on my face, and on my lips."

"Oh!" Mary Kate said. "You're a . . . a . . . ," she couldn't bring herself to say the word.

"I'm a whore, honey. You can say it," Peggy said.

"How did you wind up in a town like this? I mean aren't there . . . uh, whores in other towns?"

"Yes, but here we make twice as much money, and we don't have to put up with a bunch of laws that the city lays out, and, there are no citizens' betterment leagues trying to run us out of town. For all its faults, Purgatory is at least honest about some things, Don't forget the blueberry pie. Annie makes the best blueberry pie you've ever put in your mouth."

"Thanks."

"Now, I've told you all about this town. How about you telling me how you wound up here? And what you're doing in jail? I know you said I should know your name, but I don't."

"My father is Colonel Edward Hamilton. He is retired now, but when he was in the army, he was Major Ackerman's commanding officer. And the reason Ackerman is no longer in the army is because my father court-martialed him and he was drummed out of the service."

"You know, I've often wondered about that. Ackerman is so military about everything he does, but he isn't in the army and I was beginning to think that he was lying about ever having been in the army."

"No, he was in the army all right. I remember him. I also remember the humiliation he went through when he was drummed out. They relieved him of his command and commission, cut all the braid, rank, and buttons from his uniform, took away his saber, then because he had been broken to private, they had a corporal take charge and march him off the post."

Peggy laughed out loud. "Oh, Lord, what I would give to have seen that," she said. "Ackerman is such a pompous ass. So, you think he's holding you to get even with your father?"

"Oh, it's much more than just getting even with my father. He killed my husband right in front of me, and he forced me to come with him. He has contacted my father, demanding that he pay forty thousand dollars for my release."

"Forty thousand dollars?" Peggy said with a gasp. "Good Lord, does your father have that kind of money?"

"I don't know for sure, but I expect he does. My father is a very wealthy man."

"So he's brought you here and is holding you as his prisoner until your father comes up with the money?"

"Yes."

"That evil bastard!" Peggy said. She looked at Mary Kate with an expression of pity on her face. "I am so sorry. I wish there was something I could do for you. But the truth is, I'm about as much a prisoner here as you are. Not only me, but just about every other woman in town. You see, outlaw towns don't exactly have a lot of families living in them. In fact, there are no families at all living in Purgatory. There are only outlaws and whores. Well, present company excepted," she said quickly, putting her hand on Mary Kate's hand.

"Peggy!" a male voice called out.

"I'm still here, Marshal," Peggy replied.

Moss came into the back carrying the key to the cell. "I expect you'd better get back on over to the Bloody Bucket," Moss said as he unlocked the cell door.

CHAPTER TWENTY-TWO

There were three saloons in Purgatory: the Bloody Bucket, the Rattlesnake Den, and Pig Palace. Fong and Hood spent most of their time in the Bloody Bucket, so they knew that Casey wasn't there. The next place they tried was the Rattlesnake Den.

The Rattlesnake Den had a stuffed snake, with its rattles intact, draped around the pointed top of the mirror that was behind the bar. It was busier than the Bloody Bucket had been, with several standing at the bar and a few more at a couple of the tables. The piano player was banging away at the back of the room, though the music could hardly be heard above the sound of the many voices in conversation.

"What'll it be, gents?" the bartender asked.

At first Fong and Hood hesitated, then Fong smiled. "We got money, remember?" he said, pulling out the ten-dollar bill.

"Yeah," Hood replied, matching Fong's smile.

"Beer," Fong said.

"I'll have the same."

The bartender drew two beers and set them on the bar. "Damn, you don't have nothin' smaller 'n a ten?" he asked. "Seems like all I've been gettin' today are ten-dollar bills."

Both Fong and Hood put their ten-dollar bills away and drew out the right change for the beer.

"Has Sergeant Casey been around?"

The bartender looked up and down the bar. "He was here earlier, but he ain't here now."

The two downed their beers, then left the Rattlesnake Den and checked out the Pig Palace.

"What you want him for?" someone asked.

"Why are you askin'?" Fong replied.

"Because me 'n Casey is tight 'n if someone means trouble for him, I want to know about it. You ain't the law, are you?" He drew his pistol and cocked.

"Hold on there, Jones, these boys ain't the law," the bartender said quickly. "They been shovelin' shit down at the stable for more 'n month now. I don't think no lawman would be doin' that."

Jones kept his pistol out. "What do you want to see Sergeant Casey for?" he asked again.

"Show 'im, Mo," Hood said nervously. "Show 'im the piece of paper."

Fong reached for his shirt pocket.

"If I see a derringer come out of your shirt pocket, you're a dead man," Jones said. "Both of you are."

"It ain't no pistol," Fong said. He pulled out the sheet of paper and held it out toward Jones. "Major Ackerman, he said to give this paper to Sergeant Casey."

Jones read the paper, then smiled and put his pistol away. "Well, hell, why didn't you say so? Sergeant

Casey is over at the House of Pleasure. You know where that is?"

"Yeah, we know where it is, but in all the time we been here, we ain't never had enough money to pay 'em a visit," Fong said.

"Before now," Hood said. "We got enough money to pay 'em a visit now."

"Yeah," Fong said with a big smile. "Yeah, I reckon we do."

"Do you know Gladys?" Jones asked.

"No, who's she?"

"You know what a top sergeant is?" Jones asked.

"Yeah, I know what a top sergeant is," Fong answered.

"Well, Gladys is like a top sergeant, only, she's the top whore," Jones said. He laughed out loud, and those around him laughed as well.

"Top whore," one of the other men said with a chuckle.

"Go over to the House of Pleasure and find the top whore. Tell her you're lookin' for Sergeant Casey."

Leaving the Pig Palace, Fong and Hood walked down to the House of Pleasure, which was the last building on the left side of the Street With No Name. That was what everyone called the main street that ran through town. There were no other streets, though there were at least three crossing lanes. They weren't named, either, but they were generally referred to as the first, second, or third lane. Only the main street had graduated to being referred to by name, and by default, its name had become Street With No Name.

This was the first time either of them had ever

been inside the House of Pleasure. The wallpaper in the reception room was red, and so were the drapes. The chandelier was shining brass. There were chairs and sofas in the waiting room, but the only ones in the room were two women, appropriately dressed for the profession. They were sitting together on the sofa, playing with a cat that occupied the space between them.

"Hello, dears," a woman said, coming out from another room to greet them. Like the two women on the couch, she was scantily clad and heavily made up. Unlike the two on the couch, she was very heavy, and her huge breasts looked as if they were about to spill over. "Have you come looking for some women to pass the time with?"

"Are you Gladys?" Fong asked.

"Yes, I am, sweetheart."

"Well, Gladys, we're looking for a man."

"Oh, my, well, why didn't you say so in the first place. Hector? Come out here, dearie, you've got company."

Someone came out of a back room then, and at first Fong thought it was another woman. But as he looked closer, he saw that it wasn't. It was a man, with eye makeup, painted lips, and rouged cheeks. His hair was in a sequined hairnet, and earrings dangled from each ear.

"Oh, my," he said in a falsetto voice. "Which one of you will be first?"

"What?" Fong asked. He looked back at Gladys with a shocked and angry expression on his face. "Who is this? What is this about?"

"Well, honey, you did say you wanted a man, and

here at the House of Pleasure, we try to cater to . . .
all sorts of appetites."

"We're looking for Sergeant Casey," Fong said. "We
was told that he is here."

"Well, why didn't you ask for him in the first
place?" Gladys stepped over to the wide door that
opened into the waiting room.

"Janette, who is with Casey?"

"Amy."

Gladys smiled and turned back to Fong and Hood.
"You can have a seat. If he is with Amy, he won't be
too long. She has a way of turning them out just real
fast."

True to Gladys's prediction, it was less than five
minutes later before a man came down the stairs.

Fong had no idea if this was Casey or not, but he
took a chance. "Sergeant Casey?"

"Yeah?"

Fong smiled, then walked over to show him the
note that Ackerman had given him. Casey read it,
then nodded.

"All right, get your gear and come down to the barracks. You'll billet there."

"Barracks?" Fong looked over at Hood, who shook
his head. They had been in town for almost a month
and had no idea that there was a barracks in town.

"It's that long building, first building on the right
side of the street after you leave this place," Casey said.

"Oh, yes, I know the building. I just didn't know
what it was."

"From now on, you must always let me, or Corporal Jones, know where you are, at all times," Casey

said. "It is the same as being in the army. You go when I give you a pass to go. Do you understand?"

"Yes, Sergeant," Fong replied. "Uh, is it all right now if we . . . uh," he pointed to Janette and the other girl on the couch.

Casey smiled. "Yeah, it's all right," he said.

Fong nodded, then he and Hood went over to the couch to engage the two women.

By the time Peggy returned to the Bloody Bucket Saloon after having had supper with Mary Kate, she saw that Ackerman had already managed to take a bath and change clothes. It was easy to pick him out from the crowded saloon because he was wearing the dress blue uniform of a major in the United States Army, complete with a golden sash and saber. He was no longer authorized to wear the uniform, of course, but here, in Purgatory, there was no one who would challenge him.

"Ahh, there you are, my dear," Ackerman said to Peggy. "Did you take dinner to the lady?"

"Yes."

"Thank you."

"Why do you have her in jail, Major? What did she do?"

"It's not what she has done. It is what I fear she might do. I am afraid she might try to run away. And I can't allow that. She's worth too much money to me."

That seemed to substantiate what Mary Kate had told her, but she thought it might be best not to share any of their conversation with Ackerman.

"If she is a whore, how is she going to earn money for you while she is locked up in jail?"

"Let's just say that I need her to understand who is in charge."

Peggy smiled at Ackerman. "Honey, there is nobody around you who doesn't know who is charge."

Ackerman chuckled. "Yes, that's true, isn't it?"

"You know it is." Peggy put her hand on Ackerman's cheek, smiled, then turned to walk away.

"Where are you going?"

"I've got work to do."

"No, you don't. I've cleared it with Bart. You're all mine, tonight."

Peggy felt a chill pass through her body.

CHAPTER TWENTY-THREE

The only thing remarkable about the building was that it was here at all. It squatted alongside a road that was barely wide enough for vehicular traffic. It was constructed of gray, weathered wood, filled with pine knots, a few of which had fallen out, leaving behind holes. It was obvious that the building had expanded over the years because there were two distinct additions to it. Whoever built the additions made absolutely no attempt to blend with the original building. To one side was a half barn, with a roof and two sides, the other sides open. A couple of horses were behind a fence that kept them in the barn, and they were quietly munching hay. An empty buckboard was parked just outside the barn. A sign on the overhanging porch of the main building read simply:

GOODBODY'S
Groceries – Eats – Liquor – Beds

Falcon and his two brothers tied their horses off out front, then went inside. The building was illuminated by bars of sunlight that filtered in through dirty windows and slipped in through the cracks between the boards. Gleaming dust motes hung suspended in the air.

"Gentlemen, welcome to Goodbody's, your home on the trail. What can I do for you?" a man asked.

"We thought we might have supper if you've got anything to eat," Falcon said.

"Ham hock and beans, turnip greens, and cornbread."

"Are you Mr. Goodbody?" Falcon asked.

"I am, sir. Thaddeus P. Goodbody at your service."

"Well, Mr. Goodbody, that sounds like a good supper. We'll take it."

"Yes, sir, you just sit down over there, and I'll be right with you."

Falcon looked around the building and found it quite well stocked for being so remote. It had canned goods, a variety of fresh vegetables, flour, sugar, and smoked meats. It also had household wares from utensils to stoves, blankets, rocking chairs, and baskets.

It took but a couple of moments for Goodbody and a woman they hadn't seen when they first arrived to bring out their meal.

"You have quite a well-stocked store here," Falcon said. "Do you get much business out here so far from everything?"

"Yes, sir, I do, and I think the reason is because I am so far away from everything. People who live in the surrounding area know they don't have to go into town to buy what they need. And, I don't have any competition."

"What is the nearest town to you, and how far away is it?"

"Well, sir, I expect that would be Corvallis. It's about forty miles from here, so you can see that the local folks would rather come here than make that long trip."

"Oh, I can see that," Falcon said. "What about Purgatory? How far is it to Purgatory?"

The smile left Goodbody's face, and his eyes reflected fear. He held both hands out and backed away from the table.

"I . . . I don't know any town named Purgatory. I don't know what you are talking about."

Falcon knew, instantly, that he was lying.

"Tell us about Purgatory," Falcon said.

"Please," he said. "I don't want no trouble. You folks don't have to bother none about paying for your supper, it's on the house. I just don't want no trouble, is all."

"Whoa, wait a minute! Hold on there, Mr. Goodbody," Falcon said, raising his hand. "We don't mean to cause you any trouble. And we are going to pay for our supper. Why would you think we are trouble?"

"I told you, I don't know anything about Purgatory," Goodbody said again.

"I think you do," Falcon said. "What I don't know is why you are frightened."

"I . . . I'm not frightened," Goodbody said.

"Yes, you are. Something about Purgatory is frightening you."

"Are you men with the law? Because if you are, maybe you should know that they've got a cemetery there that's got four dead lawmen in it. Deputy sheriffs and deputy U.S. Marshals, and mostly the law don't even go there now."

"We're not with the law."

"You don't look like any outlaws I've ever seen before," Goodbody said.

"We aren't outlaws, either," Matthew said.

"Then, if you are just curious about Purgatory, take my advice and forget about it. There ain't no reason for anyone to be wonderin' about Purgatory unless you are a lawman, in which case it's too dangerous for you, or an outlaw. And you just said you fellers ain't outlaws."

"Just a minute, Mr. Goodbody, I would like to show you something," Falcon said. "But it's in my saddle-bag, and I'll have to go get it."

Getting up from the table, Falcon walked outside, leaving Matthew and Morgan at the table.

"What's he goin' to get?" Goodbody asked. "I told you men, I don't want no trouble. I ain't goin' to tell no one that I seen you, so you don't have to worry none about that."

"Why not?" Morgan asked. "We don't care if anyone knows that you saw us."

"I mean if someone's lookin' for you, why, you don't have to worry. 'Cause I promise you, I ain't goin' to say nothin' to nobody."

Falcon came back in then, and as Morgan and Matthew had suspected, he was carrying the photo-graph of Mary Kate. He showed the picture to Good-body.

"Have you seen this woman?"

Goodbody was hesitant at first, but at Falcon's

urging, he took the photograph and studied it closely for a long moment.

"Who is this?" Goodbody asked.

"This is Mary Kate McVey," Falcon said. "We are brothers," he added, taking in Matthew and Morgan with a wave of his hand. "Mary Kate is our niece. She was kidnapped and is being held for ransom."

"Oh," Goodbody said. "Well, I can see why you might be worried about her."

"Have you seen her?"

"I'm not sure."

"Either you have, or you haven't," Falcon said. "How can you be not sure?"

"Several riders came by here this morning. They didn't stop. And the funny thing was, they were all ridin' in formation, like as if they were cavalry or somthin'. But none of 'em was in uniform. And one of the riders in front was smaller than the rest and, seemed to me like, was wearing clothes just like this." He pointed to the picture.

"Riding in formation, you say?" Matthew asked.

"Yes."

"That's Ackerman," Morgan said.

"Yes, sir, that's who it was, all right. Major Ackerman. I wasn't goin' to say his name. But seein' as you already know who it is, well, I reckon me sayin' that ain't exactly the same thing as tellin' you, is it?"

"Were they going toward Purgatory?" Falcon asked.

"Yes, sir," Goodbody replied with a slight nod.

"Do you have a map?" Matthew asked. "Can you point Purgatory out for us?"

"You ain't goin' to find Purgatory on any map,"

Goodbody said. "Leastwise, not one that's been printed."

"Can you tell us how to find it?" Falcon asked.

"Look. Those people, they know that I know about them. Sometimes they are my customers. If it ever gets out that I . . ." Goodbody stopped in midsentence and looked at the picture of Mary Kate again.

"You say they've kidnapped this poor little girl?"

"Yes."

Goodbody showed the picture to his wife. "What do you think, Abby?" he asked.

"Bless her heart," Abby said. "You know the poor little thing is terrified to be there."

"Well, should I . . . ?" he left the question incomplete.

"You have to, Thad. We can't just stay here and do nothing. Not if we can help that poor thing."

"But it might put us in danger. It might put you in danger."

"There's some things you got to do, just 'cause it's right to do it," Abby said.

Goodbody nodded. "You're right," he said. Then to Falcon, "All right. Go north about another mile until you come to a creek. Follow that creek west through the pass 'til you reach another creek. Follow that creek north, always keeping it to your left until you cross three more branches. After you cross the third branch, you'll see Purgatory."

"Thank you, Mr. Goodbody."

"I ain't never told nobody before this, how to get there," Peabody said. "We got an agreement, you might say. I don't tell on them, and they don't bother me. Also, and I'll be honest with you, tellin' somebody how to find it might just be sendin' 'em out to die. There ain't never been no lawmen nor bounty hunter that went in to Purgatory what didn't get kilt there. I reckon you boys will probably get kilt there as well, so whatever you do, please keep me out of it."

"You can count on it," Falcon said.

"And if you got folks back home that'll be worryin' about you, I got to tell you that if you do get kilt in there, they ain't goin' to learn nothin' from me. 'Cause I don't intend to tell anyone I ever even seen you. I hope you understand that."

"We do understand, Mr. Goodbody. And we appreciate your help."

"Oh, one more thing," Goodbody said. "They've got 'em a marshal there, named Moss. Well, he ain't no real marshal, you understand, he's sort of an outlaw marshal. I'm just tellin' you that so's that you know if you get into any trouble while you're there and get to thinkin' that maybe you could go to the marshal and get help, well, just give up that thinkin'. 'Cause that marshal ain't goin' to help you."

"Thanks, that's good information to know," Falcon said.

"Well, I'll just go away an' let you fellas eat in peace now."

"We goin' in tonight?" Matthew asked.

"We may as well," Falcon said. "We have an advantage, and that's that none of Ackerman's raiders are likely to know any of us."

"I wouldn't count on that, Falcon. There aren't that many people who haven't heard of you."

"They may have heard my name, but that doesn't mean they know what I look like."

"Didn't you testify at Ackerman's court-martial?" Morgan asked.

"Yeah," Falcon answered with a sheepish grin. "I guess I sort of forgot about that."

"Well, you can bet your bottom dollar that Ackerman hasn't forgotten it."

"No, I don't reckon he has."

In her room over the Bloody Bucket Saloon, Peggy was totally nude, lying on her stomach on her bed, with red streaks and welts on her back and buttocks. Ackerman had whipped her with his belt, and now she lay there, whimpering, trying not to cry out loud.

"You know, on board a ship, a sailor can be brought up for Captain's Mast, stripped down, and tied to the mizzen, then flogged before the entire ship's company," Ackerman said as he was putting his uniform tunic back on. "Fifty, one hundred, one hundred and fifty lashes, with a cat-o'-nine, mind you. And that means that every stroke of the whip administers nine lashes.

"It's too bad the army doesn't have such a policy. I would very much have enjoyed watching a good lashing administered. Just think of it, Peggy, you know you would like it, too. The nude body of a young, muscular man, the skin unbroken until the moment the lash is administered. Then, seeing the red welts pop up on that smooth, unblemished skin as the lash falls across it."

"Surely, they don't still do that in the navy, do

they?" Peggy asked. She wasn't really curious about the subject, but she would talk about anything to prevent Ackerman from repeating his performance.

"I don't know, but I think a ship's captain can pretty much do what he wants. After all, when the ship is at sea, it's as if it is its own little kingdom, with the captain as the king. Ahh, I should have gone to Annapolis, rather than West Point."

Ackerman had been dressing as he was talking, and now he wrapped himself with the gold sash and put on the saber so that fully dressed again, he looked as dapper as he had when they first came up to her room.

"I won't be needing you anymore tonight," Ackerman said. "So you can go back to work and double your income."

"I . . . I don't think I can work anymore tonight," Peggy said.

"Your back is a little painful, is it?"

"Yes."

"Ah, yes, I see. Well, I will continue to teach you, so that one day you will learn that there can be as much pleasure in receiving pain as there is in giving pain. It would be so much better for you, for both of us, if you would just learn to appreciate that. But, if you've no wish to work anymore tonight, that is fine with me. I would just as soon nobody else know of our little game of giving and receiving, pain and pleasure," Ackerman said. "Part of the pleasure of giving and receiving pain, is in keeping it a secret."

"I get no pleasure from pain, and I have no intention of ever telling anyone else about it."

"That's because you aren't trying. On the other

hand, I am doubling your rate. So I suppose you'll just have to appreciate the economics of it all. Good night, my dear."

Peggy didn't respond. She heard the door close and she lay where she was, unmoving for several minutes longer. Then she got up and walked over to her vanity, where in the light of the lantern she turned her back to the mirror and looked over her shoulder to examine herself.

From her shoulder blades, all the way down to her buttocks, and even farther down to her thighs, she could see red welts. As far as she could tell, though, the skin hadn't been broken, and she was very thankful for that.

Slowly, gingerly, she began to get dressed.

When Peggy was fully dressed, she walked out into the hallway, then over to the rail where she stood for a moment, looking down onto the saloon floor below. It took her a moment until she saw who she was looking for. Marshal Moss was standing over in a corner talking to Hood and Fong. She smiled. She had only half formulated the plan in her mind, wasn't even sure she was going to do it at all, until she saw Moss here.

Now she knew that she would do it.

CHAPTER TWENTY-FOUR

Peggy went to the back of the hall, then passed quietly down the back stairs and stepped out behind the saloon into the alley. The alley reeked with the smell of the outhouse and stale beer. She heard the squeak and rattle of rats scurrying around in the piles of discarded garbage. She didn't like being out here, especially at night. There was no place in Purgatory that was really safe, but the alleyways were the most dangerous of all.

She came this way because there would be less likely a chance of Ackerman seeing her. And she, for sure, didn't want him to see her, especially not with what she had in mind.

Peggy moved quickly through the alley down to the end of the block, then she slipped between two buildings until she was standing just back off Street With No Name. She was far enough from any of the three saloons that she wasn't worried about bumping into Ackerman.

There were no streetlamps on Street With No

Name, the only illumination being that which was cast onto the street through the windows of the few lighted buildings. None of the buildings down here were illuminated, so she was able to walk right out into the middle of the street with very little danger of being seen. The biggest threat she faced at the moment would be if she were to inadvertently step into a pile of horse droppings.

"You son of a bitch!" someone shouted from the area down by the three saloons.

The curse was followed by the explosive sounds of two pistols being fired in anger, the flame of the muzzle patterns flashing bright in the otherwise black of the night.

Peggy froze, too frightened to go any farther until the situation calmed itself.

"You kilt him, Perkins," a voice said. "He's deader 'n hell."

"I told the son of a bitch!" Perkins said. "I told 'im next time he pulled an ace out of his sleeve I was goin' to kill 'im. And by damn, that's just what I done."

"Yeah, that's what you done all right. What are you goin' to do with him now?"

"What do you mean, what am I goin' to do with him? Far as I'm concerned, he can just lay there 'til he rots."

"Huh, uh. You know the rules. You kill somebody, you got to take care of cleanin' up your ownself."

After that last exchange, the conversation grew too quiet to be heard, so Peggy resumed her nighttime mission. She continued across the street, then tried the front door of the building that housed both the jail and the marshal's office.

The door was unlocked, and she was glad. She had no idea what she would have done had it been locked. Opening it, she slipped inside, then closed the door behind her. Though it was very dim inside the building, it was totally dark. There was a single lantern, burning very low and pushing out a bubble of light that extended little more than a few feet in all directions. However, it did provide enough light for Peggy to do what she felt needed to be done, so she walked over to the wall and took the marshal's ring of keys from a hook. After that she picked up the lantern and went into the back of the jail. It was good she was carrying the lantern, because there had been absolutely no light in the back, which meant Mary Kate was in total darkness.

Assuming she was still there! What if they had moved her?

"Mary Kate?" Peggy called, her voice but barely above a whisper. "Mary Kate, are you still back here?"

"Yes," Mary Kate's voice replied.

Peggy was relieved to hear her voice, and she hurried down the corridor to Mary Kate's cell, then set the lantern on the floor. "That was a pretty dumb question I asked," she said with a smile. "Where else would you be?" She didn't share with Mary Kate her fear that something may have happened to her.

There were five keys on the key ring, and Peggy started trying them, sticking them one at a time into the cell lock. The first two didn't work.

"It looks like I might have to try every one of them before I find the right one," Peggy said.

"What are you doing?" Mary Kate asked.

"What does it look like I'm doing? I'm getting you out of here," Peggy said. The key turned and the lock clicked. "Ah!" she said. "It worked!" She pulled the door open.

"Where are we going?" Mary Kate asked.

"Well, now you've asked the hard question," Peggy replied. "Getting you out of jail was easy enough. What I'm going to do with you is something else again."

"If I could find my horse, I can ride out of here."

"That's not going to be all that easy. I told you, there's nobody here but outlaws. But they are very strict with each other about some things, and one of those things is horses. They'll hang someone for stealing a horse quicker than you can whistle. So the horses are all kept in a stable, and they have guards on them, day and night."

"Well, do you have any ideas?"

"One," Peggy said. "If I can talk her into it."

Peggy opened up one of the other cells to get the mattress, then bringing it back to the cell Mary Kate had occupied, she rolled it up and pulled the blanket over it.

"I don't know," Peggy said. "If he just glances back here, he'll probably think you're asleep. That might keep anyone from knowing you are gone until tomorrow morning, at least."

Peggy closed the door and locked it, then returned the keys and the lantern to the front of the jail. She opened the front door and looked out, then signaled to Mary Kate.

"Come on."

The town, which had been fairly quiet during the day, was now alive with noise. There were at least two pianos playing, the discordant notes clashing against each other out in the street. There were the competing voices of scores of conversations and dozens of arguments, some of them louder than others. There was the occasional cackle of a woman, and the deeper guffaw of a man. There was the sound of a couple of gunshots, and Mary Kate jumped, and gasped in fear and surprise.

"Don't worry, those weren't angry gunshots," Peggy said. "More 'n likely it was just some drunk lettin' off steam."

"How do you know?"

"Believe me, honey, when you've been around this town for as long as I have, you learn to tell the difference between angry gunshots and friendly gunshots."

Peggy started walking down the street and Mary Kate had no option but to follow her.

"Why are you doing this?" Mary Kate asked. "Why are you helping me?"

"Honey, didn't your mama ever tell you never to look a gift horse in the mouth?"

Mary Kate chuckled. "I suppose she did."

"All right, it gets a little harder here," she said. "We're going to have to go back into the alley. I hate the alleys, but we need to go in through the back door."

"Go into where?"

"The House of Pleasure."

"The what?"

"It's a whorehouse, honey. I'm sorry, but in this town, that's the only place I can think to take you."

Mary Kate felt a quick sense of apprehension. Was Peggy actually trying to help her? Or was this some scheme she had worked out with Ackerman? She paused, and Peggy walked on several more steps before she realized that Mary Kate wasn't behind her.

Peggy came back to Mary Kate. "Is something wrong?"

"How do I know that . . . ?" she paused in mid-question.

"How do you know what?"

"How do I know that you aren't doing this for Ackerman?"

"I'll show you how you know," Peggy said. She reached up to the top of her dress, then pulled it down, exposing her naked breasts and skin.

"What are you doing?" Mary Kate asked in alarm.

"Like I said, I'll show you." Peggy turned her bare back to Mary Kate. "Run the palm of your hand down my back."

Mary Kate had no idea what this was about, but she did as Peggy asked. Then she felt them, the raised welts. She also felt Peggy wince in pain as her hand encountered the welts.

"Oh, I'm sorry," she said.

"Those are whip marks," Peggy said as she pulled the top of her dress back up. "From Ackerman."

"He whipped you? Why? For bringing me food?"

"Oh, no, dear, if that was all it was, I might be able to understand it. Ackerman just likes to bring pain to women."

"I had no idea. I've known him for a long time, I never knew him to . . . ," she paused, and put her hand to her cheek, remembering then that he had slapped her. "Yes," she said. "Yes, I can see now how he might be like that."

"It's not might be, he is like that. Here's the house. We'll have to go in through the back because the men will be coming in through the front."

Peggy led Mary Kate up the steps, then she opened the back door and stepped inside. Once she was in, she turned back to Mary Kate and motioned with her hand.

"Come on in," she said. "The coast is clear."

Mary Kate stepped inside with her and found herself standing in a hallway.

"We'll go in here," Peggy said, opening a door to a side room. Mary Kate went in with her, then gasped because she had expected the room to be empty. Instead there was someone here, sitting in a chair crocheting. At first she thought it was a woman, but as she looked more closely she realized that it was a man . . . but it was unlike any man she had ever seen before. He was made up like a woman, and not like an ordinary woman, but like a prostitute.

"Hello, Hector," Peggy said.

"Well, look what the cat dragged in," Hector said in a singsong, almost lisping voice. "I swear, Peggy, I haven't seen you in a month of Sundays. And who is this delightful creature with you?" Hector put his hands, or rather his fingertips, together in a prayer-like pose.

"This is my little sister, Belle," Peggy said. "Can you believe she came all the way here for me to break her into the business?"

Again, Mary Kate felt a flash of anxiety, but when she glanced toward Peggy, she realized that Peggy was just protecting her real identity.

"Belle, honey, you stay here until I see Gladys. Hector, you look out for her now."

"Oh, I will," Hector said. He held his hand out toward Mary Kate, palm down, with his fingers bent. "I am ever so pleased to meet you, Belle."

Mary Kate had no idea how to react to this man, or what she should do with that hand. Not knowing anything else to do, she lifted it to her lips and kissed it.

"Ohh!" Hector said, shuddering. "What a dear, dear, thing you are. Come over here and sit by me. Tell Hector all about yourself."

"I . . . I'd rather hear about you," Mary Kate said. It wasn't hard for her to say this; she really would rather hear about him. Never in her life had she met anyone like this person, nor had she ever even heard of such a person.

"Well, of course, I am always happy to talk about myself," Hector said. "I am what is called a sodomite. Most of the men who come here for a sexual interlude prefer to bed women." He held up his finger. "But you would be surprised at how many men in this town . . . oh, fierce outlaws, gunmen, stagecoach robbers, the denizens of the West, prefer to go to bed with another man. I provide that service for them. For a fee, of course."

"You mean like a . . . a prostitute?"

Hector laughed out loud, and even his laugh was different from the laugh of any man she had heard before.

"But of course, my dear. Only I am not *like* a

prostitute, I *am* a prostitute. But, I have to stay back here all the time, and Gladys directs my customers to a special room. You see, I can't stay out front with the other girls, because sometimes men who don't understand the delicacy of such a thing can be awful brutes. And of course, all of my customers must have an absolute guarantee of secrecy."

"Yes, I suppose I can understand that," Mary Kate said. "But, can I ask you something?"

"Oh, my dear, you aren't going to ask that dreary question, why am I like this, are you?"

"No," Mary Kate said. "But, why are you here? I mean, this whole town, as I understand it, is a place where almost everyone is running from the law."

"That is quite true, my dear. And that is exactly why I am here. I am running from the law."

"You? But what have you done?"

Again, Hector chuckled. "You are so precious," he said. "I told you, I am a sodomite. Sodomy is a felony in every state and territory in America. Indeed, in some states, it is punishable by death. So you see, being here, in this den of inequity, I am safer than I would be walking the streets of Denver, Colorado."

"Oh, I had no idea."

At that moment Peggy came back into the room. "Belle, come with me, I want you to meet Gladys."

"All right," Mary Kate said. "It was nice meeting you, Hector."

"Oh, my dear, the pleasure has been all mine. And I do hope we will be wonderful friends," Hector replied.

"I have told Gladys who you are," Peggy said quietly

as they climbed a back set of stairs. "She's a good person."

"What can she do?"

"We'll come up with somethin', don't worry. You might not like what we come up with, but I promise you, it will be better than bein' in jail. And it'll keep you safe until we can figure out some way to get you back home."

"Now you was just real good! I'll be comin' back to see you again!" a man's voice said. "But I ain't goin' to tell the others about you. I want you for myself." He laughed, a loud, raucous, laugh.

Mary Kate felt a chill as she recognized the voice of the man talking. It was Jerrod, one of Ackerman's men, and he was coming straight for her.

CHAPTER TWENTY-FIVE

Peggy acted swiftly. Stepping back into the stairs and turning her back to the upstairs hallway, she wrapped Mary Kate in an embrace and pulled her close.

"Whoowee!" Jerrod said. "Now that feller can't even wait 'til he gets to the room. He's startin' in right there on the stairs."

Mary Kate had her head pressed up against Peggy's chest and she listened to the footsteps until Jerrod went on to the back of the house.

"Come on," Peggy said quickly, grabbing Mary Kate's hand and pulling her along.

They crossed the hallway, then went in to one of the rooms. A lamp was burning on the table beside the bed, and an older, and rather heavyset, woman was sitting on the bed. Her hair was very black, but Mary Kate was sure the color came from a bottle. She had rolled herself a cigarette, and it was dangling from her lips, a thin line of smoke curling up from the tip. The smell of the tobacco was oppressive in the close room, but Mary Kate said nothing.

"So this is her?"

"Yes," Peggy said. "Gladys, we have to do something for her. We have to. We can't let Ackerman have her. He is a beast, an absolute beast."

"Oh, I agree, he's a son of a bitch, all right," Gladys said.

Mary Kate had never heard a woman say that before.

Gladys took the cigarette from her mouth and held it between her forefinger and middle finger as she studied Mary Kate.

"Tell me about it," she said.

"What do you want to know?"

"I want to know everything. How did you wind up here?"

"Ackerman killed my husband and took me as his prisoner. Now he is asking my father for a great deal of money in order to get me back."

Gladys lifted the cigarette to her lips, took a puff, then blew out a long stream of smoke.

"Is your papa just sittin' there, waitin' to make the deal?"

"No. I know that at least one of my uncles is looking for me."

"How do you know?"

"Because one of Ackerman's men was killed back in Lincoln. And it was my uncle Falcon who killed him."

"Falcon? That's his name?"

"Yes. Falcon MacCallister."

"Oh, my, I've heard of him. His is a name that

many here fear. If you are going to have someone coming after you, I would say he is a good one to have," Gladys said.

"Still, he is just one man," Peggy said. "And don't forget, Ackerman has an army."

"Yes. Well, we'll have to do something to help the young lady until her uncle comes for her," Gladys said. She squinted at Mary Kate through the cloud of smoke that had gathered around her.

"Turn around, honey, let me look at you," Gladys said.

Mary Kate didn't know what Gladys had in mind, but she turned around slowly, under the woman's observation.

"Yeah," she said. "Yeah, I think it will work. We're goin' to have to get her some clothes, and get her made up, but she'll pass as one of my girls."

"What? No, I can't . . ."

"Hold on there, honey, it ain't like you think," Gladys said. "We're only doin' this to hide you out. You aren't ever going to actually have to go to bed with anyone."

"How can I pose as one of your girls if I don't . . . uh, go to bed with someone? What if someone sees me, and asks for me?"

Gladys laughed out loud. "You've got confidence, I'll give you that. But we can take care of it. I don't know any man who wants to take a chance on beddin' a woman with the doxy's disease."

"Doxy's disease?"

"Syphilis," Peggy said. "Have you ever heard of it?"

"I'm not sure exactly what it is, but I remember the

post surgeon talked about it once to my father. He said some of the soldiers were coming down with it."

"Peggy, look through the drawers there, and see if you can come up with something for her to wear. I'll go down and bring Hector up here to get her made up."

"You want a man to make me up?"

"Oh, honey, Hector will be in seventh heaven," Peggy said. "He loves to do makeup. Here, put this on."

The dress Peggy held up, if it could be called that, was about one-third the size of any dress Mary Kate had ever worn. It had very little top and very little bottom.

"Oh," Mary Kate said. "Peggy . . ."

"Would you rather be in Ackerman's jail?" Peggy asked. "If you wear this, you will look no different from any other girl here. By the time we get through with you, your own father could be within ten feet of you and not recognize you."

"All right," Mary Kate said.

Mary Kate stepped behind a dressing screen and was still getting dressed when she heard Gladys and Hector coming back in.

"Where is she?" Hector asked.

"She's behind the screen, getting dressed," Peggy said.

"Well, heavens to Betsy, what is she hiding for? None of the other girls do."

"I think she's ready now," Peggy said.

When Mary Kate stepped out from behind the dressing screen and saw herself in the mirror, she gasped and put her hand to her mouth. Compared to what she normally wore, she looked absolutely naked.

The tops of her breasts were spilling over, and there was much more than mere cleavage, there was actual separation of the two globes.

"Oh, yes," Hector said. "It will be wonderful working with you. Sit here on the bed. Peggy, honey, could you bring that table over so I'll have a place to put my makeup box?"

Peggy complied, and Hector, after studying her face for a moment, pursing his lips, and moving from side to side, finally picked up a brush and began working around her eyes.

The night creatures called to each other as Falcon, Morgan, and Matthew stood in a small grove of trees, looking toward Purgatory. A cloud passed over the moon and moved away, bathing in silver the little town that rose up like a ghost before them. A couple of dozen buildings, half of which were lit up, fronted the street. The three biggest and most brightly lit buildings in town were the saloons.

They could hear sounds from the town, competing out-of-tune and badly played pianos, and a dog's bark. Some woman in the saloon raised her voice, launching into a tirade about something, but her angry outburst was met with raucous laughter.

"Do you think she's here?" Morgan asked.

"I'm sure she's here. But just where she might be is another question."

"Do you have any ideas? You do a lot more of this kind of thing than either of us do," Matthew said.

"We'll start with the saloons," Falcon said. "And

hope that there's nobody in there who might know one of us on sight."

"Do you think that's likely?" Morgan asked.

"Not too likely. I don't get up into this part of the country that often.

"Shall we go in together, or each one of us take a saloon?" Matthew asked.

"Let's each one of us take a saloon," Falcon said. He pointed to one. "Ha, the Pig Palace. All right, I'll take that one. You two split up the others."

"I'll take the first on the left," Morgan said.

"Let's not ride in together. I'll go in first," Falcon said.

"Falcon," Morgan called.

"Yes?"

"Let's meet out in front of the Pig Palace at eleven."

"Good idea," Falcon said.

Falcon entered this saloon as he entered every saloon, by stepping just inside the door, then moving to the side to press his back up against the wall. The saloon was brightly lit with at least two dozen lanterns, some of them attached to a wagon wheel that was hanging from the ceiling, while the others were on the wall, or on a few tables scattered around the room.

Falcon perused the room for a long moment, looking into everyone's face to see if he knew them, or if he could perceive whether or not one of them might know him. He didn't see anyone he had ever seen before, and he saw no hint that anyone in here might recognize him. He did see several who were looking at him with obvious curiosity, though.

He turned back toward the bar. "I'll have a . . ."

"Mister, you are standin' in my place," a man behind Falcon said.

Falcon looked up and down the bar and saw that there was plenty of open area, so he moved about five feet down.

"Sorry about that," he said. "I just guess I've never been in a saloon where someone had their own place at the bar."

"Now you've gone and done it," the man said. "You've took my other place."

"Billings, this fella just arrived," the bartender said. "Don't be ridin' him now."

"If he's just arrived, he needs to learn a few things," Billings said. "He needs to know that when I tell him to do somethin', he better do it. Now, mister, are you goin' to move, or not?"

"No, I don't think so," Falcon said, turning to face the man who was haranguing him. "I moved the first time out of courtesy. But you've just run my courtesy dry."

"Is that a fact? Mister, you need to learn your place. I told you to . . . ," Billings said angrily, going for his gun as he spoke.

As the gun was clearing the holster, Falcon grabbed Billings's gun hand and jerked it up, using Billings's own momentum against him. Billings hit himself in the mouth so hard that two of his teeth were knocked out, and the blood started oozing down his chin. He had been so caught by surprise that he didn't even realize that Falcon had taken his pistol away from him, and was now aiming it at Billings.

"Now, I intend to have my drink in peace," Falcon

said. He removed the cylinder from Billings's pistol, then leaned over and dropped the cylinder into a half-full spittoon.

"Why, you son of a bitch!" Billings shouted. Pulling a knife, he made a thrust toward Falcon. As adroitly as a matador dodging a bull, Falcon leaned to one side, then he reached to grab Billings's knife hand, again using his momentum against him. The knife stabbed into the side of the bar, and Falcon grabbed Billings's arm and twisted it around behind his back until Falcon heard the bone snap.

Billings let out a cry like a wounded bull, and he backed away from Falcon with his broken arm dangling in front of him. He stared at Falcon with unbridled hate in his eyes, but now, there was something else. There was also fear.

"I don't know if a town like this has a doctor," Falcon said. "But I expect you had better get that arm set, and pretty quick. Otherwise, you'll probably never use it again. Oh, and about your spot at the bar? Now that I think about it, I don't want it anyway. I'll just take my beer over to a table and enjoy it in peace."

"You low-assed bastard," Billings mumbled.

"Now is that any way to talk?" Falcon asked. "There are some ladies in this room. I think you should apologize to them for your vulgarity."

"What?"

"Your language. I think you should apologize for your language."

"What the hell are you talking about?" Billings asked. "There ain't no ladies in here. They're all whores, ever' one of 'em. Do you think they ain't never heard language like that before?"

"I said, apologize to the ladies," Falcon repeated. "Unless you want me to break your other arm."

"No, no, don't do that," Billings said, and, as a natural reaction, he tried to lift his broken arm, but the pain stopped him.

He stared at Falcon "I . . . I apologize," he said.

"Don't apologize to me, I've heard language like that before. I'm telling you to apologize to the ladies."

"To the ladies."

"Look at them so they know you are sincere."

Billings looked at the three bar girls, all of whom were watching in shock at what they had just seen. "I apologize to you whor . . . uh, ladies, for my language," he said.

"Very good. Now, I suggest that you go get that arm looked after. Really, you don't want to lose the ability to use it entirely, do you?"

About that time a man came in through the bat-wing doors, wearing a star on his shirt.

"Mickey, how about a drink for the law?" he said, starting toward the bar. Then he stopped when he saw Billings standing there with one arm dangling down in front of him. "What the hell happened here?"

"Tell Marshal Moss, Billings," the bartender said.

Billings glared at the bartender, but said nothing.

"Billings started haranguing this stranger the way he does with ever' new man that comes in," the bartender said. "Only, this feller decided he wasn't goin' to take it."

"Damn, Billings, looks to me like you better go get Doc Lane to patch you up."

"How drunk is the doc?" Mickey asked.

"What difference does it make?" Moss replied. "I've seen him pull a bullet out of someone when he was so drunk he couldn't stand."

Moss walked over to Falcon. "What's your name?"

"What does it matter?" Falcon asked.

"I guess you're right, it don't matter none," Moss said. "But try 'n stay out of trouble in my town."

"Yeah, I am going to try and do that," Falcon said.

Falcon took his beer over to an empty table and sat there, listening to the many conversations to see if anyone mentioned Mary Kate. He didn't hear her name, but he did hear Ackerman's name.

"I wouldn't join up with Ackerman no matter how much his men are getting. If I wanted to be in the army, I'd join the army."

"Hell, he wouldn't take you anyway, Meb. You're dumber than a rock, ever' body knows that."

"I ain't that dumb," Meb said.

"What kind of name is Meb anyway? I can see maybe someone changing their name when they come here, but Meb?"

"My real name is Webb. But when I went on the run, I just turned the W upside down." Meb smiled, showing a mouth full of broken and misshaped teeth. "So, who's dumb now?"

Falcon stayed at the saloon until eleven, not getting into any conversations, just listening. But except for that one mention of Ackerman, he heard nothing else of interest. And even that mention didn't tell him that Ackerman was here.

When Falcon walked out into the street, Matthew was already there.

"Where's Morgan?"

"I don't know, I haven't . . . oh, here he comes now."

"Did either of you hear anything we can use?" Falcon asked.

"I saw Ackerman," Morgan said. "He's in the Bloody Bucket, all dressed up in an army uniform looking like a dandy."

"Uniform? What's he doin' in a uniform? I thought he was out of the army," Matthew said.

"How do you know it was Ackerman?" Falcon asked.

"I heard people talking to him. He was holding court, like he was the mayor of the town, or something."

"Well, he damn near is," Matthew said. "The folks in the Rattlesnake Den were all talking about how he runs the town. I guess when you have a private army, you are king of the roost no matter where you are."

"There's a hotel in this town," Falcon said. "What do you say we get a good night's sleep and start fresh in the morning?"

CHAPTER TWENTY-SIX

When Falcon awoke the next morning, something didn't seem quite right. Then he realized what it was. In nearly every Western town Falcon had ever visited, the night sounds were of revelry; laughter, music, raucous conversation, and shouts of anger. There was gunfire as well, but most of the time the guns were discharged in fun, though sometimes in deadly seriousness. In that, Purgatory was no different from any other Western town. It was the daytime that was different.

In the daytime most towns replaced the nighttime sounds of revelry with the sounds of commerce; a blacksmith's hammer, the clump of hoofbeats, and the rolling of wagon wheels, the morning greetings and the conversation of men and women going about their daily routine.

Not so here. As Falcon lay in bed with the morning sunlight streaming in through the window, he was hearing none of that. Purgatory was strangely quiet, as if the entire town was still in bed, sleeping off the previous night's revelry.

He heard a knock on the door. "You awake?" It was Morgan's voice.

"Yeah," Falcon said. He got out of bed, then padded barefooted over to open the door. "Thanks for not calling out my name."

"I can't remember your name," Morgan said with a grin.

"That's 'cause you're old and senile," Falcon replied. "Let's get breakfast. There must be a place to eat in this town."

"I saw it last night," Morgan said. "Annie's Café."

Mary Kate spent the night in a room at the House of Pleasure. And even though she was in such a place, it was the first night of real rest she had had since she was kidnapped. She had slept in a real bed, and there was nobody watching over her. When she awoke, it was full daylight, but she heard no sounds in the house. When she got out of bed, she thought about putting her jeans and shirt back on, but realized that Peggy and Gladys were probably correct, it would be best if she put on that . . . whatever it was called . . . thing they had dressed her in last night.

Once dressed, she went downstairs where she saw two more women dressed and made up exactly as she was. Both of them looked at her with surprise.

"Who are you?" one of them asked.

"And where did you come from?" the other asked.

Mary Kate wasn't sure how to answer, but at that

moment Gladys came into the room and took care of it for her.

"Tina, Dorothy, this is Belle," Gladys said. "She arrived last night. Bless her heart, she was about to be put in jail down in Laramie for giving some soldier boy at the fort the doxy's disease."

"The doxy's disease?" Tina said, drawing back from her.

"Well, she says it wasn't her, and I believe her. But I'm not going to actually put her on the line for two weeks while we see if she has it or not."

Dorothy smiled and stuck out her hand. "Don't worry about it, honey," she said. "They accused me of the same thing in Helena, and they were going to put me in jail. I didn't have it. The funny thing, I know who it was, and they didn't do nothin' to her. By now she's probably give it to half a dozen men, or more."

"Come have breakfast with us," Tina invited.

"Thank you," Mary Kate said.

Mary Kate followed the two girls into the dining room where she was introduced to four others.

"Oh, she's too pretty, she'll take all the business away from us," one of the others said, but there was no rancor in her comment."

"Not for a while," Dorothy said. "Gladys wants to hold her off the line 'til she's sure she's clean."

"Oh, yes, well, that's good."

"Anyhow, Liz, what does pretty have to do with it?" Tina asked. "Most of the men who come here are so drunk they can't tell one of us from another."

"Unless they wind up with Hector," another girl said, and they all laughed. They were still laughing when Hector came to the breakfast table.

"Did I just hear my name uttered in vain?" Hector asked.

"Hector, girl, we would never say your name in vain," Liz said.

"Well, I would certainly hope not," Hector minced.

It did not escape Mary Kate's notice that Liz had referred to Hector as "girl," nor did she fail to notice that he made no reaction to it.

A short, skinny, black man came into the dining room pushing a cart on which were several bowls and platters of food, including scrambled eggs, bacon, and stacks of pancakes.

"Oh, Black Lib, it looks wonderful," Dorothy said.

"Black Lib?"

"His real name is Black Liberty. He was born just after the Emancipation Proclamation, so that was what his mama named him," Dorothy explained. "But we just call him Black Lib. He's our cook, and he's the best cook in town."

Black Lib put the plates on the buffet, and the girls started moving through the line, filling their plates.

"Why are you living in Purgatory?" Mary Kate asked, just as she spooned on some scrambled eggs.

"Oh, I was cookin' for a minin' camp, and some of the men started to funnin' me, only it wasn't fun for me. So I poisoned them. I put arsenic in the scrambled eggs."

"What?" Mary Kate said.

Black Lib and the others laughed.

"Don't listen to him, he tells that story to every new girl that comes in here," Liz said. "He did kill one of the miners, but he shot him, he didn't poison him."

"So unless you see him come in here with a gun, you don't have to worry," Dorothy added.

Mary Kate laughed this time, and as she sat down to eat, a cat came in and jumped up on her lap.

"Oh!"

"That's Mr. Trouble," Dorothy said. "He's just checking you out."

Mary Kate began petting the cat. "Whose cat is he?"

"Oh, you don't own cats," Dorothy said. "They just sort of hang around wherever they want to be."

Satisfied with her inspection, Mr. Trouble jumped down, then went over to eat his breakfast. Mary Kate looked around the table and felt strangely connected to the other girls.

Moss had spent the night with one of the girls at the Bloody Bucket. He went downstairs where he stuck his hand down into one jar of vinegar to retrieve a hard-boiled egg, then in the other jar of vinegar to pull out a pickled pig's foot.

"Want 'nything to drink this mornin', Marshal?" Bart asked.

"You got 'ny coffee made?"

"Yeah, I'll bring you a cup."

Moss sat at a table next to the stove to have his breakfast. It was not cold enough for the stove to be used, but the faint aroma of burnt wood, a residue from its last use, wrapped a cloud around it. He was halfway through his second pickled pig's foot when he remembered that he had a prisoner who would need feeding.

Returning to the bar, he again stuck his hand

down into each of the two big jars and, with vinegar dripping from the fingers that clutched the two breakfast items, he left the saloon and walked back to the marshal's office.

"All right, girlie, I've got your breakfast here," he called as he opened the door into the back. "Are you awake back there?"

Moss walked to the end of the corridor and saw what he thought was his prisoner asleep.

"Wake up," he called.

When there was no movement he looked more closely and saw that she wasn't there. He pulled on the cell door, but it was locked.

"I'll be damned," he said aloud. "How the hell did you get out of there?"

There was a small house alongside the barracks. This was the commandant's quarters, and like the house he had rented outside Feely, this was made up like a post headquarters, complete with desk, wall map, and, unlike his rented house in Feely, in this case, he also had a flag standing in a brass holder.

When he awakened this morning he put on his uniform, choosing this time the undress uniform with shoulder boards, rather than the formal uniform with epaulets and gold fringe. He strapped on his pistol, then examined his image in the mirror. He saluted his image, then stepped outside. That was when he saw Moss walking quickly toward him.

"Good morning, Marshal Moss."

"She's gone, Major," Moss said.

"She's gone? Who's gone?"

"The woman you had me put in jail yesterday."

"What?" Ackerman shouted angrily. "What do you mean, she's gone?"

"I mean she's gone," Moss said. "When I looked into her cell this mornin', she wasn't there."

"Well, when did she leave?"

"I don't know. Like I say, I didn't even notice that she was gone 'til this mornin' when I went back to take her some breakfast. At first I thought she was in bed, 'cause I seen somethin' under the blanket. But then I seen it was just another mattress from one of the other cells."

"Did you leave the cell door unlocked?"

"No, I didn't leave it unlocked. As a matter of fact, it was still locked this mornin'."

"Well, if it was locked, how the hell did she get out?"

"I don't know, Major. I had her locked up, and like I said, the cell door was still locked this mornin'."

"There's something fishy about this."

"Yes, sir, there purely is, 'cause I don't have the slightest idea how she could have got out of that jail like she done."

"Bugler!" Ackerman shouted. "Bugler, report!"

A minute later Powell, still not fully dressed, came running from the barracks.

"Yes, sir?"

"Sound 'Recall'!"

"Here, sir? In town?"

"Yes, here in town! I have no idea where everyone is, but I want them here!"

"Yes, sir."

"And you, Moss, that woman is worth a lot of money to me, and I'm telling you now, if we don't find her, you are going to answer to me. And it isn't going to be pleasant."

The bugler began playing "Recall."

"Damn!" Smith said to Waters. "Is that 'Recall'?"

"Yeah, what's he playin' it in the middle of town for?"

"I don't know, but I expect we'd better go see what it's about."

Corporal Jones was also away from the barracks when "Recall" was sounded. He was still in bed, having spent the night with one of the whores at the Pig Palace. He groaned when he heard the music.

"What's that fella playing the bugle for?" the woman in bed with him asked.

"I don't know," Jones said. "But if he's just drunk an' doin' it on his own, I'll make him eat that damn thing."

At Annie's Café, Falcon, Morgan, and Matthew were sitting at a table when they heard the bugle.

"That's a bugle," Morgan said. "What's that he's playing, do either of you know?"

"He's sounding 'Recall,'" Falcon said.

"What for?"

"I expect that Ackerman is calling all his men together for some reason."

At that moment, Annie approached with a pad in her hand.

"Good morning, gentlemen, and welcome to my

café. I don't believe I've seen you boys in here before, have I?"

"No ma'am, you haven't," Falcon said.

"You called me ma'am. How sweet," Annie said with a broad smile. "Now, what'll it be?"

"Do you have any flapjacks?" Matthew asked.

"I certainly do. I have the best you ever tasted," Annie replied.

"I'll take half a dozen flapjacks," Matthew said.

"Half a dozen? My, you must like flapjacks. All right, half a dozen flapjacks."

"Half a dozen pieces of bacon, and half a dozen sausage patties," Matthew added.

"Oh, I see. You are ordering for all of you, aren't you?" Annie said. She chuckled. "You had me going for a moment."

"Better bring me half a dozen eggs, over easy, and some fried potatoes," Matthew said. "And, do you have any gravy?"

"Yes."

"Better bring me half a dozen biscuits and gravy, too."

"Oh, my, you gentlemen do have big appetites," Annie said. She turned away from the table.

"Wait a minute, ma'am, you haven't taken our orders yet," Falcon said.

"What?" Annie gasped.

"Never mind," Falcon said. "Just bring some extra plates, we'll share his."

Annie laughed. "You had me going for a minute there."

When Annie brought the food out—it took her several trips—Falcon waited until the last trip, then he held up his hand. "You said welcome to your café. Does that mean you are Annie?" he asked.

"I am."

"Annie, we're looking for our niece. We have every reason to believe that she was brought here against her will. Would you know anything about that?"

The sudden and frightened expression on Annie's face was all the answer Falcon needed.

"No," she said quietly. "I wouldn't know anything about that. Will this be all?"

"Yes, thank you."

Annie walked away, and as the food was distributed, Falcon spoke to his two brothers.

"Did you see the expression on her face when I asked the question? She knows something."

"Yes, but she's too frightened to tell us anything," Morgan said.

"She's told us that Mary Kate is here," Falcon said. "She wouldn't have reacted like that if she didn't know."

A few moments later Annie returned to the table. "I like men with a good appetite," she said. "Here's your bill." She put a piece of paper down in front of Falcon. The total cost of the breakfast was four dollars and fifty cents. But that wasn't the only thing written on the bill.

She is in jail.

"Thank you, Annie, that is the best breakfast I've eaten in a long time," Falcon said as he paid her. He didn't share her note with his brothers until they were outside.

"I met the town marshal last night," Falcon said. "I think it's time I introduced you to him."

The three men walked down the street to the marshal's office, then went in. The office was empty.

"Anyone here?" Falcon called.

Matthew pointed to a door at the back of the office. "That must go to the cells," he said.

Falcon opened the door and stepped into the corridor. "Mary Kate, are you here?" he called.

They walked up and down the corridor from one end to the other. Every cell was empty. Mary Kate was nowhere to be found.

CHAPTER TWENTY-SEVEN

"Now, why do you suppose the major is blowin' that trumpet like that?" Tina asked.

"It isn't a trumpet, it's a bugle. And the major doesn't blow it, he has somebody else blow it," Dorothy said.

"If he's really a major, what's he doin' here in Purgatory?" Janette asked.

"He's not really a major," Amy said.

"Well, he goes around wearin' that uniform all the time," Janette said.

"I hear he got kicked out of the army," Tina said.

"What for?"

"I don't know, I've never heard."

So far Mary Kate had not spoken one word, because she was sure she knew why Ackerman was having the bugle blown. She knew that, by this time, her absence from jail had been discovered.

Another girl that Mary Kate had not yet seen came into the dining room then. Picking up a plate, she walked over to the buffet.

"Good morning, Jolene. We didn't think we would see you this morning," Liz said.

"I wasn't goin' to come down to breakfast, but when that horn got blowed this mornin', Bobby said that was 'Recall,' and that meant he had to report back to the barracks."

"Bobby?" Amy asked.

"Jerrod," Jolene said.

Mary Kate shivered at the thought that one of Ackerman's men had been so close.

"Who is this?" Jolene asked, looking toward Mary Kate.

"This is Belle," Dorothy said. "She's just joined us."

"Welcome to the House of Pleasure, Belle," Jolene said with a smile. Her plate filled now, she sat at the table with the others. "I wonder what the major has planned? Bobby said they were all going to make a lot of money, soon."

"If you would excuse me, I'm not feeling very well," Mary Kate said. "I think I'll go up to my room."

"It was awfully nice meeting you, Belle," Dorothy said. "And I hope you enjoy being here with us."

Every man in the Raiders was standing in formation in front of the barracks, including Hood and Fong, who had only just joined. In uniform, and carrying a baton, Ackerman paced back and forth in front of the formation.

"Men, our incompetent marshal allowed our woman to get away during the night. Jerrod, I want you and Smith to ride back south along the trail to see if you can find any trace of her. Baker, you and

Waters go north. Go no more than five miles, then return. I just checked, and her horse is still in the stable, so it is my belief that she is still in town. So we are going to begin a search. I want every room of every building in town searched. Sergeant Casey?"

"Yes, sir."

"Get the men started, then come with me."

"Yes, sir," Casey said.

Casey divided the men who remained after the four riders left, put half on one side and half on the other, instructing them to look for the woman.

"Me 'n Hood have never seen her," Fong said. "We don't know what she looks like."

"You've been in town long enough to know that there are no women here except whores, haven't you?" Casey asked.

"Annie ain't no whore," Hood said.

"All right, it's easy. Just look for a woman that ain't a whore and ain't Annie," Casey said.

With the assignments given, Casey joined Ackerman, and they walked out into the middle of Street With No Name, halfway between each end. Ackerman pulled his pistol and shot it, three times, into the air.

"Listen to me!" he shouted at the top of his voice. "Everyone, come out of the buildings and listen to me!" He fired three more shots into the air. "Everyone, out of the buildings and listen to me!"

"All right, girls," Gladys said. "You heard the man, out onto the balcony."

"Well, what do you think he is up to now?" Tina asked.

"I'm sure he'll tell us," Gladys said.

Mary Kate looked over at Gladys with a frightened expression on her face.

"Belle, come over here for a second before you go out, would you? I need your help with something," Gladys said.

The other girls, paying no attention to Mary Kate and Gladys, went out onto the second-floor balcony, as much from curiosity as from being ordered to appear.

"Honey, you need to go out there so that none of the girls get suspicious," Gladys said. "But don't worry, with that getup and your makeup, your own mama wouldn't recognize you."

"Are you sure?"

"Trust me. I've been in this business for more than thirty years now. I know what I'm talking about."

"All right, I trust you," Mary Kate said hopefully.

Cautiously, and with no small amount of trepidation, Mary Kate went out onto the balcony to join the other girls. The others, curious as to what was going on, crowded the bannister and strained to get a good look. Mary Kate stayed back away from the bannister, as did Hector.

"Aren't you curious, my dear?" Hector asked.

"Not particularly. I haven't been here long enough to be curious."

"Well, it isn't that I'm not curious but, someone of my particular uh, predilection, has no business being seen in public. It can only bode evil for me."

"Well then, we shall keep each other company, shan't we?"

"Indeed, we shall," Hector said.

* * *

Gradually people began coming out of the saloons, the café, the hotel, the barbershop, the livery, the leather shop, the gun shop, and the general store. They stood on the boardwalks that lined both sides of the street and looked out toward Ackerman, who was now replacing the cartridges in his pistol. He looked up when he saw everyone had come out.

"Sometime during the night, a woman prisoner escaped from jail," Ackerman shouted. "I want her back, and I want her back unharmed. I will pay two hundred dollars to anyone who finds her and brings her back to me."

"Two hunnert dollars?" one of the men shouted.

"Two hundred dollars," Ackerman repeated. "Now, start searching!"

Jones and Jerrod went over to the House of Pleasure and, looking up, saw all the girls out on the balcony.

"Gladys," Jones called. "Get all your whores down in the reception room now."

"Why do you want us there, honey? We're all out here now."

"Because I said so," Jones said.

"All right, girls, you heard the man," Gladys said. "Let's go down to the reception room."

Mary Kate took a deep breath and folded her hands into fists. Gladys sensed her tensing up and walked over to put her arm around her. "Honey, just act natural, smile a lot, and everything will be all right. Trust me."

Mary Kate bit her bottom lip, then followed the other girls back downstairs and into the parlor. A moment later Jones and Jerrod came in. Mary Kate knew both of them very well, having been with both of them night and day from the moment she was taken.

"All right, are you sure ever' one is in here?" Jones asked. "We aim to search ever' room, and it'll go hard on anyone who ain't in here."

"We're all here, Sweetie, even I," Hector said. "But when you're all through searching, you might want to come back and see me. I can give you a real good time."

The other girls laughed, including Mary Kate, who was thankful to Hector for giving her something to laugh at.

Jones and Jerrod make a quick perusal of all the girls in the reception room and, satisfied, began their search of the rest of the house. Mary Kate relaxed, noticeably, and again Gladys came over to her.

"You did well," she said quietly.

Falcon, Morgan, and Matthew were standing out in front of the jail looking over the street, which was unusually crowded. "What do we do now, Falcon?" Morgan asked.

"It's not like we can go around asking people about her, is it?" Falcon said. "The whole town is looking for her. And since Ackerman insisted that she be returned unharmed, we may as well let them do the work for us. I suggest we go have a beer. But not at the Pig Palace, I wasn't that impressed with it last night."

"I can't say much for the Rattlesnake Den, either," Matthew said.

"The Bloody Bucket wasn't the best saloon I've ever been in," Morgan said. "But it wasn't the worst."

"All right, the Bloody Bucket it is."

At that same moment, Peggy went into Annie's Café.

"What's all the excitement, the horn blowin', the shootin', and the yellin' about?" Annie asked.

"You remember the woman I told you about last night? The one that I took supper to?"

"Yes, indeed, I remember."

Peggy smiled. "Well, she escaped from jail, and Ackerman is having a conniption fit. He's got the whole town out lookin' for her, and he's put a two-hundred-dollar reward out for her."

"I know where she is," Annie said.

"You do?" Peggy was surprised by Annie's pronouncement.

"Yes, her uncles found her and have taken her somewhere."

"What? What uncles are you talking about?"

There was nobody else in the café at the moment, but Annie looked around anyway before she spoke.

"I probably shouldn't have done this, and please don't tell anyone," Annie said. "But the girl's three uncles were here for breakfast. They were such nice men, such a departure from the men that we have here, that I told them."

"You told them what?"

"I told them that their niece was in jail. Please tell me that I didn't make a big mistake."

Peggy grinned. "You didn't make a big mistake, but you did make a mistake."

"What do you mean?" Annie asked anxiously.

"She wasn't in jail this morning because I let her out last night."

Now a big smile spread across Annie's face. "You did? Oh, how marvelous! But, where is she? No, don't tell me, I don't want to know," Annie said, holding out her hand. "I'm just the kind of addle head that might say the wrong thing at the wrong time. Just tell me that Ackerman's men aren't going to find her."

"They aren't going to find her," Peggy insisted.

"Oh, but her uncles are still looking for her."

"What do her uncles look like?"

"Big men, all three of them. Strong looking, if you know what I mean, with broad shoulders. They're all good-looking men, too. If I was thirty years younger . . . oh, never mind," Annie said with a laugh. "Listen to an old woman goin' on about being thirty years younger."

"I wonder if they are still in town," Peggy said.

"I expect they are," Annie said. "They don't look to me like the kind of men who give up very easy."

"I must try and find them."

"You two!" a couple of men shouted as they came in through the front door.

Turning toward them, Peggy recognized Mo Fong and Harvey Hood. They were easy to recognize, as they had been in town for nearly a month and had spent most of their time in the Bloody Bucket.

"What do you want, Fong?" Peggy asked.

"What do you mean, what do I want? Haven't you heard? Major Ackerman brought a woman into town yesterday, and durin' the night, she escaped."

Peggy laughed. "That's the thing about some men," she said. "They can't hang on to their women, even if they have 'em locked up in jail."

"It ain't funny. The major is some upset about it, and he wants her back. We're searchin' the whole town."

"Well, you can easily see that she isn't here," Annie said. "So go somewhere else to search," she added with a dismissive wave of her hand.

"We ain't goin' nowhere 'til we search real good. That means we're goin' to look into the kitchen."

"Don't you go into my kitchen, you filthy things!" Annie said.

Both Fong and Hood pulled their pistols. "We're goin' into your kitchen," Fong said.

Annie and Peggy watched helplessly as the two men went into the kitchen. They could hear them moving pots and pans around, sometimes obviously throwing them onto the floor.

"Be careful in there!" Annie called.

At that moment Falcon came in through the front door.

"Hello, Annie," he said. "My brothers and I were wondering . . ."

"That's him!" Annie gasped. "That's one of them! One of the girl's uncles."

At that moment Fong and Hood came back out of the kitchen, still holding their pistols.

"All right, she ain't . . . ," Fong started, then he saw Falcon. "MacCallister!" he said. He and Hood both raised their pistols. "Major Ackerman said you would be comin' after the girl he brung with him, and here you are."

"I'll just bet you didn't expect to ever see me 'n Mo again, did you, MacCallister?" Hood asked.

"As a matter of fact I didn't. I thought you two were in prison down in Colorado," Falcon said.

"We was, but we broke out," Fong said. "Just like you must 'a broke out that girl that Major Ackerman is lookin' for."

"You know what, Mo. I'll bet if we take him down to Major Ackerman, he could make him talk."

"I don't want to take him down to Ackerman," Fong said.

"What do you want to do with him?"

"I want to kill him," Fong said, a broad smile spreading across his face. He put his thumb on the hammer of his pistol to pull it back.

CHAPTER TWENTY-EIGHT

Fong and Hood didn't get the hammers pulled back on their pistols. With a draw that was so fast it was a blur, Falcon pulled his gun and shot twice. The shots were so close together that it sounded like one, even to Peggy and Annie, who witnessed it, and, seeing both Fong and Hood go down, knew that he had shot twice.

"Are they the only two in here?" Falcon asked, smoke still curling up from the gun in his hand.

"Yes," Annie said. "How did you do that? Both of them had their guns out and were about to shoot."

"I just got lucky, I guess."

"You are Mary Kate's uncle, aren't you?" Peggy asked.

"Yes. Do you know Mary Kate? Do you know where she is?"

"Yes, I'm the one that let her out of jail last night. I have her somewhere safe."

"That's good to know," Falcon said. "Keep her safe for me. It will make my job easier."

"What job?"

"Cleaning out this town."

"What? How do you propose to clean out this entire town all by yourself?"

"I'm not by myself," Falcon said. "I have my two brothers with me."

"Still, Ackerman has a lot of men with him. These two you just killed didn't even join him until last night. He has a whole army with him."

"Do you know exactly how many he has?"

"Well, I can figure it out," Peggy said. "He has Casey, Jones, Boyle, Smith . . ."

"He doesn't have Boyle anymore. I killed him back in Lincoln."

"All right, I won't count him. There's also Waters, Baker, Jerrod, and Powell. That's how many? Seven"

"Except for Ackerman himself, I don't think any of the others you named would recognize me on sight."

"You forgot the Hastings," Annie said. "That's two new men he picked up since he was here last."

"Hastings?"

"Yes, they're brothers," Annie said.

"Oh, if they are who I think they are, they would also recognize me."

"And he'll have Moss with him, for sure," Peggy said. "So that's at least nine, ten counting Ackerman. And I expect he may pick up a few more from town. He's got the whole town under his thumb."

"Annie, would you bring me a piece of paper and a pencil?" Falcon asked.

"Yes."

Annie brought the paper and pencil, and Falcon sat down at the table to write a note.

Ackerman.

I have killed two of your men. You will find them in the middle of the street in front of Annie's Café. Now I'm coming to kill you and your entire army.

Falcon MacCallister.

Falcon folded the note over and handed it to Peggy.

"Give me time to get these two bodies out of here, then give this note to Ackerman if you would, please."

"All right," Peggy said.

Morgan and Matthew rushed in then, with pistols drawn.

"Oh!" Peggy gasped.

Annie put her hand out to touch Peggy. "Don't worry," she said. "They are his brothers."

"Ackerman's men?" Morgan said, seeing the two bodies lying on the floor.

"Yes, but they were a couple of men I had run across before, so they recognized me. Show my brothers the note, Miss," Falcon said.

Peggy handed the note over to Morgan, who read it, chuckled, then handed it to Matthew.

"You don't think you might have discussed this with Matthew and me before you decided to take on his entire army?"

"Do you see any other way of handling it?" Falcon asked.

"No." Morgan smiled. "I guess that was discussion, huh?"

"I guess it was. Help me drag these two carcasses

out into the street," Falcon said. He looked over at Peggy. "What's your name?"

"Peg . . . ," she started to say, then she smiled. "My real name is Agnes Bennett. But everyone here calls me Peggy."

"All right, Miss Bennett, if you would please, deliver that note to Ackerman."

"Hello, my dear," Ackerman said when Peggy approached him. "I suppose you know what is going on here."

"You are looking for the woman that I took supper to last night."

"Yes. You don't have any news of her for me, do you?"

"No," Peggy said. "But some man gave me this note to give to you."

"Really?" Ackerman smiled. "Maybe he has found her and wants a reward. Well, let's just see what . . ." Ackerman had been unfolding the note as he spoke, now he read the message. "What?" he said. He glared at her. "What is this?"

"Like I said, Major, this note was just given to me."

"He says he killed two of my men."

"Yes, he killed Fong and Hood."

"How do you know who he killed?"

"Because I saw him do it. I was in Annie's Café when Fong and Hood came in to look for Mary Kate. When Mr. MacCallister came in, they recognized him and they tried to kill him. But he killed them instead."

"How do you know the girl's name is Mary Kate?" Ackerman asked, his eyes narrowed.

"She told me her name when I took her supper to her."

"Well, now I know what happened to her, at least. MacCallister has her." He looked at the note. "And he's going to kill me and my entire army, is he? We'll just see about that. Moss?" he called.

Moss, who was across the street at the time, came over in response to the call. "What do you want?"

"Two of your citizens were just killed by the same man who broke the girl out of your jail. I want you to get up a posse and go get him. But don't kill him unless you have to. I'll be needing him to tell us what he did with the girl."

"What makes you think I'll need a posse?" Moss asked.

"The man's name is Falcon MacCallister. Have you ever heard of him?"

"Yeah, I've heard of him," Moss said. "I ain't never seen him, but I've heard of him."

"You'll know him if you see him. He's a big, mean-looking son of a bitch. He's also very good with a gun. I think you should take at least four men with you."

"I'll get some of your men to go with me," Moss suggested.

"No. Get them from town. Tell them I'll give them fifty dollars apiece to go with you."

"What about me?" Moss asked.

"Bring him back to me, and I'll give you a hundred dollars."

"What if I have to kill him?"

"I'll still give you a hundred dollars. I just need him to be out of my way, right now."

Moss smiled, took his pistol from his holster, checked the loads, then put it back.

"All right," he said. "I'll take care of MacCallister for you."

Peggy watched as Moss went around recruiting his posse.

"Burke, Pell, Hanlon, Bivens, with me," Moss called.

Moss and the four men he recruited started down the street, Moss in the middle, and two men to each side of him. The rest of the town, having heard what was going on, watched as well.

"Hey, who's them two lyin' dead in the street up there?"

"What Moss said was they was Fong and Hood."

"Who?"

"Fong and Hood. You know, them two that swept out down at the Bloody Bucket. They hadn't been here too long."

"What happened to 'em?"

"Moss said MacCallister kilt 'em. That's why Major Ackerman is givin' fifty dollars to them that's goin' down to take care of him."

"Hell, I'd almost give fifty dollars myself to see MacCallister killed," one man said.

"Yeah, I've heard of the son of a bitch," another said. He laughed. "Once we kill him, it would put Purgatory on the map. If we wanted to be on the map."

A few others laughed as well, as they took up positions on either side of the road to watch Falcon MacCallister get killed.

* * *

"MacCallister!" Moss called. "MacCallister! I'm callin' you out! Come out in the street, you yellow-bellied bastard!"

Ahead, Falcon, Morgan, and Matthew came out of Annie's Café, then walked out into the middle of the street. They spread out to face the five men who were coming toward them.

"There . . . there are three of you," Moss said. "Which one of you is MacCallister."

"We're all MacCallisters," Falcon said.

"Kill 'em!" Moss shouted, and he and the others fired. Street With No Name echoed with the sound of gunfire. In all, ten shots were fired. Five of the bullets missed, five of the bullets found their targets. When the gun smoke rolled away, Moss and all four of his posse lay dead in the street. Falcon and his two brothers were still standing, unscratched.

"Bugler! Sound 'Recall'!" Ackerman shouted, his voice on the edge of panic.

Ackerman blew the bugle and, within a minute the Raiders began returning.

As Ackerman's men were regrouping at the barracks, Falcon, Morgan, and Matthew were dragging the bodies of Moss and his deputies into the center of the street. Now they were all lined up, side by side, seven bodies in a row.

It was so evident that a gun battle was about to take place and those who had gathered to watch Moss and the deputies were now off the street. Most of them were gathered in the Bloody Bucket Saloon, and they were having a discussion as to what their course of action should be.

"Hell, I say we do nothin', a man named Cassidy said. "Ackerman has been cock of the walk around here, this is his problem, let him handle it."

"What if the MacCallisters win? What will happen to Purgatory?" another asked.

"Nothin' will happen to Purgatory. The way I understand it, they just want the girl back, is all."

"Where is she?"

"Hell, if I know'd that, I would 'a already collected my two hunnert dollars."

"Anyway there's only three of the MacCallisters. Ackerman has what? Ten men?"

"Ten, countin' him."

"Twelve," one of the other men said.

"Twelve?"

"I seen Baddy Thomas and Angus Bligh goin' over to join up with Ackerman."

"Thornton and Givens went over there, too."

"That makes fourteen of 'em. Fourteen against three. I'd say the shootin' is more 'n likely goin' to be over pretty damn quick."

"I want a sharpshooter with a rifle posted in the loft of the livery," Ackerman said.

"Hell, Major, they's fourteen of us and only three of them," Givens said. "What do we need all that for? Let's just go down there and shoot the bastards and get it over with."

"Nevertheless, I want you to do what I said. I want one man on the balcony of the whorehouse, and another on the roof of the barracks. We don't have time to dig rifle pits, but Casey, I want you to get some men behind the water trough."

Bligh laughed. "What's all the fuss, about, Major? You act like we was about to get attacked by an army, or somethin'. Sharpshooters, rifle pits. You sure you don't have a couple of cannons hid out somewhere?"

"Believe me, if I had them I would use them," Ackerman replied. "And as far as you're concerned, the MacCallisters are an army. A three-man army."

"Shit. They ain't no different from anyone else. We got 'em so bad outnumbered, I don't know why we don't just face up to 'em. And anyway, when it comes right down to it, I'd be willin' to bet that they put their pants on one leg at a time, just like ever'one else." Bligh laughed at his comment.

"How do you know that, Bligh?" Ackerman replied. "Have you ever seen any of them put their pants on?"

"Well, no, but . . ."

"I didn't think so. Falcon MacCallister isn't like everybody else, and though I don't know his brothers, I doubt that they are like anyone else, either."

"Major, you ain't a'feared of MacCallister, are you?"

"Fear doesn't enter into it. I am an army officer and, in making plans for any battle, the first dictum is to do whatever it takes to make certain that you have an overwhelming advantage. That is what I am doing. Now, get to your assignments, all of you."

"All right, you heard what the major said," Casey called out. "Jones, you're the best marksman with a rifle we've got, you get up into the loft of the livery. Jerrod, you get out onto the whorehouse balcony, and Smith, you get on the roof of the barracks. Waters, you 'n Baker get to either end of the water trough over there on the other side of the street. Hastings, you two get behind the water trough on this side. Now all of you, get."

"What about me 'n Thomas, 'n Thornton, 'n Givins?" Bligh asked.

"Well you was talkin' so all-fired brave, I figure maybe you can just sort of take a stroll down the middle of the street toward 'em. There's four of you, and only three of them. You should make out all right."

"What? Wait a minute! What about you 'n the major, 'n him?" Bligh asked. He pointed to Powell.

"Don't worry, we'll be right behind you," Casey said. "And Powell is the bugler. He stays with the major and Jones."

"Little brother, I don't know about you," Morgan said, "but I'm not all that sold on the idea of just walking down all bunched up in the middle of the street. I think we need to find a better way to approach them."

"I think you're right. Morgan, you get over there to the right side and stay close to the buildings as you move down the street. Matthew, you stay on this side and do the same thing. But . . . keep an eye on the buildings you are following, make certain nobody shoots you from inside."

"Great, one more thing to worry about," Morgan said with a smile.

"Where are you going to be, Falcon?" Matthew asked.

"I'm going right down the middle of the street. And I'm counting on you two to keep me covered."

"We'll do it."

"Are you both ready?" Falcon asked.

Both of his brothers nodded.

"All right. Give me a wave as soon as you are both in position, then I'll start down the street. You two keep up with me."

Morgan and Matthew hurried into position, then, after a wave from each of them, Falcon started forward.

Morgan saw somebody kneeling in the open window of the loft over the livery. Whoever it was had a rifle in his hand. Morgan whistled and when Falcon looked toward him, Morgan pointed to the open loft window. Falcon looked around just as someone was raising a rifle to his shoulder. Falcon fired first, and the man dropped his rifle, grabbed his stomach, then fell forward, flipping over onto his back before he hit the ground.

The next person to shoot was Dale Hastings. He got a shot off before Falcon or Matthew, who was on his same side, saw him. The bullet fried the air by Falcon's ear, but Falcon didn't return fire. He didn't have to shoot back because Matthew took Dale Hastings out with one shot.

"You son of a bitch! You kilt my brother!" Travis Hastings yelled, and in his anger he stood and fired at Matthew. Matthew managed to duck into the doorway of the building he was by, and Travis missed. Matthew wasn't in position to return fire, but Falcon was, and he shot Travis, who tumbled forward into the watering trough, where he lay with his face down in the water.

Morgan shot next, killing Waters. Baker got up then and started running back toward Baddy Thomas, Bligh, Thornton, and Givens, who, while they were in the middle of the street, had not advanced toward the MacCallisters. As Baker ran, he fired back at Falcon, and one lucky shot creased Falcon's arm. Falcon returned fire, hitting Baker, who sprawled belly down in the street.

"Shoot him, shoot him, shoot him!" Bligh yelled, and all four started shooting. After a rapid exchange of fire, all four went down.

Falcon was trying to remember how many shots he had fired. He had reloaded after the encounter with Moss and his posse. But he had shot three rounds before these four had come after them. And he had fired two at these four. He only had one round left, and he had no idea how many bullets his brothers had, but he believed they had fired at least as many times as he had, and maybe more.

There were three men remaining, though Falcon recognized only Ackerman. Suddenly one of the three men started running away, and Ackerman turned toward him.

"Powell! Come back here, you cowardly son of a bitch!" Ackerman shouted, and he fired, hitting Powell in the back of the head. Powell went down.

"You shouldn' of done that, Major. Now there's just the two of us left."

"Jerrod is on the balcony of the whorehouse, remember," Ackerman said.

* * *

Up on the balcony of the House of Pleasure, the girls, frightened, had all gathered in the back room. Mary Kate, however, realizing that her personal fate depended on what happened here, couldn't stay back there. She went into the hall, then moved quietly up to the alcove just before the balcony. When she looked out, she saw Jerrod taking a bead on Falcon. From here, he couldn't miss!

Suddenly two shots rang out, and Jerrod fell back. Mary Kate saw that the two shots had come from either side of the street, one from her uncle Morgan, and the other from her uncle Matthew.

"Damn, they've kilt 'em all!" Casey shouted. Pulling his pistol, and with a loud shout, he started charging toward Falcon, shooting as he ran. Both Morgan and Matthew stepped out into the street to shoot at him, but in both cases, their hammers fell on empty chambers. Falcon shot Casey, the bullet hitting him in the middle of his forehead. He fell, and Falcon turned and pulled the trigger as he pointed his gun toward Ackerman. But like his two brothers, he was out of ammunition.

Ackerman pulled his pistol, and with a big smile aimed at Falcon. "How dare you come into my town after me," he said. "And just so you know, when I find that little bitch, I have no intention of ever taking her back to her father." He pulled the hammer back. "So this is where the great Falcon MacCallister meets his . . ."

That was as far as he got. There was a rifle shot from the balcony of the House of Pleasure, and Ackerman went down. Looking up toward the sound of the shot, Falcon saw one of the whores holding a smoking rifle.

"Thanks!" Falcon shouted. Quickly, he began reloading, and he saw his brothers doing so as well.

"Uncle Falcon! It's me!" Mary Kate shouted.

Falcon looked up again and saw the young woman, the one he thought was a whore, waving at him.

"I'm coming down!" she said.

By now Falcon's two brothers had joined him, and the rest of the town were coming out of the buildings, moving slowly up Street With No Name, taking a count of the dead.

Mary Kate came running up to her uncles and hugged them all. "I knew you would come after me," she said. "I knew you would. Even if you aren't riding a white horse and wearing shining armor."

"What?" Morgan said.

Falcon chuckled. "You wouldn't understand."

By now more than half the town was gathered in the area in front of the barracks and the House of Pleasure, and they were talking among themselves, pointing out the dead bodies that were strewn all up and down the street.

"Damn!" one of the men said. "Twenty-one! They's twenty-one lyin' dead in the street."

"I ain't never seen nothin' like this in all my borned days," another said.

"Who the hell are you people?" a third man asked.

"We aren't the law, and we've got what we came after," Morgan said, putting his arm around his niece. "We would just as soon be leaving now, unless you think there's a need for some more killing."

"You ain't goin' to have no trouble from me," one of the men said.

"No, nor me, neither."

"Good. If there's no more trouble, we'll just be going on our way," Morgan said.

Matthew had been staring at Mary Kate, and finally he couldn't hold it in any longer.

"Mary Kate, what in the world are you doing in that getup?"

By now several of the other girls had come out from the House of Pleasure, including Gladys.

"I put her in it," Gladys said. "I thought it would be a good way to hide her from Ackerman."

"It worked, too," Mary Kate said with a smile. "Jerrod came in and looked at all of us when he was looking for me. I was right there in the room with the rest of them, and he didn't even recognize me."

"I hope you don't mind," Gladys said.

"Mind?" Falcon said. "Why should we mind? I think that's one of the smartest ideas I've ever heard."

"Gentlemen," Dempster called to the others of the town who were gathered in the middle of the street. "I think it's time we organized."

"Organized what?" one of the others asked.

"Organized ourselves into a real town," he said.

"Wait a minute, Hodge, they's some of us come here to get away from the law. Are you sayin' we won't be safe here, no more?"

"Those whose crimes were most egregious are lying dead in the street," Dempster said. "As for the rest of us, I think a fresh start is in order."

"The first thing we should do is change the name of the town," Peggy said. "Purgatory has an evil connotation."

"You got 'ny ideas what to call it?" Dempster asked.

"Yes," Peggy said. She looked at Mary Kate and smiled. "I think we should call it McVey."

"Any objections?" Dempster asked.

No one objected.

"You know what you have just done?" Falcon asked.

"What?"

Falcon smiled. "McVey has just held its first democratic town meeting."

EPILOGUE

From the *Helena Independent*, April 23, 1889:

WE WILL BE A STATE!

STATEHOOD APPROVED

November 8, 1889, the Date

John Kemp Toole, First Governor

The preamble of our new state constitution, approved in convention in Helena, reads thusly:

We the people of Montana, grateful to Almighty God for the blessings of liberty, in order to secure the advantages of a state government, do in accordance with the permission of the enabling act of Congress approved the 12th of February, 1889, ordain and establish this constitution.

Much is owed to Edward Hamilton of Deer Lodge, and Hodge Dempster of McVey, who toiled long and hard to secure statehood for Montana. Now all citizens of

Montana will be able to gaze upon that
Star Spangled Banner and know that one
of the stars represents us. Long may it
wave, and long live the state of Montana.

A celebration of statehood was held at Brimstone.
Falcon, Morgan, and Matthew were there, as was
Mary Kate, who had remarried to Mark Worley, a
lawyer from Deer Lodge. Mark had been very active
in helping put together the statehood convention, his
contribution so valuable that Governor Toole had ap-
pointed Mark as his chief of operations.

At the moment, Edward and Megan Hamilton,
Hodge Dempster and his wife, Peggy, Mark and Mary
Kate, Falcon, Morgan, and Matthew, were all out on
the patio behind Denbigh Castle. Mary Kate's twin
sons, Johnny and Edward, were playing in the back-
yard. A pig, being rotated over an open fire, filled the
air with an aroma that promised a delicious dinner to
be served, later.

"You know, Falcon, Governor Toole offered Mark
the position of U.S. Senator, but he turned it down,"
Edward said.

"Why did you turn it down?" Falcon asked. "That
seems like a pretty powerful position."

"I suppose it is, but I would have to spend too much
time in Washington. And I love this territory . . ."

"Soon to be a state," Dempster said.

"Soon to be a state," Mark corrected with a grin,
"too much to leave it. I wouldn't be very good in congress, I would be homesick for Montana. Look at this."

Mark took in the purple vista of the mountains.
At this hour of late afternoon, the mountains were

limned with a golden glow from the sun that had gone down behind them. "Can you imagine anyplace more beautiful? Certainly nothing like this in Washington."

"No, nor anywhere I've ever been," Edward agreed.

"Falcon, I've always wondered why you never got into politics," Megan said. "You've certainly made a lot of friends. I think you could be elected to any office you aspired to."

"I've made a lot of friends, yes. But don't forget, I've also made enemies," Falcon said.

"Not that many enemies," Matthew suggested. "It's not healthy to be one of your enemies. They either wind up dead, or in prison."

"Matthew," Megan scolded. "That's not a nice thing to say."

"I mean nothing untoward about it, Megan. Everyone who knows Falcon, knows that he has always been on the up and up."

"And lest someone forget, Falcon, and you two," Dempster said, taking in Morgan and Matthew with a wave of his hand, "not only saved Mary Kate, you also freed a town. And speaking as mayor of McVey, our town will always be grateful to you. To all of you."

"But my mother-in-law is right, Falcon. You could be elected to any office you might want," Mark said.

"But what would I do with my shining armor, and my white horse?" Falcon teased.

"What?"

Only Mary Kate knew the joke, and smiling, she walked over to give him a kiss.

"Use it to save damsels in distress," she said.

Turn the page for an exciting preview!

USA TODAY BESTSELLING AUTHOR
WILLIAM W. JOHNSTONE
with J. A. Johnstone

THE BROTHERS O'BRIEN
The Explosive New Series from the Authors of
The Family Jensen

FOUR BROTHERS. ONE DREAM.

From William W. Johnstone, the master of the epic
Western, comes a bold new series set in the harsh,
untamed New Mexico Territory—where four
brave-hearted brothers struggle to work the land,
keep the peace, and fight for the dream of America.

THE SAGA BEGINS . . .

The War Between the States has ended.
Now, driven from Texas by carpetbaggers, former
CSA Colonel Shamus O'Brien sets off for a new
frontier—New Mexico. There, where land is cheap,
bandits shoot to kill, and rustlers rule the night,
it takes more than one man to run a ranch.
So he offers a partnership to his eldest son, Jacob,
with equal shares going to his sons Sam, Patrick,
and Shawn. Together, the brothers O'Brien will
defend their homestead, the Dromore, in this
violent, lawless land . . . and when necessary,
administer their own brand of frontier justice.

On sale September 2013
wherever Kensington Books are sold.

CHAPTER ONE

West Texas, May 28, 1866

Texans are a generous breed, but they do not confer the title of Colonel lightly on a man. He has to earn it.

The two men who sat in the sway-roofed sod cabin had earned the honor the hard way—by being first-rate fighting men.

Colonel Shamus O'Brien had risen though the ranks of the Confederate Army to become a regimental commander in the Laurel Brigade under the dashing and gallant Major General Thomas L. Rosser.

O'Brien had been raiding in West Virginia when the war ended in 1865, and thus escaped the surrender at Appomattox, a blessing for which he'd thank the Good Lord every single day of his long life.

He was twenty-three years old that June and bore the scars of two great wounds. A ball ripped through his thigh at First Manassas and a Yankee saber cut opened his left cheek at Mechanicsville.

By his own reckoning, Shamus O'Brien, from County Clare, Ireland, had killed seventeen men in single combat with revolver or saber, and none of them disturbed his sleep.

The man who faced O'Brien across the rough pine table was Colonel Charles Goodnight. He'd been addressed as colonel from the first day and hour he'd saddled a horse to ride with the Texas Rangers. A Yankee by birth—yet the great state of Texas had not a more loyal citizen, nor fearless fighting man.

"Charlie," O'Brien said, "it is a hell of a thing to hang a man."

Goodnight stilled a forkful of beans and salt pork halfway to his mouth. "Hell, Shamus, he's as guilty as sin."

"Maybe the girl led him on. It happens, you know."

Speaking around a mouthful of food, Goodnight said, "She didn't."

"She's black," O'Brien said.

"So, what difference does that make?"

"Just sayin'."

Goodnight poured himself coffee from the sooty pot on the table.

"Shamus, black, white, or in between, he raped a girl and there's an end to it."

O'Brien let go of all the tension that had been building inside him, words exploding from his mouth, his lilting Irish brogue pronounced. "Jesus, Mary, and Joseph, Saint Peter and Saint Paul, and all the saints in Heaven save and preserve us! Charlie, he's a Yankee carpetbagger. He's got the government on his side."

"Yeah, I know he has, but I don't give a damn. He's

among the worst of the carpetbagging scum and I've got no liking for him. He called me a raggedy-assed Texas Reb—imagine that. I mean, I know it's true, but I don't need to hear it from a damned uppity Yankee."

"Is that why you're hanging him, because he called you raggedy-assed?"

"No, I'm hanging him for the rape of a seventeen-year-old girl."

"Charlie, you're not a Ranger anymore. You don't have the authority to hang anybody."

"So the government says. A Union general in El Paso told me my enlistment ran out at Appomattox. Well, I don't see it his way. The Rangers didn't tell me I'm done, so as far as I'm concerned I still have a sworn duty to protect the people of Texas, men, women, and children."

O'Brien was a big man, sturdy and well built, with the thick red hair and blue eyes inherited from his ancestor Brian Boru, the last High King of Ireland. His pine chair creaked in protest when he leaned back. "They'll come after us, Charlie, I'm thinking. And the gather just completed."

Goodnight considered that. He scraped his tin plate, the noise loud in the silence and stifling heat of the cabin. Finally he said, "By the time the Yankees give up their plundering and get around to investigating we'll have the herd across the Pecos and be well on our way north."

"They look after their own, Charlie," O'Brien said.

"And so do I, by God." Goodnight pushed his plate away, leaned back, and sighed. "That was an elegant meal, Shamus."

His poverty an affront to his Celtic pride, O'Brien said, "I am shamed that my poor house had so little to offer. Salt pork and beans is not a fit repast for such an honored guest."

Goodnight stepped lightly. "The food was excellent and freely given. You did indeed do me great honor, Shamus."

O'Brien and Goodnight were Southern gentlemen of the old school, and the mutual compliments were accepted without further comment.

"Will you hang him, Charlie?" O'Brien said. "I mean, after all that's been said."

Goodnight consulted the railroad watch he took from his vest pocket. "Yes, at noon, fifteen minutes from now."

O'Brien listened into the morning, his face grim. "He screams for mercy. You'll hang a coward."

"He's a carpetbagger. He was brave enough to throw women and children off their farms, but he's not so brave in the company of men." Goodnight's eyes hardened. "God, I hate his kind."

"What's his name?"

"Do you care?"

"Not really. I'm just curious."

"Dinwiddie is his last name. That's all I know."

"Ah, then he's not a son of Erin."

"No, he's a son of a bitch."

CHAPTER TWO

His name was Rufus T. Dinwiddie, and he was not prepared to die well.

When Goodnight's drovers, Texans to a man, dragged him toward a dead cottonwood by a dry creek, he screamed and begged for mercy, and his broadcloth suit pants were stained by the loosening of his bowels and bladder.

Dinwiddie was a small man with pomaded hair and a black pencil mustache. His brown eyes were wild, filled with terror, and they fixed on Shamus O'Brien's wife, who stood beside her husband, a ragged parasol protecting her from the hammering sun.

"Save me, ma'am!" Dinwiddie shrieked, the dragging toes of his elastic-sided boots gouging parallel furrows in the dirt. "In the name of God, save me."

Saraid O'Brien was pregnant with her second child. Her five-year-old son Samuel stood at her side, frightened, clinging to her skirts.

She turned her head and glared at Goodnight. "Will you hang such a man, Charles?"

Goodnight said nothing, but the shocked, sick expression on his rugged face spoke volumes.

"He shames you," Saraid said. "He shames all of us here."

The rope was around Dinwiddie's neck and the little carpetbagger's screams had turned to hysterical shrieks that ripped apart the fabric of the young afternoon like talons.

Goodnight had seen men hanged before, but all of them, scared or not, had at least pretended to be brave before the trap sprung. A man who died like a dog was outside his experience and the last thing he'd expected.

He stood rooted to the spot as the drovers threw Dinwiddie on the back of a horse and then looked at him expectantly.

The man was no longer screaming, but he was heaving great, shuddering sobs. Still he pleaded for mercy.

Saraid rounded on her husband. "Shamus, if you hang that miserable wretch today you'll never again be able to hold your head high in the company of men."

She grabbed Goodnight by his upper arm. "And that goes doubly for you, Charles."

He looked like a man waking from a bad dream. "Saraid, he raped a girl."

"I know, and she stands over there by the cottonwood," the woman said. "She is the wronged party, so let her say what the justice is to be."

Goodnight shook his head. "I did not expect this, not in a hundred years."

If Saraid heard, she didn't respond. She said only

one word that held a wealth of meaning—the name of her husband. "Shamus." Her green eyes glowed like emeralds.

O'Brien said nothing. He drew his .36 caliber Colt Navy from the holster on his hip and strode toward the cottonwood. "Take him down."

The hands were confused. "But, Colonel, the boss says to hang him."

"I know what he said, but this man isn't worth hanging," O'Brien said.

The punchers looked toward Goodnight, but the man stood frozen where he was, Saraid's slim hand still on his arm, as though she was holding him in place.

"Get him down from there," O'Brien said again.

The men did as they were told.

To O'Brien's disgust, Dinwiddie let out a loud wail and threw himself at his feet. He kissed the toes of O'Brien's dusty boots and slobbered his thanks. O'Brien kicked him away.

Rape was a serious offense and there was still justice to be done. "You men, put his back against the tree and hold him," the colonel said.

As he was hauled roughly to his feet, Dinwiddie cried out in alarm. "What are you doing to me?" he squealed.

"An eye for an eye, me lad." O'Brien's face looked like it had been carved from rock.

The black girl, slender, pretty, wearing a worn gingham dress, stood near the cottonwood. Her face was badly bruised. When O'Brien got closer he saw the arcs of a vicious bite on her neck.

He pointed the Colt at Dinwiddie. "Is he the man who raped you?"

The girl nodded. Her eyes were downcast and her long lashes lay on her cheekbones like ragged fans. "He hurt me, mister." She didn't look at O'Brien. "And now I'm afeared I'll be with child."

About two dozen men, women, and children had gathered from the surrounding shacks to see the hanging. They called the dusty settlement a town because of its single saloon and attached general store, but within a couple years the place was destined to dry up and blow away in the desert wind.

"Nellie works for me as a maid, Colonel," a fat woman said, stepping so close to O'Brien he could smell her sweat. "I examined her after she was undone, and she's tore up all right, fore an' aft if you get my meaning."

Tears trickled down the girl's cheeks and sudden anger flashed in O'Brien. Suddenly he wanted to smash his fist into Dinwiddie's face.

"Hey, ain't you gonna hang him?" the fat woman said.

O'Brien ignored her. He grabbed Nellie's arm and said, "Come with me, girl."

A breeze had picked up, lifting veils of yellow dust. Near where Saraid and Goodnight stood, a dust devil spun, then collapsed at their feet like a puff of smoke. Insects made their small music in the bunchgrass and the air smelled thick of sage and the new aborning afternoon coming in clean.

Goodnight watched O'Brien, as did the crowd.

The residents of the town had come to see a hanging, but Dinwiddie's cowardice had spoiled it for everybody, especially the women. The ladies expected the condemned man to make the traditional speech blaming loose women and whiskey for his undoing, though he had a good mother. That always went down well at a hanging. It gave wives the opportunity to glare at their cowering husbands and warn darkly, "You pay heed, or this could happen to you."

But the spectators, their rapt attention fixed on Shamus O'Brien and the colored girl, had decided that not all was lost, for a fine drama was unfolding.

At least that's how it looked to Saraid. Why else would the people stay and brave the noonday sun to see a poor, cowardly wretch suffer for his sins, grievous though they were?

O'Brien led the girl called Nellie to within six feet of the cottonwood. A couple grinning punchers held Dinwiddie's arms, so his back was against the trunk.

The little man's eyes widened when he saw the Colt in O'Brien's fist. "What the hell are you going to do?"

O'Brien ignored him, thumbed back the hammer, and passed the heavy revolver to Nellie. "Shoot him."

Dinwiddie's expression went from fear to disbelief and back again. He glared at the girl. "Pull that trigger and I'll see you hang, missy."

The girl held the Colt in both hands. She started to lift the revolver, hesitated, and looked at O'Brien, her brown eyes afraid.

"Go ahead," O'Brien said. "He can't hurt you now."

Dinwiddie made an appeal to the crowd. "Stop this!" he screamed. "Are you going to stand there and see a white man get shot?"

No one moved or said a word, their collective stares on Nellie and the wavering blue Colt.

Goodnight stepped beside O'Brien. "This ain't gonna work, Shamus. Damn it, we'll put cotton in our ears and string him up."

But Nellie surprised them.

She raised the Colt in both hands and pointed it at Dinwiddie's head.

The man screeched and tried to break free, his eyes wild. The punchers held tight to his arms, strong men who quickly subdued his puny struggles.

The muzzle of the revolver trembled, then Nellie let it lower slowly, her skirt slapping against her legs in the hot desert wind.

O'Brien thought she was done. That she couldn't go through with it. He heard Goodnight curse under his breath and a collective sigh raise from the crowd.

The girl stopped the Colt's descent when it pointed at Dinwiddie's crotch, and pulled the trigger.

The ball slammed into the little man's groin and he screamed in pain, his mouth a startled O of shock.

Nellie fired again. Same place.

Stunned, the punchers dropped Dinwiddie's arms. The man's knees buckled and he sank slowly to the ground.

"All right, he's had enough," O'Brien said. Almost gently, he took the Colt from the girl's shaking hands. "Go home now, girl."

She buried her face in her white apron and stumbled away. The fat lady stopped the girl, put her massive arm around her shoulders and led her toward home.

"You done good, girl," she said as they walked away.

Dinwiddie was traumatized, his pinched, narrow face white. But, no matter how shocked a groin-shot man may be, he'll always rip open his pants and check on his jewels.

Dinwiddie did—and what he saw made him shriek in horror.

Unbelieving, he looked around the crowd, then at O'Brien and Goodnight. "It's gone," he wailed. He looked down at his groin again. "All of it."

"Then you'll never again rape another woman," O'Brien said.

"Help me," Dinwiddie wailed. "Get me a doctor."

O'Brien deliberately turned his back on the man. He said to Goodnight, "I've got a bottle of Old Crow in the cabin if you want to get the bad taste of Dinwiddie out of your mouth."

"Shamus, we should've hung him," Goodnight said.

O'Brien smiled. "Well now, all things considered, I'd say he's suffered a fate worse than death."

VISITOR

Name: Clay

Date: 3/5A   3/3

THE EAGLES SERIES BY
WILLIAM W. JOHNSTONE

__Eyes of Eagles
   0-7860-1364-8   **$5.99**US/**$7.99**CAN

__Dreams of Eagles
   0-7860-6086-6   **$5.99**US/**$7.99**CAN

__Talons of Eagles
   0-7860-0249-2   **$5.99**US/**$6.99**CAN

__Scream of Eagles
   0-7860-0447-9   **$5.99**US/**$7.50**CAN

__Rage of Eagles
   0-7860-0507-6   **$5.99**US/**$7.99**CAN

__Song of Eagles
   0-7860-1012-6   **$5.99**US/**$7.99**CAN

__Cry of Eagles
   0-7860-1024-X   **$5.99**US/**$7.99**CAN

__Blood of Eagles
   0-7860-1106-8   **$5.99**US/**$7.99**CAN

Available Wherever Books Are Sold!

Visit our website at **www.kensingtonbooks.com**